FOR WHAT IT'S WORTH

Sarah,
Sometimes climbing mountains is worth it ;)
love
J. PRESTON
Jo Preston xxx

For What It's Worth
Book 2 in the False Start Series

The moral right of J. Preston to be identified as the author of this work has been asserted by her in accordance with the Copyright, Designs and Patents Act 1988.
All the characters in this book are fictitious, and any resemblance to actual persons living or dead, is purely coincidental.

Copyright © 2021 by J. Preston

All rights reserved. No part of this publication may be reproduced in any form or by any electronic or mechanical means, including information storage and retrieval systems, or transmitted in any form or by any means without the prior permission in writing of the copyright owner, except for the use of quotation in book reviews.
To request permission, contact jo@authorjpreston.com.

Edited by: Adora Dillard
Cover Design: Ashley Santorro

Published by DIRTY TALK PUBLISHING LTD
www.dirtytalkpublishing.com

To those who are getting over a heartbreak. Your sunshine is just around the corner.

Author's Note

Thank you so much for picking up my novel and supporting me in this exciting adventure. Your kind words and love for these characters are what keeps me motivated to write. So if you enjoy the book please consider leaving a review

FOR WHAT IT'S WORTH PLAYLIST
Music is a huge part of every book I write.

To listen head over to Spotify just scan or click the QR code

I hope you love this book as much as I do.

Jo, xoxo

Prologue

Carter

Christmas Day - One year ago

Fucking Christmas spirit, my ass. Who's to say Christmas is supposed to be the time of happiness and tinsel shit, anyway? Not this guy. How can you live through the happiest time of the year when your heart has been stomped on? How the fuck are you supposed to be smiling through presents, food, and family stuff when the person you're in love with is all loved up... With someone else. Yup, I'm that sucker. The guy who falls for his best friend then watches her fall in love with another dude.

It didn't happen instantly. Don't get me wrong, Jenny, or as I like to call her, Grasshopper, is gorgeous and clever and out of this world funny, but I have my qualities too. And my qualities, well...they bring all the girls to the yard, and this yard ain't discriminating. So it took me a while to get my head out of my ass and realize that the girl I'm crazy about was worth fighting for. Needless to say, I was a little too late, and Grasshopper was currently loved up in London with my other best friend. Fucking cliche.

What can a guy do in a situation like this but get himself out of this world drunk? Nothing.

"One more shot!" Hayley shouts, pouring the whiskey into our shot glasses as Frank Sinatra sings '*Jingle Bells*' over the speakers.

It's funny how small the world is. One minute you think you're drowning your sorrows all by yourself, the next a friend from college, located three hundred and sixty miles away, sits down next to you and demands you celebrate Christmas in style. Hayley, Grasshopper's best friend, is in L.A. for a modeling gig or something, and they chose tonight to come out on the town. To the same bar I always go to when I visit home. When all I wanted to do was be alone and mope. Call it fate. Call it shit luck. Call it whatever. I'm done caring.

"To misery." I raise my shot glass, liquid sloshing over the rim. Hayley narrows her eyes at me but lifts her glass to mine.

"To freedom." Sydney, the girl sitting with us, clinks her glass with mine and, without thinking, downs the whiskey in one go. I follow suit, not wanting to be left behind. That will make it...six shots? Maybe. Maybe eight. Hayley gets up and makes her way towards the bar. She's steady on her feet, which I find impressive. You have to admire a chick that can hold her liquor. As she leans over the bar and starts chatting to the bartender, I turn my head and face Sydney.

"Why freedom? Aren't we all free? Isn't that what America stands for? Land of freedom?" I ask, pouring another shot. She cocks her head and picks up her glass.

"I'm English. Why misery?" She deadpans, then downs her shot.

"English-shminglish, you're in America, babe. Did you just get out of prison?"

"No, and you're changing the subject."

"Who cares, anyway? I'm miserable, and I'll drink to that." I lift my shot glass to my lips. Her gaze doesn't waver, so I sigh and put the shot down. "I seem to be suffering from a serious disease called badassery." She doesn't bite, so I lift the shot again and throw it back. Slamming it down on the table, I smile. "I'm the jackass who's in love with his best friend."

"I assume it's not reciprocated?" She pours two more shots. Good girl.

"Would I be drinking myself into a stupor if it was?" I pluck one of the shot glasses from her hand and, as our fingers touch, an electric shock runs through me. My eyes meet her blue ones as, simultaneously, we down the shot. I'm probably not going to remember much tomorrow, but I sure as hell hope I'll remember her. She's fucking beautiful. Like, should be on the covers of magazines type of beautiful. Who am I kidding? Given her employment, she probably *is* on the covers of all the magazines. Her hand brushes my leg, interrupting my thoughts.

"You know, the best way to get over someone is to get under someone else." She winks at me. I fucking knew it. God must have been giving out lottery tickets today, and yours truly has hit the jackpot. I'll be sure to say a couple of Hail Mary's in thanks for this miracle.

"Oh, yeah?" I reach for the bottle, but her hand gets there first, and as she lifts the whiskey to her lips, her gaze not leaving mine, my dick stirs in anticipation of what's to come. I smile at her then take the bottle out of her hands. She lifts her eyebrow and, not breaking my gaze from her, I take a long swig. "Want to go somewhere where they're not trying to brainwash us with Jingle Bells' subliminal message?" I ask.

When she nods, I stand up and reach for her hand. She takes it without hesitation. As we weave through the crowded bar, I look over at Hayley to wave goodbye. She's busy kissing the bartender, so I don't bother interrupting.

"I don't do relationships," I say once we're in an Uber. I want to get this out of the way before we get any further.

"I didn't ask for one. I just want to fuck." The driver's mouth opens. Yes, dude, I'm the master of the universe. This hot as fuck woman wants to have sex with moi!

"Lovely." I lean in and nuzzle her throat. She smells floral and fucking arousing. I lick at the spot on her neck where her vein pulses and am rewarded with a gasp.

"That, that there, now go lower," she whispers. The whiskey starts hitting me, so I wrap my fingers around her short, sunshine-colored hair and pull it.

"Patience, Sunshine." I nip at her earlobe as the Uber pulls up in front of her hotel.

Drunkenly, we make our way to the room. It's not pretty, but who the fuck cares? Carter *is going to get some*. When the key card clicks and the door opens, we tumble to the floor. My hands are all over her, rough and exploring. She tears at my clothes, ripping my t-shirt in half.

Fucking hot.

"Mmmm, nice, just what I was hoping for," she mumbles, stroking my chest up and down. That's all the invitation I need. In one swift motion, I lift her up and stumble to the bed, dropping her on it unceremoniously. The world is spinning full force now, but I'm a man on a mission. A mission to get my dick wet. Sunshine lifts on her elbows, her crop top riding up, and I am graced with a sight of glorious underboob. The view is so incredible I lick my lips, already imagining my mouth on them. Clumsily, I lean over her and pull her top up, exposing her pert nipples. As I circle my tongue around one, then suck it into my mouth, I lose my balance and fall to the side, catching my face on her shoulder.

"Fuck!" she yelps.

"You okay?" I slur.

"Yeah, I think so, You?" My eye is throbbing something fierce from the impact, but that's not going to stop me.

"Yeah."

"Great, now take off your jeans," she commands drunkenly. "We're breaking my dry spell."

Fuck yeah, we are. I stand up and unzip my jeans, but the fucking zipper catches on my boxers, so it takes some serious pulling for the fucker to go down. With a little force, I manage to unzip them. There's a hole in my Calvin Kleins', but I don't need them right now anyway. Eagerly, I pull my jeans and underwear down at the same time, and it's the wrong fucking move. I'm such an idiot. I stumble and—unable to catch my balance with my legs caught in this self-made denim trap—fall on my ass, banging my head on the leg of a chair in the process.

I think I'm dying.

I'm pretty sure I am, or at least I'm bleeding out.

Possibly, it might just be a big bruise, but it hurts like a motherfucker.

Sunshine's head peeps over the edge of the bed. Her eyes zero in on my cock, which is standing to attention despite the amount of whiskey I have running through my veins and injuries I have sustained. She licks her lips and slides off the bed, pulling her skirt down and lifting her top over her head, leaving her in just her panties. She goes to her knees, runs her hand up my leg, and all thoughts of bleeding out are instantly forgotten. When her fingers graze my balls, I nearly die. It feels like it has been forever since anyone touched me, and it has been. Truthfully, I haven't been with anyone since I kissed my best friend and realized I might have feelings for her. My stomach tightens. I close my eyes, trying not to think about Grasshopper, but it's the wrong move. The world just won't stop spinning. I'm half-aware of Sydney's hand wrapping around my cock, but the asshole is not cooperating, probably enjoying his time on the carousel much more than I am.

I open my eyes. Sydney is above me, my dick still in her hand. One look at her, her body, her face, her hair is all it takes to get me ready. I flip us around, Sydney landing underneath me. "Condom," she demands, wriggling down her panties. I couldn't be more on board with that demand. I reach down to my ankles, where my jeans still are, and pull a condom out. Sydney's eyes are half-closed, her lips parted as I pull it on.

I lean down to kiss her. The moment our lips connect, an electric current goes through me. Her arms wrap around my neck as she molds into me. The kiss is slow and deep, unhurried. She tastes like whiskey and mint, and her lips move against mine like they were made for each other. At the back of my head, I have a nagging thought, but I can't quite grasp it. When I pull away, her eyes are closed, lips tilted up in a small smile, a smile that spreads warmth around my body. I trail kisses down her jaw and neck before coming back up to nibble on her earlobe. As much as I want to fuck her, something urges me to make it last, make it count. My dick has other ideas and, as it brushes against the inside of her thighs, I can't help myself. Her legs open even more for me as I position myself against her heat. I push, no, slide into her in one go. She's so wet, so fucking wet. And tight and so fucking warm. The thought keeps coming almost within my reach, but I still can't quite grasp at it. I slide back out and push again. God, she feels so good. So fucking good. Like she was made just for me. I lift my head to look into her face and freeze. Sydney's eyes are closed, mouth parted. Her breaths are steady and deep.

A little snore escapes her.

The fuck?

She snores again, and I instantly pull out. What. The. Fuck? Did she just fall asleep while my dick was in her? I'm not being funny, but it's not like Carter Junior is a small guy. One does not simply fall asleep while my dick is inside them!

Sydney makes a content sigh and tries to turn to her side. I slide off her. Who is this devil? I lift her up and put her on the bed, then I go to the bathroom to discard the condom. How did this go from me putting the fucking thing in to her asleep in the next five seconds? I splash some cold water on my face, trying to get the world to stop spinning, but the world's not cooperating, so I go back into the room and slide in beside Sydney. Wrapping my arms around her, I nuzzle her hair and close my eyes. *Mine,* crosses my mind. Huh? *It's her, it's always been her.* I shrug the thoughts off and fall asleep.

When the sun wakes me up in the morning, I have a black eye, the room is empty, and Sydney is gone.

PART I

It'll Never Be Me

You say 'Nothing's changed' but in my heart
I know it'll never be the same
My hands in my pockets, I can't reach out
Can't touch your face
Inside my head the rain is falling
Everything's turning grey
Then you smile at me and suddenly
The color's back again
And when you cry, did you know
My heart cries with you
All I want is you to be happy
And if that means that
It'll never be me
So be it
My hands in my pockets, I can't reach out
Can't touch your face
So I turn around and walk back in
To the life where everything is not how it seems
It's not me
Now is not the time
It'll never be me

Chapter 1

I'll Owe You Big Time

Carter

One year later

Your life can change drastically from one day to the next, trust me. I'm a prime example of that. Last year my best friend shared a video of me singing, and the thing blew up. I went from your average heartthrob next door type of guy to...not so average. Huh. Joking aside, I never lacked attention from women; they'd just fall into my lap, and things would go from there, usually ending up in a sweaty but satisfying finish. I like my women well sated and thoroughly fucked before I send them on their way. So what the hell has been fucking with my mojo this past year? For I, Carter Kennedy—also known as Casanova, as my best friend likes to call me—have not had sex in almost a whole year. Three hundred and fifty-two days, to be exact. It's absolutely unheard of for me. After the failed one night stand with Hayley's friend, Sydney, I tried again. I really did.

We were having a great time, we drank, we talked. There was chemistry between us, so we went back to my place. Katie was great. She had a dirty mouth and a banging body, and as soon as we got back to my place, she undressed herself and went down on her knees, unzipping my fly. A true sign of a keeper, that's a no brainer, right? So why, when I went to brush her brown hair out of her face so I could watch her lips wrap around my dick, did it go flaccid? For the rest of the night, I couldn't get it up, and trust me when I say it has *never* happened before. Never.

It was the worst night of my life. Katie didn't get anything out of it either. I tried, I really did, but she was... wrong, just wrong. I can't explain it. Maybe it was the Grasshopper thing, perhaps it was something else, but it allowed me to take a good, hard look at myself and realize that fucking my way through college might not be the best career choice. So after that, I did what I thought was best. I pretended I didn't have feelings for Jenny and poured all my emotions into writing songs. Songs which I then recorded and posted online. Songs that got me where I am today. It didn't hurt that I already knew how to play a guitar and string together some chords. Who am I kidding? When I was fourteen, it was my dream to be a singer songwriter, a dream which would have been a reality had it not been for the stage fright I experienced at a talent show I entered. Yes. Yes, I did. No, seriously, I did! I puked my guts out, ran away, and never looked back, I swear. I know it's hard to believe, but it's true. Yours truly has a weakness. Unfortunately, that weakness proved stronger than my desire to sing. Until last year, when that fire was lit again. A fire that was now burning stronger than ever, and it didn't hurt that, this time around, all I had to do was sing in front of the camera. No audience, no drama. But that was all about to change.

"Are you excited?" Jenny asks, plopping down in my chair as I stuff a t-shirt into my bag.

"Sure." I rub my temple. I'm not. I'm terrified, but I just need to man up and face my fears. That's exactly the reason why I'm taking this trip. I'll drive home from Starwood with a few stops on the way. The trip that would typically take me no longer than five and a half hours will take about a week.

"Itinerary is sorted?"

"Yes."

"How many stops are you making again?"

"Just a few. It all depends." I grit my teeth. Talking about this does not help my nerves. At all.

"You'll be fine, Carter. You were born for this, and I'll see you on New Year's Eve." Grasshopper grins at me. "Stop stressing, you nutter. You'll be amazing. I've watched every single one of your videos. Hell, I recorded some. And you, Mr. Miyagi, you rock!"

She's right. I need to stop getting stressed about this. This is just the test run. If I can't do it? No biggie. I'll just need to figure out something else to do with my life. I might go back to fucking my way through college. Sighing, I hug her.

"Thanks, Grasshopper. You're right, I'll be fine. Now go and make us some popcorn." She walks out of the room, and I shout after her. "Two bags, please. I would actually like to eat some this time!"

When the credits roll, Grasshopper is asleep, breathing softly, her head resting on my shoulder. I turn my face to her hair and breathe in her strawberry scent. It still hurts, watching her relationship with Aiden blossom and having to keep my feelings to myself.

"Is she asleep?" Aiden whispers from the doorway. I nod, embarrassed, pretending I wasn't just sniffing his girlfriend's hair. "You okay, mate?" I nod again. He knows I'm not, but he's not going to press. What could he say to a guy who's fallen for his girl? "I'll take her home." He walks over and lifts Jenny up. Her arms wrap around his neck on instinct, and she nuzzles his throat. Jealousy eats me up inside. I want to be him so badly, to have that sort of connection with her...with someone.

It doesn't take a genius to notice that I haven't been myself this past year. I don't know if it was Jenny, Sydney, Katie, or the combination of the three. I feel like I've just been going through the motions, smiling and talking where appropriate, but not really feeling anything. Except when I'm writing, then my emotions pour out and things are more clear. But it leaves me drained and in a zombie-like state. The whole process is a vicious circle.

I stand up and walk Aiden to the door, watching him put Jenny gently into the passenger seat and clip the seatbelt in. After his car accident last year, he became a stickler for rules, never going past the speed limit, always making sure everyone was buckled in. I don't blame him. I wave him off and walk back to the living room to tidy up, then to my bedroom. My phone is on my nightstand and, like every night, I battle with myself. I want to scroll through my contacts and call one of my sure things to end this miserable dry spell. But, like every night, I don't. It's not about fucking anymore. I'm missing that *something, that spark, that magic.* As much as it sucks, I want to find it.

I grab my phone and walk over to the bathroom to brush my teeth when I see a message notification.

Hayley: *Friend emergency. I have a huuuge favor. Please say yes.*

Me: *The answer is maybe. What's up, cutie?*

Hayley: *Friends' car broke down and they need a ride to LA. Can you please, please help?*

I hesitate. This trip was meant to be soul searching, in part. I don't know if I want a tag along.

Hayley: *They're quiet as a mouse, you won't even notice they're there.*

Hayley: *Pleeeeaaaase. I'll owe you big time.*

I sigh. Fuck it.

Me: *Tell them to be at mine at 10 am. If they're late, I'm leaving by myself.*

Hayley: *OMG thank you! You're the best! I shall be forever grateful.*

I get into bed, take a snap, and post it on my Instagram, wishing my followers a good night.

I close my eyes and take a deep breath. I hope I won't regret this.

Chapter 2

Greyhound It Is

Sydney

I can't believe this is happening to me!

Thanks, life. Throw some more shit my way, why don't you?

I suppose I should have seen it coming, having bought this piece of crap car for five hundred dollars from a sleazy looking dude in downtown San Francisco. I just really wanted to do this drive. Something about an American road trip spoke to me. It excited me, the prospect of driving the short route and making it a bit of a journey, stopping at different locations, experiencing the rural side of California. It was a brilliant idea. *'You'll find yourself, Sydney'*, I told myself. *'You'll find some inspiration'*.

Now, I was five hundred dollars out of pocket with no way of getting back to LA since all the flights were either full or their prices were astronomical. Serves me right for having a bright idea. You probably think this isn't a big deal, Sydney. *Just call your family*, you'd say. Impossible. I don't even know where my mum is. She only calls if she needs something from me. And my dad? The only thing I know about him is the city he screwed my mother in. The city I'm named after. Needless to say, family values were not on the priority list when I was growing up. Having my mother remember to buy food and school books was.

From early on, I learned to take care of myself. Not to rely on anyone else. It's my motto. *'The only person you can count on is yourself'*.

Well, *myself* just royally screwed me over.

I thought I had it all figured out. After graduating from University early, I came to America—like Eddie Murphy, full of hope and excitement. Although my reason was for a modeling gig and not to find a suitable wife. The jobs kept coming, so I stayed in LA on a working visa.

How did I end up in Starwood? My latest shoot was in San Francisco, a short drive from Starwood, where one of my close friends from the industry lives. I came to visit her for the weekend to have a mini, pre-Christmas celebration. Neither one of us spent Christmas with family, so we adopted each other, a tradition which started last year.

"Have you called a tow truck?" Hayley asks while I stare at the engine under the hood of the rusty Honda I purchased, hoping that it'll speak to me. Explain what the hell is going on.

"Ugh, no." I throw my hands up in the air. "It's going to be at least another hundred bucks, and then God knows how much they will want to get it fixed."

Hayley looks over my shoulder at the engine, cocking her head to the side. "I don't know what else to suggest," she says. "We tried jump-starting the thing, checked the fluid, oil... This is where my car knowledge ends, I'm afraid."

"Right? Do you think it would be better to just scrap it?" I huff, covering my face with my hands.

"Uhmm, maybe." Seriously, just my luck. I'll have to take a nine-hour Greyhound bus just to get back home, at this rate. "Although..." Hayley's finger touches her chin. "One of my study buddies is doing engineering, he might have some friends. I can ask around and see if anyone could help?"

"You think they could have it ready by tomorrow?" Hope sparks in me.

Hayley laughs. "God, no! They're not actual mechanics, just a bunch of car-obsessed engineers. It's better than scrapping it, though, isn't it?" I nod, and Hayley walks away to make phone calls.

It is definitely better than getting rid of the car altogether. Years of scraping by on little food and wearing clothes that never quite fit and were always a bit too old made me into a bit of a tight arse. As in, if I can help it, I'll barter for it. If I can avoid spending money on something, you bet your sweet arse I will. Hence, I've only just bought a car. Yes, I've been using buses to travel around LA. Yes, I'm crazy. But also, I kinda love it. There's nothing better than sitting on a bus people-watching, imagining the sort of lives they led or the problems they might have. It's my favourite game, actually.

"I've got good news and bad news," Hayley says, walking back. I really don't want to hear any more bad news, but I look at her expectantly, waiting for her to elaborate. "One of my friends loves fixing cars, is good at it, and he's up for the challenge." A big smile spreads across my face. "But, he won't be back until just after Christmas." My smile drops. Fuck. Greyhound it is.

"No worries, I'll just take the bus back."

"Here's the thing, a friend of mine is already going to LA in a car. Actually doing a road trip of sorts, stopping at different locations and staying places overnight. A sort of *'find yourself'* trip, but also going to open mic nights to sing..." I look up at her. This is exactly what I had in mind, minus the singing. I can't sing for shit! "And I may have asked if you could tag along," she smiles.

"And?" I close the hood of the Honda and turn to fully face her. I'm not getting ahead of myself, but the excitement is growing.

"The answer is yes!" Holy fucking Christmas spirit and a Hallelujah! I squeal and jump up. Something is finally going right! "You'll need to be there at ten in the morning tomorrow ready to leave."

"I fucking love you, Hayls." I give her a hug. "But what about the car?" I kick the tire for good measure.

"You can leave it in the parking lot for the time being. Then, once it's fixed, I'll drive down to see you," she grins.

"Jesus Christ, woman! No, sorry, you're not Jesus Christ. You're a Mother Teresa. Who made you this awesome? I want a name and address so I can write a thank you note."

Hayley laughs and pulls me by my hand towards the dorms. "Come on crazy, let's get to bed. It's late and you have to be up early tomorrow for your road trip."

"*Say you're leaving on a seven thirty train and that you're heading out to Hollywood... I go crazy, crazy baby, I go crazy!*" I sing at the top of my lungs. Hayley jumps to me and covers my mouth, laughing as we walk inside.

The road trip is on. I can't wait. And if this girl I'm going with is even half as awesome as Hayley, I'll have a blast.

Chapter 3

Jeepak Chopra

Carter

It's five to ten, and the asshole is still not here. My bags are in the trunk, snacks and drinks are all laid out for the first leg of the journey, and my 2003 Jeep Cherokee is warmed up. I know, I know. *Carter? What's going on with the car choice? Where's the Tesla, the Audi, or at least the BMW?* Chill out. Jeepak Chopra was my first car. I bought it myself, with my hard earned, grass cutting money. Have you ever tried to cut two acres of grass? I *Can't Buy Me Loved* the shit out of that gig. Dad paid well too, so it only took one summer for me to earn enough. But I still value my girl above all others. I'll always have love for her. Love and respect. That's why she was the only car I could think of when deciding on this road trip. She was it, the one who'd always been there for me. And she was going to be there for me again. I had my music queued up on my phone, a general idea of where I wanted to go, and I was ready.

Now, if this dude could hurry up, I'd be forever grateful.

Me: *Is he still coming?*

I text Hayley, then look up. A gorgeous blonde is walking my way, her eyes glued to my house. I can't look away. The way she moves, it's like she belongs in a movie. You know, the one where a woman walks by and all the guys turn their heads? Her long, blonde hair is down, moving with each step. She's wearing ripped blue skinny jeans, a white tee, and a black leather jacket. On her feet, she's got a pair of Timberlands. Even with those, she's tall, with legs for days. Her gait is fast and, as she gets near, I can see her eyes framed by long, dark lashes and brows currently scrunched up in concentration. Her lips are full and plump, ones you'd only dream of but are never a reality. It clicks then. I have dreamt of those lips; I have kissed those lips. I know her.

"Sunshine?" I hesitate, stepping away from Jeepak. She tears her gaze off my house and looks at me; her face pales. "Sydney." My smile grows. Devil knows why she's dropping into my arms after a year of silence, but I'm not letting her go without an explanation. "It is you!"

"Hey," she sighs, looking around. "I'm really sorry but I'm in a hurry."

Oh no, she doesn't. "Where're you going, beautiful?"

"I'm meeting someone." My face falls. Of course she is. The phone buzzes in my hand.

"A boyfriend?" I ask, not sure where the question is coming from.

"What? No!" Her cheeks flush. I smile, teeth and all. "I'm catching a ride down to LA," she says. It's then I notice the large backpack. She fiddles with one of the straps, looking around, her gaze landing on my front door again. A thought crosses my brain. I look at Sydney, then back down to my phone. A text message is waiting for me. I tap the screen.

Hayley: *omg, he's a she! And she should be there already! Her name is Sydney. You met her last year when we* *bumped into you at Christmas, remember? I'll text her and see where she's at.*

"Sydney," I say, my voice wavering. Her phone buzzes. I look up at her as she pulls it out and reads the message, her face draining of all color. "I think you're catching that ride with me."

"But," she starts. "But, you're a guy."

I grin and wink. "You bet your sweet ass I am. A full-blooded male. With a large appendage to prove it, should you need convincing." I waggle my brows at her while she rolls her eyes at me.

"What I meant was that I thought I was catching a ride with another girl." Sydney crosses her arms and takes a few steps toward me. "And you're right, I've already seen it. Not much to write home about. In fact, from what I remember, I fell asleep, so couldn't have been all that exciting either," she says, straight-faced. Her jaw ticks, though, and I know the little vixen is playing me. This is going to be fun.

I take her arm and gently turn us, pressing her against my car. She's tall enough that I don't need to bend down much to face her. She inhales sharply when my lips touch her ear.

"Oh, sunshine, I can assure you it's exciting. If you want, I can show you, and this time you definitely won't do any sleeping," I whisper, inhaling the fresh coconut scent of her hair. Sydney shivers.

"No, thanks." Her voice is strong and clear. If I couldn't feel the sharp rise and fall of her chest, I'd think she was unaffected. But I can. So I'm not buying it. "Been there, tried to do it, got the t-shirt. I'm good."

"Ah well," I push off, smiling. "Was worth a try. You ready? I'm on a schedule." I open the car door and slide in.

"Jerk. I'm going to kill her," I hear her murmur as I shut the door. Yup, this is definitely going to be fun.

Sydney is one pissed off bunny. I can tell by the way she forcefully closed the trunk after stuffing her backpack in there, and by the way she slammed the car door once she finally got in the passenger seat. It wasn't fast either. She paced outside for at least five minutes, throwing her hands up now and then, huffing and muttering to herself. She gave up in the end, and after a few minutes of furious typing on her phone, the spectacle was finally over. That's when she decided to take it out on Jeepak and manhandle my poor girl. Like the good host my mother raised me to be, I did not say a thing. I just let her get on with her little breakdown, set the music to '*Only Real*', and waited patiently, tapping my finger on the steering wheel.

"I'm sorry," she says, then bumps the back of her head against the headrest. "I just wasn't expecting it to be you. It threw me for a bit of a loop, I suppose. I shouldn't take it out on you though, you're being kind enough to let me tag along."

"No worries." Like a gentleman, I brush it off then pull out of the driveway. "I wasn't exactly expecting you, either. I thought you were a guy." She snorts with laughter.

"I'm starting to think Hayley did this on purpose. Do you think she has enough knowledge to break a car?"

"What?" I laugh.

"My car, the reason I'm tagging along. I bought a car a few days ago and it just died on me last night," she exhales.

"Did you take it back to the dealership to see if they can

help?"

"Ah. Not quite. I didn't buy it at a dealership. I saw a bargain and just went for it."

"Just how much of a bargain are we talking about?"

"Five hundred dollars." Her lips lift in a weary smile. "The one time in my life I was spontaneous..." she trails off. "Well, the second time." I barely hear the second part of the sentence. But I do, and I fight the smile. I think she's talking about the time we met.

"There's your answer. I really don't think a five hundred dollar car would need to be tampered with much in order to die a disgraceful death."

"Yeah, I figured. It's just hard to believe that all this would be a coincidence, I guess." She looks out of the window, deep in thought. "Oh well, never mind. Let's make the best out of this. Hayley said you were planning a bit of a road trip, just like me?"

"I sure was. Wanted to spend some time on my own, do some reflecting—"

"Ah, shit. I'm sorry," she interrupts me. "I totally shat all over that plan, didn't I?"

"Nah, it's all good. It might be nice to have a friend along the way. I need some entertainment, snacks, and music can only take you so far."

"Blasphemy!" she exclaims. "Snacks and music are life! What world would we live in without them?"

"A sad, sad world," I confirm.

"Exactly. So now that we've got that sorted..." She shifts her weight and angles her body toward me. "Where are we going first?"

"Well, Sunshine"—I flash her a smile—"our first stop is the mountains. I hope you've got some warm clothes with you, cause we're going snowboarding."

Chapter 4

Road Tripping

Sydney

Hayley stitched me up, no doubt about it.

Well, to be fair, she didn't say whether I was meant to travel with a guy or a girl. I just assumed it was going to be a girl. But to put me in an enclosed space with Carter? The guy I lost my mind for last year, basically jumped his bones but then was too drunk to actually have sex with? So embarrassing!

I had to sneak out at the arse crack of dawn with a raging headache and properly smudged makeup. Thank goodness I was already packed! All I had to do was check out then get to the airport and wait for eight hours until my flight left. Classic Syd flight mechanism. Thankfully, I was going back to London and didn't have to face him. And, once I got back, I hoped he would have forgotten that English weirdo who fell asleep on him mid-sex. I mean, who does that? Apparently, I do.

And now we're going snowboarding. The guy wants me dead. Obviously, he's holding a grudge and the only way he can exact revenge is by pushing me down a mountain strapped to a piece of wood. Goodbye dreams of making something of myself. Goodbye life. At least I won't have to fix my car.

We're only twenty minutes in, and I can already tell this road trip will be nothing like what I imagined. No relaxation, no finding yourself; instead, trying to survive Carter is the new theme.

As I fiddle with the stereo of his Jeep, Carter's hand shoots out, and he grabs my hand, putting it down and holding it hostage. An electric current runs through my arm as his skin touches mine.

"What do you think you're doing?" he says, still holding my hand down. "Jeepak does not need any more manhandling." Jeepak? Who the hell is Jeepak?

"Sorry," I mutter. I was only going to check out his music.

"She's a delicate girl and you need to treat her as such." Jesus Christ, he's talking about the car, isn't he?

"Your car is a she?" He nods. "And you named it Jeepak?"

"*Her*. Named *her*. And yes, her name is Jeepak Chopra," Carter replies, his damn hand still on mine. I try to wriggle it out to no avail. He just tightens his grip.

"I'm not even going to ask..."

"Rightly so. You should never question genius."

This guy. I shake my head, trying not to laugh.

"Right... So, snowboarding? Really?" I change the topic to what's been on my mind.

"Yes, sunshine. Snowboarding." Should I tell him I have no clue how to snowboard or ski? London isn't exactly the best place to learn that when you barely scrape by and your only goal is to get out of your mum's and her flavour of the month's way. It taught me to take care of myself, though, and that the only person I can rely on is me. Had my first job at twelve, mopping the floors of a chippy shop. I lied through my teeth about my age to get that gig. But it came with free food and drink and a place to do my homework when our flat was otherwise occupied. The fact that I smelled like fried food didn't deter me, even though I'd get called names at school. *Sydney Buyer is a Fryer* was one of the gems they came up with. Seriously. Those idiots will be in charge one day. Makes you sad for the country.

As time went by, my boobs developed and I got taller and taller still. Must have been after my sperm donor father because my mother was vertically challenged. I spent most of my free time at the chip shop, doing any job I could. It was better than being at home where the stares from male visitors morphed from uninterested to curious. I did not want those arseholes curious. So I avoided home like the plague, sneaking in when I knew everyone was passed out and tip-toeing out before they woke up.

Somehow, I was still making it to school on time, getting my homework done, and getting good grades. But it wasn't until I turned sixteen that my life changed. By sheer luck, the editor of a fashion magazine was out with some friends, and one of them had a hankering for a chicken burger with chips, which led them to where I was. It was a weird encounter. I had no clue who they were, so the looks they kept giving me really creeped me out. I was glad when they left, exhaling breaths I didn't know I was holding practically the whole time they were there. One of them came back the next day, though; a lady close to my mother's age. She ordered water then just left. And the next day, she came back with a man. This time, after speaking in hushed voices for ten minutes, they turned to me and walked towards the counter I was standing behind. The hair at the nape of my neck stood on end as the woman began to speak. She told me her name was Ines Bergman and that she was an Editor-in-Chief for one of the world's most popular fashion magazines. The guy next to her was called Francois, and he was the Creative Director. And I? I was their next cover.

I didn't think I was anything special. At sixteen, I was too tall, too long, and too skinny; at least, according to my peers. My clothes never fit me, always too short or just a bit too tattered. My hair, although naturally blonde, felt dull and matted. But that day, Ines and Francois made me believe I was not just another scruffy kid from Hackney. They made me believe I could be something, something other than an afterthought for my mother. Since I was no longer a minor, things started falling into place. And before I knew it, I had a career; a career that paid enough for me to be able to move into shared accommodation, finish sixth form, and save up enough money to go to University. My shitty childhood was all in the past.

Carter pulls into a parking lot, breaking me out of my thoughts. We are not in the mountains. At least I don't think so, since I don't see any in front of me. It's one in the afternoon, so we've been on the road for just under three hours. Maybe he just wants to stretch his legs?

"Pit stop number one!" Carter grins, looking at me. His eyes crinkle at the sides, the afternoon sun shining behind him. He looks so damned handsome. I can't help but stare. I remember I thought he was beautiful when we met. There was this magnetic force between us that kept pulling me closer to him. If circumstances were different, maybe we'd be together. Maybe. But I did not want a relationship then, nor do I want one now. I don't need anyone else. It's the Syd show; always has been. And from what I remember, he didn't want a relationship either. In fact, wasn't he in love with his best friend? I'm pretty sure that was the case. Love is messy, and I just don't need that type of mess in my life.

"Need the toilet?" I ask. I'm not gonna lie, I wouldn't mind getting some fresh air and some space from the hot devil next to me. I open the door to the car and he follows suit. It's freezing, my jacket not doing anything to keep me warm. But Carter is one step ahead. He pulls a big puffy jacket out of the trunk and proceeds to dress me into it.

"Sydney. Sydney, Sydney, Sydney. You've yet to learn so much about the ways of the world. There's no such a thing as road tripping without stopping for some of the best attractions America has to offer. The land of beauty and freedom and...caves. We're going into a cave," he says, bopping my nose.

"Whoa, whoa, whoa." I fist his shirt, my hand coming into contact with a firm pec. "A cave?" I do not like dark and enclosed spaces; it's not my thing.

"Don't worry, Sunshine. I'll be right there with you, holding your hand if you need me to." The smile he gives me has me relaxing a little.

"I don't know about this." I hesitate.

Carter's eyes light up. "I swear you won't regret this. It's supposed to be amazing inside. The stalactites and the drapery calcites are out of this world." I try to contain my giggle, but Carter's nerd just came out and, honestly, it's super sexy. If he had dark rimmed glasses on, I could not be held responsible for my actions. I'd probably jump him again.

"All right," I agree, wanting to see some more of this sexy nerd he's been hiding. I still have a bad feeling about this, though.

The cave is damp and thankfully large, the air warmer here than on the outside. Light seeps through the entrance, illuminating the red clay surrounding us. It's actually quite beautiful. The formations on the ceiling look like red seaweed floating in the air upside down. Carter grabs my hand and pulls me towards the metal staircase. Reluctantly, I follow him deeper into the cavern.

"This cave is made of limestone," he says as we descend. The natural light is gone now, and there are a few lamps scattered around, casting artificial light. My chest gets tighter and breathing gets harder. "The formations on the ceiling are stalactites. Do you see the water that drips off them? That basically means that the cavern is active." He leads me through a tight passage. My steps are rigid as the light disappears behind me. I can't breathe. I'm trying to move, get out of the enclosed space, but my body is suddenly consumed with violent shakes.

"Mummy, please, no!" I cry as she slams the door to the small cabinet in the kitchen and locks me inside. "I'll be good, I promise."

"Little whore," she spits out. "Where did you get that chocolate bar from?"

"Mummy, please, please don't lock me in!" I cry again.

"Where?" she shouts. "Did Julian give it to you? What did you do? Did you promise to suck him off?" Julian is mum's current boyfriend, and I try to avoid him. His stares make me uncomfortable.

"No mummy, I swear!" I plead. She kicks the door to the cabinet, making me cry out. I know what 'sucking off' means only because I hear her talk to her boyfriends. Julian is

particularly vocal about what exactly he likes her to do to him.

"Look at you, eleven years old and already prostituting yourself. You're a disgrace! I should have gotten rid of you when I had a chance. Should have known you'd be nothing but an arse ache and a disappointment." Her voice is getting distant.

"Mummy, please don't leave me in here!" I shout as tears run down my cheeks.

"You'll stay there as long as I see fit." My tears are choking me, and I struggle to breathe. I'm scared, so scared. This isn't the first time this happened and it won't be the last. At least I no longer soil myself from fear. But the fear is still there.

"Please," I mumble. "Please, please, please..."

"Think about what you've done, Sydney!" she shouts from another room. "Sydney!"

"Sydney?" The voice is distant and strange. "Sydney, baby, answer me! Please, Sunshine. Sydney." I'm still shaking, but the fear is no longer crippling. "You're okay. I'm here." I'm being rocked gently back and forth. Back and forth. The motion soothing me. My face is pressed against a hard chest, and my trembling fingers are gripping onto a shirt. I inhale the unmistakable scent of Carter. His cologne makes my knees weak, so it's probably best that I'm in his lap. He strokes my hair, murmuring that everything is okay, slowly calming me down. As the adrenaline leaves my system, I start to notice things. Like the fact that my face is wet, as is Carter's black t-shirt; the fact that I'm in his lap surrounded by his strong arms; and, for the first time in my life, I feel safe. Not scared or trapped. "I'll get you out of here,

Sunshine," he whispers. Then, in one swift motion, he gets up with me still cradled in his arms.

There's no chance I'm letting go until we're out of this hellhole. But Carter doesn't insist on it; in fact, his grip on me tightens as he walks us out of the first cave, through the narrow passage, and then up the stairs to the main cavern until we're outside and I can feel the sun on my face.

He opens the car door and sits us in the back seat, me still in his lap.

"Are you okay?" He sounds concerned. I open my eyes and look up from his chest into his golden brown eyes. I probably look like I just went through a tornado, eyes puffy, snot running down, but that doesn't stop the magnetic force the instant our eyes connect. His fingers connect with my cheek and he strokes it gently as his other arm tightens around me. A car honks in the distance and I look away, the spell broken.

"I think so... I'm sorry."

"Don't be silly. You have nothing to be sorry about. I should have listened to you when you said you didn't want to go in." He shakes his head.

"To be fair, I didn't realise my deep-rooted childhood memories would rear their ugly head," I try to make light of the situation.

"I heard you call your mom..." he trails off.

"Yeah, well, she was never very maternal," I sigh. "Let's not talk about it... please."

He nods. "One day, Sunshine. You're going to tell me everything, okay?" I try to scoff, but something in his voice stops me. I don't know him very well, but I have this feeling, deep in my gut, that I can trust him. That I want to trust him. I nod reluctantly. "Good, now let's forget about the caves and just go straight to Bijou."

Chapter 5

She's Shy

Carter

"This is incredible." Sydney's eyes widen as we get out of the car. It's late afternoon and the sun's begun to set, bathing the lake and mountains in pink and orange hues, making it *look* iridescent. I inhale the crisp winter air and reach for our bags in the back of the car. I love winter and everything associated with it. Christmas, cold dark days, snow. When I decided on doing this trip, there was no question about veering off course to go to the mountains and getting some one-on-one time with my board and the powder. But that's tomorrow. Tonight, I've got an open mic to attend. I grab my guitar case and sling it over my shoulder. With our bags in one hand, I lock the car and pull out my phone. Opening Instagram, I start recording a story.

"Hey there, California!" I grin at my phone. "So, we've arrived in South Lake Tahoe, and it looks amazing out here." I do a three-sixty to show the view. "We're going to head to our apartment, but we'll see you tonight at Whiskey Dick's, and tomorrow night, we'll be in Nevada. Don't worry, only a mile or so away." I wink at the camera. "Don't forget to tune in later on! I'm going to try and rope in my travel buddy, Sydney, into doing a live. Say hello, Sydney!" I turn to show her on camera, but just as she comes into view, she ducks behind Jeepak. "Oh well, she's shy." I smile. "Anyways, I'll see you all later! And remember, Edward never goes green!" I shout and post to my stories.

"Who's Edward?" Sydney catches up behind me.

"A loaf of bread."

"Huh?" Her confused expression has me doubling over in laughter.

I wipe the tears away. "About two years ago, my buddy found a loaf of bread in his kitchen in a house that hadn't been lived in for years, so the loaf was old. Like ooold-old. We started betting on when it was going to go green, moldy. Before we knew it, the whole campus was invested, and now, it's all over Insta too. People love it."

"Why Edward?" she asks as we walk up the stairs to the apartment we will be staying at for the next couple of nights.

"The bread that never dies." I shrug. "Edward, like in Twilight, cause it's immortal."

She snorts. "Do you name everything?"

"Most things." I smile and open the door. I drop our bags and turn around. "Home, sweet home." The smile on my face drops as soon as I look at Sydney. Her face is ashen. "Are you okay?" I rush to her. "Is it another panic attack? I know it's small, but it's not *that* small."

She cracks a smile. "That's what he said."

"What's wrong, Sunshine?" I step to her, lifting my hand to stroke her cheek but stopping myself at the last minute. That's too forward, isn't it? I might have seen her naked once—more if you count my fantasies—but we barely know each other.

Sydney sighs. "There's only one bed." I slowly turn

around and look at the apartment. It's more of a large hotel room with a couple of chairs, a desk, a wardrobe, and a kitchenette. In the middle, there's one Queen size bed.

"So? It's not like we haven't slept in the same bed before. No big deal," I retort.

"No big deal," she says in a small voice before moving past me and locking herself in the bathroom. I will never get women.

When we finally unpack and get ourselves together, we have just enough time to grab a bite to eat before I'm due at Whiskey Dick's. The temperature dropped below forty after the sun went down, so Sydney commandeered my spare jacket. I don't mind. She looks damned cute in it. And as we walk down the Boulevard, she inches closer to me, explaining that she's freezing, so I wrap my arm around her to keep her warm. Before long, we find our destination: a small pizza place.

"You want to share a big one?" I ask, checking over the menu once we sit down at the table, my guitar leaning on the wall next to me.

"Uhmmm, I would, but..." she trails off, scrunching her nose. What? She can't even share a pizza with me? "I don't eat meat." Well, I wasn't expecting that. "I used to work at this chicken shop and, ugh, I don't know, it just turned me off meat for life."

"Do you eat cheese? Eggs? Dairy?" She shakes her head at each. Well then, pizza might not have been the best idea.

"It's okay, really. You just order what you want and I'll have some fries and maybe some garlic bread or something."

Oh, hell no! She's barely eaten all day and now all that checking of the labels on all the snacks makes total sense. She wasn't looking at calories, but at ingredients, making sure she could eat them.

"Hiya, Sugar," I smile at the waitress when she comes over to our table. For some reason, my accent decided I'm from the South, but I just go with it. "We have an unusual hankerin'. Would you mind fixin' us a large pie and loading it with just the sauce and all the veggies you have? No cheese and no meat."

"No problem, hon. And to drink?"

I look at Sydney. "Are we allowed beer?" I raise my eyebrow. She nods, trying to contain her laughter. "Two beers, sugar."

"Anything else?" Sydney shakes her head, covering her mouth.

"We're finer than a frog hair split four ways." The waitress doesn't blink, just nods and walks away.

Sydney bursts out laughing. "What the hell are you—"

"Hush now, you're louder than a one-legged rooster at dawn."

"I-I, I can't," she gasps out then beats her palm on the table, laughing so hard tears start streaming down her face. I grin and join in.

"It just happened," I say. "I couldn't stop it. Once I'm in the zone, the zone takes over."

"Oh my God, Carter. I love you!" She laughs. My heart stops and my chest constricts. I know she's joking. Even so, it just feels... My heart starts up again and I shake myself out of the confusion, pretending like nothing out of the ordinary just happened.

We laugh some more and, soon, our pizza arrives. I take a photo to post it on my feed then add a caption that I've decided to go vegan for the time being. Time being the next 15 minutes, or however long it will take me to get my hands on some bacon. But honestly, if it makes Sydney more comfortable, I really don't mind not eating meat when I'm with her. Not that she'd ever ask me to do it.

As we eat, Sydney tells me about some of the weirder outfits she's had to wear on her photoshoots, and I guffaw when she talks about having to wear a full-on bear costume for an animal rights campaign.

"Are all shoots like that?" I ask.

"No." Her face grows serious and her jaw tightens. She takes a drink of water just as our waitress comes over with a check.

"How was that for you?" she asks.

"S'wonderful, I'm full as a tick now!" I exclaim. Sydney spits her water all over me.

"I'm so sorry," she laughs, mirth in her eyes. "Went down the wrong tube." She punches her chest.

I drop two twenty dollar bills on the table and grab my guitar, my shirt soaked, but I can't be mad. For some odd reason, making Sydney laugh feels really good.

"How much do I owe you for the pizza?" she asks, putting on my jacket.

"Don't worry, Sunshine, this one is on me." I grab her hand and we make our way outside. "There is one thing you can do to pay me back." She stiffens. "Get your mind out of the gutter, woman! I'll pay for all our food on this trip if you'll be my cameraman. Much of my fanbase is online, and that's how I spread the word. The gospel of Carter Kennedy. Anywho, record my open mics, stream stuff live, take cute photos of me, and we'll be even."

"Sounds good," Sydney agrees. "We can work out the details later, but I'm paying half for accommodations."

"Sorry, doll, no can do. All the accommodations are free. Friends, family, and fans are letting me stay at their places."

"Seriously?" I nod. "Huh, what about petrol?"

I roll my eyes. "If you must pay for something, you can pay for road snacks. I wouldn't know what to get for you, so you can buy the lot."

"Thanks, that's really sweet." She blushes. "Alright, it's a deal."

"Yaay! I always wanted to have my own crew. It'll be like our very own Real Housewives, except less drama. No, wait! Let's have more drama!" Sydney fights a smile, so I pick her up and spin us around. With her arms locked behind my neck, she throws her head back in a laugh. "Thanks, Sunshine," I say as I slide her down my body, placing her back on the ground. Her arms stay around my neck, and her blue eyes focus on mine. "It's a tremendous help. I really mean it," I breathe. Her proximity makes my body hum with electricity despite the many layers between us. She exhales, the air forming a frosty cloud between us as our breaths mingle. As if pulled by force, I lean toward her. Closer, closer, and closer still. My lips are mere inches from hers.

"We shouldn't do this," she whispers.

"We definitely shouldn't," I agree as her arms tighten around me. My lips almost touch hers.

"Get a room!" Someone shouts behind us, and a group of people starts laughing. Sydney snorts, and I swear to God, that snort is one of the sexiest sounds on earth. Or at least my dick thinks so. I smile and step away from her warm embrace, instantly feeling the chill. I grab Sydney's hand, and we run the two blocks to the bar.

Chapter 6

Down, Syd!

Sydney

This motherfucker is going to kill me. It hasn't even been a full day and he already makes me want to throw all caution to the wind. *Down, Syd,* I keep telling myself. *Keep it in your pants, Syd. Remember, it's you against the world.* Well, my brain might be listening, but my vagina has other ideas. Every time Carter smiles or winks at me, I get fanny flutters. I had to resort to constantly looking at my shoes for fear of jumping on his arse and mauling him.

And don't even get me started on him with a guitar in his arms. All he did was whip it out, and my ovaries sang 'Hallelujah'. Imagine the tune they were singing when he started tuning the damned thing.

'WAP', they were singing 'WAP'... They apparently have a thing for guitars.

The dude hasn't even started singing yet! It certainly doesn't help that my dry spell never got broken. That night with Carter was the most action I got in two years. I still remember how his lips felt on mine, how his touch ignited my skin, and how incredible his cock felt in my hand. *Down, Syd!*

I'll never forgive myself for falling asleep on him because, although we were both seriously drunk and sloppy, it somehow felt really right, like he knew exactly what to do at each moment. He played me like a guitar, strumming the right chords at the right time, making my body sing along the way. And now? Now he's walking up onto the stage, a single chair and a mic in the middle. I check my phone and press record on a live stream. Just before he went on stage, Carter downloaded the app on my phone then logged himself in so that I could be his 'social media manager', as he put it. Now, I have access to his DMs from all the women propositioning him. Splendid. Just what a girl wants to know when she's got the hots for a guy. That she's one *of* a million.

Carter clears his throat and sits down on the chair, placing his guitar on his lap. He looks pale, his eyes searching the bar's audience until they stop on me. I wave, and he smiles, taking a big breath.

"Good evening South Lake Tahoe." The voice that comes through the speakers is clear, confident, and has a rasp to it. Carter's gaze is still on me as he goes through his introduction. His soulful voice hypnotises me where I stand, and he hasn't even started singing yet. It took everything in me to get out of the haze. I barely manage to catch the last bit of his speech. "This song is to all the guys that had their hearts broken. We've got it." He strums the first chords, and I instantly recognise 'Baby Jane'. His voice is perfect, and I find myself singing along to his slow version of this classic. When he gets to the chorus, I'm entranced. This guy belongs on the stage singing to millions of people. He is beyond talented—just another reason as to why we could never work.

"When I fall in love next time, I know," he sings, his eyes never leaving mine. "It's gonna last forever." I'm barely breathing. It's like he's singing to me, but surely it's only because he's looking at me. With a strength I didn't know I possessed, I tear my eyes away from his and look at the phone, making sure I'm getting all of this. The bar is silent, all conversations on pause as Carter holds the audience captive. *One of a million*, I remind myself and exhale. I'm a nobody and this guy is going places. Places I don't want to go. No matter how attractive I find him, our goals are different. He wants to sing and be famous. I want to just...be. Away from the limelight. I cannot afford another Darius in my life.

Carter sings a couple more covers, the audience eating right out of his hand. When the next song stops, he doesn't start a new one. Instead, he leans over to the mic and, in his raspy voice, he says, "How about an original?" The bar explodes in excitement, making Carter laugh. "Okay." He smiles. "This one is called 'It'll Never Be Me'. I wrote it about a year ago. Let me know what you think." He leans back and starts strumming his guitar. A haunting melody fills the air and, as he opens his mouth and starts singing, his voice is sad and full of emotion. "You say nothing's changed, but in my heart, I know it'll never be the same," he starts as my heart beats out of my chest. "My hands in my pockets, I can't reach out, can't touch your face." His eyes are still on me, but with the next verse, he closes them. "You know that I, all I want, is you to be happy. And if that means that it'll never be me, so be it." My heart breaks at the pain I hear in his voice, and I know. I just know this song is about his best friend. The one he told me he was in love with. And if the ache in his voice is anything to go by—still is. Fuck me.

As the song reaches its crescendo, he whispers in a broken voice, "It'll never be me." I can feel tears streaming down my face, not quite sure if it's because of the emotion in the song or because I just realised, I might have hoped he was over her.

"Oh my God, that felt incredible," Carter laughs as we walk out of Whiskey Dick's and make our way back to the apartment. "The adrenaline, the vibe... Sydney! God, Sydney! I feel like I'm on top of the world!"

"You were amazing," I laugh, despite the weird feeling in my chest.

"And you!" He turns on the spot and faces me, his warm hands cupping my cheeks. "You were astounding, Sydney." What? I mean, I held the phone up pretty steadily, but let's be honest, anyone could do *that*. "Sunshine, just when I was drowning, you threw me a lifeline, pulled me out of the depths. Anchored me." I blink, melting in his hands. Fucking musicians. They always have to spew poetry your way, making your brain turn to mush. "I was petrified, the stage fright taking over. Then I spotted you, and you waved at me, smiling. Fuck, Sunshine. Who knew? You were all I needed; my lucky charm." He leans forward and boy, oh boy, he's going to kiss me. Yes! Let's do this. Let's have another go at this one night stand business. I'm ready. And this time I've only had one beer, so no chance of me falling asleep. Unless he's really bad at sex, but that's impossible if the way my body responds to his touch is anything to go by.

And then he kisses me.

On my fucking forehead.

"Thank you," he murmurs, then lets go of my hand.

"No probs," I squeak, voice a bit too high. I clear my throat as we start walking again. "So that was really great, by the way. You're really good. Like really, really good." He rubs the back of his neck with one hand as the other reaches for mine. I've noticed Carter is very tactile, and, as someone who has been starved of loving touch from a young age, I can't complain. In fact, I love how openly warm and affectionate Carter is. "Oh, and the 'live' went really well. We had about twenty thousand people tune in. Lots of likes and comments." The comments were mostly about how amazing the show was, but there were quite a few on how hot Carter looked and some suggestions that if he's coming through their town he should give them a call. I decided not to go into details.

"That's awesome. I can't believe twenty thousand people would want to watch me."

"I can. You were great. It's like you belong on the stage," I say as we climb up the stairs to our apartment. Carter blushes, then opens the door. "I mean it, Carter." I grab his sleeve. "You were born for this."

"Thank you," he mumbles. "Hey, you want the bathroom first?" I snort at the unsubtle change of subject and nod. Shrugging off Carter's jacket, I walk over to my backpack and dig for something to sleep in, coming up empty.

"Uhmm, Carter." I bite my lip.

He turns to face me. "Hmm?"

"So, I may need to borrow a t-shirt to sleep in." I have a limited number of clothes with me, and if I'm honest, I sleep naked, so I haven't even thought to bring sleeping clothes with me, all my t-shirts are either very tight or very see-through. Consider me educated on road tripping etiquette. "I'll buy something to sleep in tomorrow, I swear. It's just for tonight."

Carter's lips spread into a smirk. "Don't be silly, I don't mind you sleeping in my stuff." He reaches into his bag, pulling out a t-shirt and throwing it my way. "Do you need boxer shorts too?" I bite my lip, considering, but before I even form a coherent thought, a pair of Calvin Klein's land on my face. I shake my head and walk to the bathroom, muttering thanks.

I quickly shower then towel off, loosely braiding my wet hair. Sleeping with wet hair is the last thing on my 'Things I love to do' list, but I have no clue if there's a hairdryer around here; plus, I don't want to take even more time. Face scrubbed and teeth brushed, I tentatively open the door.

The room is dark except for the light that streams in from behind me. Carter sits in one of the chairs in the corner, scrolling through his phone. His eyes lift and he stills.

"The bathroom is all yours," I say timidly. "Sorry if I took too long." I take a step toward where he's sitting, right next to my backpack. He stands up, rigid, and rushes past.

"It's fine." I hear before he slams the bathroom door. Okaaay.

I put my things away then look at the bed—no time like the present. I slide in under the covers, the sheets cool on my skin, and close my eyes as the sound of the shower coming from behind the bathroom door lulls me to sleep.

Chapter 7

Cutosaurus

The morning light gently wakes me up and, as I lie there on my back with Sydney still asleep next to me, her palm on my chest, I think back to last night. The open mic, how stage fright nearly won over me. How Sydney, with one look, one smile, grounded me. How she brought me calm and focus. The walk back to the apartment. How I almost kissed her but chickened out last minute and placed a kiss on her forehead instead. How she looked when she came back out of the bathroom, wearing my t-shirt and boxers. Her hair wet and face pink. How her dark lashes framed her big blue eyes. How she sucked in her bottom lip when I looked at her.

And when she spoke, her voice soft, it took all that I had in me not to just tackle her to the floor. Instead, I rudely walked past her then quietly jerked off in the shower. Not one of my finest moments.

Sydney's small hand tightens around my t-shirt. And she starts mumbling in her sleep. "No, please, no!" I stiffen. "I don't want to... You're hurting me..." I jerk up in shock, her fist still clenching my t-shirt, and pull her into my lap, shushing and rocking her. My thoughts instantly go to the darkest of places.

"Shhhh, baby. It's just a dream. Shhh." I stroke her hair. Her face is wet on my chest. And as she slowly wakes, she tenses up in my arms. "It's okay, Sunshine."

She relaxes, putting her face in her hands. "Oh God, you must think I'm such a spaz." I don't say anything. Instead, I just keep holding her. I need to know she's okay and safe. "It hasn't even been twenty-four hours, and it's the second time I've freaked out. I'm really sorry. You didn't sign up for a total psycho to join you on this trip. I swear I usually don't cry this much, or at all."

"Sydney," I start. She tries to get off my lap, but I hold her tighter. "It was a bad dream; you can't help that." She sighs. "Sunshine, I need you to be honest with me. You talked in your sleep, and what you were saying..."—my jaw starts ticking—"it sounded a lot like someone was forcing you to do something you didn't want to do. I need you to tell me, okay? Was it a nightmare or bad memories?" She doesn't speak, her silence breaking my heart in two. Her hand twitches just like it did after the cave incident when she was holding back. "Sydney, I know we haven't known each other long. I'm normally a happy go lucky kinda guy, don't take myself too seriously, and just let things slide. But baby, I need to know the truth because, if it was a bad memory, I need to find this fucker and I need to kill him."

She snorts.

I wasn't going for funny. I was absolutely serious. But I guess Sydney laughing is better than Sydney crying.

"Why do you call me Sunshine?" she changes the topic. "Is it my sunny personality?" A laugh escapes her. My lips lift into a small smile.

"The night we met," I say. "Your hair. I couldn't stop staring at it. It just made me think of the sun."

"So, what you're saying is that my hair is yellow?" She giggles.

I shake my head. "You know it's not. It's more giving me vacation vibes. Sunshine, beach, surfing. Hence the 'sunshine' nickname."

"I like it. Thank you. I've never had a cute nickname. Most of them weren't cute," she chuckles. "Unless you think that Fryer, Chippy-Whippy, or Gigantosaurus are cute."

"I don't even know where to start my questions."

"I used to work at a chip shop in London, hence the first two, and the last one because I was the first one to get a growth spurt in my year. One that didn't finish until I reached five-ten."

"For what it's worth," I say. "I like your height. And I think you're more of a Cutosaurus, but who am I to throw nicknames about? I only have a degree in nicknames and naming things." I place a small kiss on the top of her head.

"Thank you," she whispers.

"There's nothing you need to thank me for."

"There's so much..." she trails off.

"Will you tell me what the dream was about?" I ask. She takes a deep breath and nods almost imperceptibly.

"I guess working in the modeling industry isn't all glamour, amazing clothes, and parties. Well, some of it is... But some is assholes trying to take advantage of young girls. You'd think with the *#metoo* movement this would change, but it hasn't...much." I grip her tighter as she continues. "When you start modeling, it's like a different world, you know? Suddenly, you're thrust into designer clothes, doing photoshoots in beautiful places, catwalks in Milan, Paris, New York... You get swept up in it all and you don't question things. At least, not at the beginning. Yes, it might feel uncomfortable changing your clothes in front of the entire crew and their mothers, but all the girls are doing it, so it must be fine..." She takes a large breath. "There was this one photographer. I never worked with him alone, but he always gave me the creeps. His eyes would linger when I'd be changing. He'd touch me for just a little too long when positioning me, his hand slipping places it shouldn't be near. Pushing me out of my comfort zone when I'd say I didn't want to shoot nudes, then somehow, I'd wind up naked. The worst part was he'd say these sleazy things like 'don't worry, these are not going to be published', you know? Why the hell would he take them then?"

"Sick bastard," I mutter.

"Yeah... So about two years ago, I was doing fashion week in Milan and Darius—that's his name—showed up out of the blue. He kept following me everywhere, saying he had a shoot in the area, that he kept bumping into me by coincidence so it must be fate. It felt really off. So I told him to get lost and I guess he didn't like that. He followed me back to the hotel and tried to attack me." I can't breathe. "He...he pushed me around and tried to assault me, but one of the other guests must have heard me fight back, or scream, or maybe they saw him barge into my room because someone called security and they got in just in time."

"Sydney," I exhale. "I'm so sorry. This should have never happened to you. Assholes like that should not exist."

"I know. But I was okay. I got a restraining order against him and he got a slap on the wrist. I suppose that happens when you're a well known photographer and tell everyone that the girl you tried to assault was the one coming onto you and that it wasn't an assault at all. I didn't fight it. I stopped doing catwalks for fear of him finding out the lineup and finding me again. I make sure I never have shoots with him and just stay away. Life goes on. I guess yesterday's panic attack brought on some emotions, and that caused my nightmare. I'm sorry."

"Sydney, you've got nothing to be sorry about!" I exclaim. "You did nothing wrong, and I can't believe that bastard is still running loose. If I ever see him, I swear to God, I will hurt him."

She lifts her head off my chest and looks at me, cracking a smile. "Deal. Now I'm going to go brush my teeth and get ready."

I rub my thumb against her cheek and nod. "Wear something warm and breathable." She stops in her tracks and looks at me, dumbfounded. "I'll just lend you something," I laugh and head for my bag.

"Carter?" she says as she stops at the bathroom door. "Thank you for listening. I've never told anyone this story. Never felt comfortable enough to admit to it."

"You can tell me anything." In four steps, I'm right in front of her.

"I'm beginning to see that." She smiles then disappears into the bathroom.

I don't know how, but in the last twenty-four hours, Sydney has managed to make herself at home in my heart. With everything that happened since yesterday, I honestly care for and feel protective over her.

"I'm going to die, aren't I?" Sydney looks at me bleary eyed. Her feet are strapped to a snowboard, her hands covered in hard gloves, and on her head is a woolly hat with a large blue pompom. She looks fucking adorable. She also looks scared, even though we're on the smallest hill known to man. And for a brief moment, I consider if I should take her back home. The last time I pushed her, she ended up having a panic attack. She looks around and says, "I'm only joking. I mean, I'm terrified but also quite excited." She grins goofily, and I exhale, the knot that was forming in my chest loosening.

I stand my board up in the fresh mound of snow to the side and grab her hands. "All right, I've never actually had to teach anyone how to snowboard, but it shouldn't be too hard. It's kinda like sex."

Sydney's eyes go wide. "How so?"

"You might not know exactly what you're doing, but you get the general idea and just go along with it. Plus, it's all in the hips."

She snorts with laughter, throwing her head back, then loses balance and starts tipping backwards. I grab for her hand, but I'm a bit too late and end up falling on top of her.

"You see? The power of love has toppled us over. You'll be an ace at snowboarding."

"Ugh, I don't think so. Can you forget snowboarding? I'm pretty sure I forgot sex. I haven't really had any in two years, not counting our failed attempt..." She bites her lip. My gaze zeroes in on her plump mouth, and I can't for the life of me remember what we were talking about. I don't understand the pull she has on me, but I'm starting to think it's stronger than my resolve to focus on my music alone. "Uhm, Carter?"

"Yes?" My voice comes out hoarser than I'd like, my eyes still on her lips.

"Do you think we can get up now?"

I grunt and stand up, pulling her up to me. I'm such an

idiot. She's clearly been through things, and all I can think about is getting my dick wet.

"Okay, so like I was saying, it's in your hips, but also your knees and your feet. Even though you are strapped to the snowboard, you hold the power. The trick is to remember that the main movement is like a hip thrust forward and backwards." I demonstrate, spreading my legs into a correct stance. "When you move your hips, you'll need to steer with your front foot, edging it to your toes or your heel, depending on the side you want to turn."

"Edging," she repeats the word softly, her eyes focused on her feet. And in that moment, I cannot think of anything that I want to do more than to bring her to the edge of climax then not let her come until she can't remember her name. God, I want her. I had no clue just how much. But a year of spanking the monkey to the memory of her gripping my cock makes a guy a bit frustrated, you know? "Okay, let's do this," she says, and it takes me a lot longer than I'd like to admit to comprehend she's talking about snowboarding and not me eating her out. *Get your mind out of the gutter, you horn dog!* I berate myself.

I walk to Sydney and take her gloved hands in mine. "No time like the present, Sunshine." I smile at her, silently thanking Billabong for making snowboard apparel that hides the huge hard on I'm currently sporting.

Chapter 8

I'm In Trouble

Sydney

"Holy shit, I can't believe I'm snowboarding!" I exclaim as we finish another ride and stop by the lifts to take us up the mountain. It has not been easy, but honestly, it hasn't been too hard, and three hours into walking up the hill then sliding down, I was finally ready to go onto a bigger slope. The feeling I get from riding down is akin to nothing I've ever felt before. It's freedom, exhilaration, adrenaline, and bliss all tied into one. I did not realise I could love a sport so much. But I do.

Carter has been an amazing teacher. From walking with me as I slid side to side to teaching me my first turn and then snowboarding alongside me, holding my hands. We fell so many times my butt and knees are probably permanently bruised, but honestly, I have never felt this happy, and I know that no small part of this feeling is because of the company. I can't lie to myself anymore. Carter gets hotter and hotter with every minute. And each time he opens his mouth, my brain finds all the possible sexual innuendos in what he is saying. I have not been this turned on in a long, long, looong while. I'm not sure if he feels the same, but I hope he does, and, from the looks he gives me every so often, I can tell he finds me attractive. The question is: *do we do anything about it?*

I haven't figured out the answer yet. Even if my vagina has. That bitch wants it bad. But hey, 'Brains before sex gains'.

Carter grabs my hand and pulls me towards a bar situated next to the ski lift. Skis and snowboards are sticking out of the pile of snow in front of it. It looks so cool, probably because I've never seen anything like it before outside of a movie, and let's be honest, 'Ski School' is not the best portrayal of how things work. However, it didn't lie about places like this. It's dazzling. A large hexagon chalet made out of pinewood with enormous windows all around, giving the surrounding space a light and airy feel. There's a huge log burner in the middle to keep everyone warm, and people are milling around it in their undone ski boots, awkwardly carrying trays with steaming hot drinks. The place is abuzz with conversations and laughter, the smell of hot dogs and warm drinks assaulting my senses. The atmosphere here is infectious as I find myself bopping my head to the loud music coming from the speakers. It takes me a second to recognise it. 'Jingle Bells', just like the last time I was with Carter at a bar. I should probably stay away from alcohol this time.

"Welcome to après-ski!" Carter shouts over the noise. "May I interest you in some vegan hot chocolate?" I nod, salivating instantly. I didn't realise how parched I got from all this snowboarding. But now that I'm no longer moving, the thirst hits me full force, along with hunger.

Carter walks off towards the bar, and I find us a place to sit in front of the large window. I take off Carter's jacket and hang it over the stool, sitting on top of it. Somehow, everything I'm wearing today—except for my bra and knickers—belongs to Carter. I don't even know where he packed all this stuff, but somehow, when I got out of the bathroom this morning, he was wearing a big cheshire grin and had a full snowboarding kit, including shoes, waiting for me. I questioned him, but all he said was that he managed to get it sorted last night after I fell asleep. He must have found a place that rents stuff out.

I spend the next few minutes doing my favourite thing: people-watching. I'm entranced by a young family. A woman and a man skiing down with a toddler in between them. He can't be older than four. Carter sits down next to me, sliding a tray in between us, but I can't look away. They look so happy. A mum, a dad, and a baby.

It hits me at the most inopportune moments.

The longing for someone to love me. And the feelings of inadequacy.

The toddler speeds ahead and, at the last minute, breaks sideways, causing a slurry of snow to rise in the air. He's giggling, and when his parents reach him he jumps up and down with glee. He grabs the ends of their ski poles and they drag him to the lift. Happy, loving... That's what a family is supposed to look like.

"Your hot beverage, madam." Carter breaks me out of my melancholy.

"Why, thank you, good sir," I reply and look at the tray. There are two cups of hot chocolate and two hot dogs.

"All vegan, beautiful." He smiles at me and my heart swells. I can't believe this guy. He's so unapologetically crazy, never thinks twice about what someone else might think of him, yet always puts others first. His best friend is one stupid woman to pass on a guy like him. Carter is hilarious, and lovely, and hot, and caring... And, oh fuck. I'm in trouble.

If only he wasn't in love with his best friend and my heart wasn't scared to open up.

"Thank you." I pick up one of the hot dogs and take a bite. It's delicious. I quickly stuff some more in my face then lick the juices that drip down my hand.

"Fuck," Carter mumbles. I almost missed it. I look up and am met with amber brown eyes, darkening with every second. "So, what are we doing?" he rasps out. And I don't know if it's me or is this question loaded with subtext.

I swallow. "People watching." He nods and picks up his hot chocolate, taking a sip. His eyes go huge.

"Hey, this is really good!" he exclaims, taking another sip. "It's really, really good!"

"It's hot chocolate, of course it's good," I laugh.

"Well, yeah, but without the cows."

"That's what makes it so good," I tease.

"Maybe..." He genuinely looks like he's giving it some thought. He takes a bite of the hot dog and pulls it away from his mouth. "It's not disgusting. It's actually quite tasty. Hmmm."

I smile and take a sip of my hot chocolate. A loud moan escapes me. "Carter, call the coroner cause I'm dying right here, right now. I've had a nice life, did a lot of things I'm proud of. And this hot chocolate? Icing on the cake. I don't need anything else. Mouthgasm." I take another sip, closing my eyes.

"Bathroom," Carter mumbles and rushes off. I continue the sweet seduction of my insides with the world's best hot chocolate. I honestly would die a happy woman. Well, I could do with one last actual orgasm. But if I can't have that? I'll settle for a mouthgasm.

Too soon, my drink is finished, and I resume my people watching until Carter comes back. He finishes his food and drink in silence then gets up and puts his hand out for me to take. I don't hesitate. My body's reaction is automatic. Like it knew what to do before my brain even thought about it. Together, we walk out and head for the lift again. This time when we get off, rather than go back down, we take another lift, then another, and another one. Until I lose count and have no idea where we are.

Carter grabs his board under his arm. I follow suit, then he takes my hand in his again, walking uphill for a good fifteen minutes, away from the signposted pistes, through a small area filled with trees where our boots dig in the snow. I start thinking he brought me here to push me off the mountain—the psycho finally coming out—when he stops. We're on the other side of the trees, and I lose my breath at the sight. Carter flips his board upside down and sets it in the snow then does the same to mine. He walks around them, my hand still in his, and sits us down. The view is spectacular. Far in the distance, I can see Lake Tahoe and the surrounding mountains. The sun is slowly coming down, bathing them in orange and pink tones.

"Wow," I finally manage to say. Carter keeps staring at the view.

"When I was thirteen, I thought I was the king of the world, especially on these slopes. I knew every track, every tree, but somehow, one day, I got lost. The snow got too deep and I kept digging in, so I had to unstrap and wade, constantly falling in. I'm not going to beat around the bush. I was terrified. I thought I was going to die and that I'd never see my family again. That a bear would come and eat me," he chuckles. "Then I stumbled upon this place, in all its untouched glory. From here, I could see Lake Tahoe and knew which way was home. It kept me calm, it made me feel like I could get back down the mountain safely." He turns to me. "This is how you made me feel last night when I was on stage, Sydney. This is how you keep making me feel. I know that, in the grand scheme of things, we haven't known each other long, and I don't know what it is between us, but I know it's something. Something really strong. Because, Sydney, I just... I can't..." He looks into my eyes, searching, and then he kisses me.

Fuck, does he kiss me.

Chapter 9

Nope!

Carter

Fuck it.

I crush my lips to hers, and when she doesn't push me away, I take her face into my palms. She tastes sweet, faintly of the hot chocolate she drank earlier. I probe, nipping and licking her top then bottom lip, and when she opens for me, I don't hesitate; instead, I push my tongue against hers, desperate to feel her. Tasting her, I groan, annoyed at all these unnecessary layers between us. Without breaking the kiss, Sydney straddles me and wraps her arm around my neck, digging her fingers into my hair and pulling it sharply. I can't help it. I grind up into her, desperate for friction. She moans as I assault her with my mouth. I break away and trail kisses down her jaw to her earlobe, biting and licking at it. I want her so badly.

I rip a glove off my hand and, without thinking, I fumble to get underneath her jacket. She helps, lifting it up, and my palm glides against her bare skin, scalding my fingers. It's been a long time coming. I've thought of this moment so many times over the last year. She's as desperate for this as I am. When my hand reaches her glorious tits, I squeeze one, eliciting a grind against my straining cock. I flick a nipple then slowly, leisurely trace my fingers down, down, down, undoing a button of her pants.

I can't stop myself. I want to feel her. Want to touch her. Sydney doesn't protest. Instead, she gasps as my hand slips against her pubic bone. I want to savor it, take my time, but she is bare, fully waxed, and I lose my goddamn mind. She grinds against my hand as her lips find mine. Her kisses are hungry, frantic as I trace one, two, three circles around her clit, then slip my finger into her soaking pussy, taking it out and repeating the process.

"Fuck, Carter, this feels so good. I need you to keep fucking me with your fingers. Just. Like. That," she groans against my lips. And I'm hanging on by a thread. My girl likes to talk, and I'm all for it. I slip another finger into her pussy and stroke in and out, curling them, hitting her g-spot.

"Tell me how you like it, baby. I'll fuck you so good. God, if you didn't have all these clothes on, I'd spank you so hard for your filthy little mouth," I rasp, pumping my fingers harder.

Sydney moans louder. "Oh God, yes. Harder, fuck me harder." My thumb connects with her clit while my fingers pump in and out. She pulls her mouth from mine and starts sucking at my throat, grinding. "Oh God..." She shudders as I grip her ass through all the layers.

"Not God, baby. Just me. Say my name." She moans, grinding harder. "Say my fucking name." I bite her earlobe.

"Carter!" she explodes around my fingers. I keep pumping, letting her ride the high all through to the end.

Her breathing slowly evens as she places her forehead against mine then moves her lips and kisses me hard. My fingers are still inside her, so I stroke her clit and push them in deeper. She shudders against me then clenches and starts coming again. I fucking lose it. She's too hot. And if things continue this way, I'm going to blow a load in my pants.

I look into Sydney's aqua-blue eyes and gently pull my fingers out. Then, ever so slowly, I put them in my mouth and suck her juices off them, never breaking the connection our eyes hold.

"Fuck, Carter. That's so hot," she says as I savor the taste of her. She tastes like nectar, and, in my head, I imagine a thousand ways I will make her come with my mouth on her sweet pussy. My cock keeps straining in my pants, and I groan, so aroused I can barely think. Sydney reaches for my zipper, but I stop her.

"No, Sunshine. When I come, it's going to be inside you." She bites her bottom lip and nods while I try to think of something that will get me out of this lust-induced haze. Kittens, puppies, animals, animals fucking, fucking Sydney like an animal. Nope!

Family, holidays, Christmas, egg nog, mistletoe, drunkenly fucking Sydney under the mistletoe. Nope! Nope! Nope!

Let's try this again. Mom, Dad, Aunt Bertie... Nice, this is finally working. I manage to get myself into a head space where my dick does not want to poke a hole through my pants and break free. Standing up, I reach out to help Sydney up. She stands, and I pull her into my embrace, kissing her again. Now that I've started, I can't seem to stop. I don't think I'll ever get enough.

"We should make our way back. I have a gig to attend," I say against her lips.

"We should," she agrees, but doesn't move a muscle.

Instead, she nips my bottom lip, then licks it, soothing the sting. This woman is trying to kill me.

"We could go into town too. I need to do some last-minute Christmas shopping."

"We could."

"We could go get some food."

"We could. Are you hungry?"

"Ravenous," I reply, then kiss her, stroking my tongue in and out.

"Mmmm."

"Or..." I start. "We could go back to the apartment and I could show you just how hungry I am."

"Mmmm... I like that idea." She deepens the kiss, wrapping her arms around me. Then, after a few minutes, she breaks away. "Lead the way, Mr. Kennedy." I sigh and strap on my board then help Sydney strap hers on. I give her a few pointers then slowly guide her down through the terrain to where we started walking.

"You want to catch a lift back down or snowboard?" I ask.

"Are you kidding me? Of course I want to snowboard! It's so much fun!" My heart soars at hearing her words. At the fact that she loves this sport as much as I do.

Seeing her grin when she snowboards, no matter how carefully, does something to me. And I find myself not minding having to go slow, not even a little bit. By the time we reach the bottom of the mountain and load our boards onto Jeepak, it's late afternoon. We're silent as we drive back to the apartment. I'm not quite sure how we get there, but we do. And then it's the stairs. The door. And we're inside.

My breaths are uneven as I stand in front of her, taking her in. I know she's gorgeous, but there's so much more to her that makes her extraordinary. The freckle on her right eyelid. I can see it when she closes her eyes and sucks in a breath as I unzip her jacket. The dimple on her left cheek, the one that only appears when she really lets go and laughs, loudly, unabashedly. The ridge at the top of her ear. I gently stroke it. Her cute nose that's got just a little bump on the top. Those eyelashes; they're so long they don't even look real. And those damned aqua-blue eyes with flecks of gold strewn across them, surrounded by a dark blue circle.

I gently cradle her chin, lifting her face up to mine, and kiss her. It's not rushed. We've got all the time in the world, so I just want to savour her. She opens up for me, her lips inviting mine to explore. I take the hint and slip my tongue in, probing, stroking, tasting. I could kiss her for days, just kiss and never stop. Who needs food, anyway? She and her perfect kisses can be my food.

There's an annoying sound coming from somewhere, a vaguely familiar one. I ignore it and keep kissing Sydney as she unzips my jacket and helps me shrug it off. The sound continues. Getting louder as Sydney reaches into my pocket and pulls out my phone. Fuck. My. Life.

"Hello?" My voice comes out hoarser than I'd like, but whoever is on the other side can draw their own conclusions.

"Carter, it's LolaJean. From Lola's." She pauses, waiting for my response. LolaJean is the owner of Lola's, the bar I'm supposed to be performing at tonight.

I pinch the bridge of my nose. "Hi LolaJean, is everything okay?"

"Not quite. The band that had the set before you caught some nasty bug. They're all sick." For a second, I genuinely am excited about the prospect of her cancelling the whole event. The things I could do to Sydney if we had the entire night. Then the guilt comes in. Someone is seriously ill, and I'm here almost celebrating the fact. "The thing is, I saw what you can do. I've seen your clips on YouTube. I watched the 'live' last night, and Carter, if you would be interested, I'd love it if you could come in earlier and perform the whole set. The full hour and a half. If you want, that is. I'd pay you double obviously—" I zone out for a second. She wants me to WHAT? This is huge! I'd need to think of the songs and the order, but this is truly a dream come true. And a test of my skills. Can I do it? "We can also have a backing band for you. Keys, drums, and bass."

"Yes," I blurt out. "I'll do it." I turn to Sydney with a huge grin on my face; she's grinning right back. She must have overheard the conversation. I want to run up to her, spin her around, then throw her on the bed and fuck her for as long as we have before we need to be at the bar.

"That's great! Can you be here in half an hour?"

The fuck? "Half an hour?" I parrot, the meaning of the words not quite computing.

"Yes, we need to do a soundcheck, and it would be great if you could rehearse with the band, make sure you're on the same page."

"Sounds good." I smile through the despair, knowing full well that my dick will hate me for the rest of the night. "Can we make it forty-five? We just got back from the mountain and I need a quick shower before the show."

"Perfect, I'll see you soon, Carter. Can't wait to see you in action!" In my head, I'm already running through a set list. I say my goodbyes and walk over to Sydney.

"Sunshine..."

"We'll pick this up after your gig." She smiles and gives me a quick kiss. "Now go shower, you stinker." I spank her and walk towards the bathroom, removing my top with one hand then unbuttoning my snowboard pants and sliding them down. Just before I reach the bathroom, I turn my head back to Sydney.

"To be continued." I push my boxers off then walk into the bathroom and close the door behind me.

Chapter 10

One Of Many

Sydney

As Carter's shapely arse disappears behind the bathroom door, I can't help but groan at the unfairness of the situation. Don't get me wrong, I'm ecstatic for him, and the opportunity this gig presents for him is huge. A fact I can't dismiss, especially since he confided in me about his stage fright.

But...

But.

BUT!

Does it really make me a selfish cow that I wanted that call to be a cancellation? The thought of having Carter to myself, of finally having sex after so long of a dry spell. With him. And this time, hopefully *not* falling asleep... Well, that thought had me really excited.

After what happened on the mountain, that's all I could think about until reality came crashing down with a phone call. And since he didn't let me reciprocate back there, he must be feeling pretty wound up. He had said, *'when I come, I want it to be inside you'*. I pace back and forth.

I could...nah. I mean, he wouldn't say no, but...no. It could take the edge off... Surely he wouldn't mind that.

And a mouth...That would technically be inside me, wouldn't it?

Fuck it. I decide it's worth a try. I start removing my clothes to go join Carter in the shower when the bathroom door swings open and out comes a specimen of male perfection. Carter is so hot; I start salivating as I take him in. His dark hair is wet and sticking every which way. Droplets of water slide down his perfectly sculpted chest and abs, glistening, a road map to the V barely covered by a white towel. Yup, he's definitely trying to kill me. I swallow loudly, looking at the outline of what's beneath his towel. And what's beneath his towel grows the longer I stare, making it even harder to look away. I lick my lips.

"Sunshine, if you don't stop staring at my cock, I'm going to have to introduce the two of you. And he likes very long and very tight hugs. So..." My lips twitch, and I clench them tight, trying hard not to laugh. His words work, though, because I finally look up and straight into his dark brown eyes. Entranced, I walk over to him. We're almost chest to chest when my hand tentatively reaches out and traces his peck. He inhales sharply and closes his eyes. As much as I want to follow through with my initial plan, and I can see in his eyes that his mind is going the same way, I can also see the desperation. He's struggling, it's clear. I sigh and take my hand back, my fingers still tingling from touching his skin. I walk past him and do the same thing he did to me. Well, almost. I undress down to my bra and panties, then shoot him a smirk and walk into the bathroom.

Twenty minutes later, we head out of the apartment, the atmosphere between us too thick, too charged to be able to stay in an enclosed place for too long and not do something in time. The crisp air clears my fuzzy, Carter-filled head until he takes my hand and an electric pulse charges through my body. As he pulls me in the direction of Lola's, I war with the emotions I'm feeling. I don't understand what's happening. I have never felt this way about a guy. No one has ever gotten me so wound up, so desperate. If one look from him can get me all hot and bothered, I can't wait for what his hands can do to me.

Hands which are currently dragging me down the Boulevard. I try to look around where we're going, but Carter's step quickens and, although my legs are long, I find myself having to run after him. I know we're in a rush, but this is crazy.

"Car—"

"Shhh," he interrupts me. "Trust me." I nod, realising that I do. I trust him.

I suppose he's given me no reason not to, except the fact that he might still be in love with his best friend. But who am I kidding? We never said this was anything more than road trip fun, so I can't hold it against him. It's what we both want, isn't it?

The last time we talked about what we wanted from each other was last year. And we both were after one thing. Scratching an itch. An itch that definitely needs scratching right now.

Carter pulls me harder and breaks into a run. The hours I spent hating life on the treadmill are finally coming in handy. Without them, I'd be sweaty and out of breath by now because, with God as my witness, cardio is the devil's way of giving me a middle finger.

Carter looks back at me, a huge grin on his handsome face, and I can't help but grin back. He takes a sharp left and takes us down a side street. He turns a few more times until he suddenly stops and walks through a line of trees and bushes.

"Where are we—"

"Shhh," the bastard shushes me! "We need to be really quiet." I shush, but let it be known I'm not happy about it. When we finally get through the thicket, I've got snow behind the collar of my jacket and I'm a less than happy bunny. I'm about to let the beast holding my hand know just how unhappy I am when he stops and whispers.

"Look." He points at the ground. There's an empty swimming pool in front of us. A deep layer of snow is covering the bottom and sides. I raise my eyebrows, unimpressed. He tsks. "Have faith, Sydney. Have I ever led you astray?" I cross my arms. The cave comes to mind, but to be fair, he didn't know I was riddled with issues.

I try to show some enthusiasm. "What are we looking at?" He nods excitedly then hops down into the swimming pool and kneels into the snow. I look around, apprehensive that we're trespassing as he starts furiously digging in the snow, swiping it away.

"Come on," he urges me. I shrug my arms. It's not like I've got anything better to do. I might as well join in on the crazy. I hop in and start digging, wondering if we're about to discover a dinosaur fossil. But when we finally get to the bottom, it's not dinosaur bones I see. Instead, there is a thick line with one word on each side. I stare at it. "Cool, eh? Want to put your foot on each side?" he asks. When I don't reply instantly, his face starts to fall. My brain catches up to my emotions, and I squeal.

"Are you fucking with me?"

"I wish," he mutters, the smile slowly coming back onto his face.

I grin back and skip from one foot to the other, going from California to Nevada each time.

"This is the coolest thing on Earth," I say excitedly. "Look, look!" I jump to one side of the line. "I'm in California." I jump to the other side. "And now I'm in Nevada. Fast as lightning." I karate chop the air like a first-class dork. He laughs out loud, making me giggle so much I slip and fall on my butt and laugh even harder. I lie down on my back, my body in California, and Carter follows suit, his head next to mine but upside down and on the Nevada side. The thick state line between us.

"I was hoping you'd like it." He pulls his phone out and snaps a picture of us.

"It's awesome." I turn my head to face him. "Thanks for showing this to me."

"I like to impress my ladies." The corner of his lips lifts as my mind zeros in on the term 'ladies'. Yeah, Syd. You're just one of many, many women. Keep the walls up. Don't forget, the devil always wears a disguise. I'm about to reply when we hear a patio door open and hurried steps crunching in the snow. Shit. I scramble up and ready myself to parkour out of this swimming pool any minute. Carter grabs my hand and puts his finger on his lips, telling me to stay quiet before motioning for us to move to the edge of the pool. I try to move as silently as possible, but the deep snow doesn't help; plus, anyone with eyes can see the enormous hole we dug in the snow.

"Hey!" someone shouts from above me, and I freeze. "What are you doing here? This is private property!" Shit, shit, shit. I guess it's about time my ass landed in jail. I just hoped it would have been for something a little bit more exciting than trespassing, like grand theft auto or armed robbery. Well, not really, but you get my drift. Something cooler than this. Carter turns to the dude who is surely calling the cops by now, I assume, because I'm kind of scared to look up.

"Hey, Dyl. Sorry, man. Was just trying to show my girl your genius idea." My head whips up and my eyes narrow. That little monster—well, not so little since he's towering over me. But still!

"Carter?" The dude called Dyl, or whatever, comes to the edge. "Hey, man!" His whole face lights up at our sight. "Long time no see! What have you been up to? You here for long? We should do a run together!" He goes a million miles a minute, clearly excited to see Carter. My head slowly swivels to the side. Carter beams, and once again, his smile is so infectious that I can't help but copy him.

"Aww man, I wish. But we're heading out tomorrow morning. Got a gig at Lola's tonight, though. Stop by?" He gently leads me to the side of the pool and we take the snow-covered steps out. Dyl is waiting there and, as soon as we're out, he pulls Carter into a huge bear hug. "We probably should be going. I'm supposed to be there for rehearsal in five. Sorry we trespassed, man." I hear Carter's muffled voice, his hand is still clutching mine despite having the life squeezed out of him by his mate.

Dyl lets go, a pout on his face as he steps away. "Awww man, with the baby. I need more notice to get a sitter, but next time call me as soon as you even think of coming to Lake Tahoe! And you can bring your woman here any time! You should come in the summer, so we can actually use the pool."

"Hell yes!" Carter exclaims. "We're definitely coming back in the summer; it's a completely different place." My

For What It's Worth

heart skips a beat at his words, but deep down, I know he's only saying this to get rid of Dyl. There's no chance that he wants to bring me here in six months' time. This is just a fling. "Right, we really do have to go, but maybe see you tonight?" Dyl nods enthusiastically as Carter starts walking in the direction we came through. Ah, so we're going through the bushes again. Lovely.

After a few steps, he halts. "Shit, I'm such a dick," he mutters, then turns back and shouts, "Dylan, this is Sydney. Sydney, that's Dylan. We go way back."

"Nice to meet you, Sydney," Dylan shouts as Carter starts pulling me through the bushes.

"You too!" I shout just as a snowy brunch brushes my face, but I honestly have no clue if he heard me.

Carter's hurry pays off because, somehow, we arrive at Lola's on time. We go to the back door, and a middle-aged woman with curly platinum blonde hair wearing leopard print leggings, high heels and a neon pink top opens the door and ushers us in.

The place is dark, except for a dim light above the bar. The woman reaches behind the bar and flicks a switch, illuminating the whole place. I'm instantly drawn to the picture-covered walls. As Carter starts talking to LolaJean, my legs move of their own accord, taking me closer to the wall. I gasp as my eyes move from one picture to another, more and more awestruck. Instantly, I'm glad the earlier call was not a cancellation because it's clear as day that this gig is a huge deal and that this place is a lot more important than I thought.

Faces stare at me from the pictures, ones you can't help but recognise. Seems like anyone who's ever made it in music has been here. Not only been here, but played here too. The photos are of bands and famous singers, all on the small stage that I can see out of the corner of my eye. Dire Straits, Prince, Jimmy Eat World, Bob Dylan, Eagles, Bon Jovi, AC/DC, Kings of Leon, Lorde, Chainsmokers. There's more: all people who went on to be famous, all looking young and like they were at the start of their career. In some of the pictures, there's a middle-aged man standing next to the performers. In others, he's with a blonde woman, looking at her like she hung the moon, in some they're joined by a small girl, then a teenager. Some feature the bands with LolaJean. I can't take my eyes off them.

"That's my dad," LolaJean says from behind me as I examine a photo of the man laughing with his arm around Morrisey. "And that's my mom," she points at a young woman standing next to a band I don't know. "She was a backing singer for one of the first bands that performed here. It was a whirlwind romance. They knew each other for a weekend before they drove to Vegas to get married. When they got back, my dad changed the name of this place from Rico's Joint to Lola's." I look back at the pictures. "That's her name," she continues. "I've never seen two people more in love than those two. Still very much all over each other," she laughs, and I smile with her.

"All these bands?" I look at her in question.

She shrugs. "I guess we got lucky. Most of the bands were in their baby stage when they performed here. Some were passing by, some came for vacation, some came for an open mic night. Word spread around and we became a sort of lucky charm."

"That's amazing." I look at the stage where Carter is talking with three guys as they set the equipment up.

"Those are my daughter's friends. She's the one who told me about Carter and convinced me to invite him here. We're very strict on who we invite to perform."

"Carter is amazing. You won't be disappointed." I nod.

"I know that, hon. He's a star waiting to shine his bright light on the world. You have an exciting journey ahead for the two of you." My face doesn't move, but inside, my heart clenches because I know I'm just here for the week and, even if I wasn't, this lifestyle is not for me. After what happened with Darius, I want to be as far away from the limelight as possible. That's why I've been busting my arse for the past two years. I took every photo gig offered to me, got my BA in English Lit., and, in any spare moment I had, I wrote. Last month, I finally got a literary agent who believes in me. Part of the reason for this trip was trying to find inspiration for my future books. Carter was never the plan. Not him, not his sexy voice and body, not the career he surely has ahead of him. He's a distraction, one I need to shake off before the end of this trip.

I look at Carter while he's tuning his guitar, getting ready to start the soundcheck. As if on cue, his head whips up and his eyes meet mine. He winks at me as his mouth spreads into a wide smile. He's so fucking handsome it's unfair to the rest of the male population. I turn back to LolaJean and think of the days we have left together, my heart beating fast. I don't know what Carter's plans are for the journey, but I'm going to let someone else take over and lead me for once in my life.

"Thanks, LolaJean. It's going to be an adventure. But I'm looking forward to it."

I used to think being in a band was hard work. I wasn't wrong. Although Carter made it look easy, I could see the stress and strain pouring off him as the drummer lost the beat or the bass got a bit out of hand with one of Carter's originals. While watching them rehearse, I took pictures and posted them on his Instagram, drumming up excitement for the upcoming event. I also took a lot of pictures of Carter, his face, his hands holding the microphone, his forearms... I'm a sucker for forearms, and Carter's do not disappoint.

Now, sitting by the bar and sipping my water, I watch as bodies start trickling into the space. Apparently gig night at LolaJeans happens only once every couple of months, and people come from around both states in hopes of seeing the next big thing, so the expected turnout is large. This place will be packed. Carter must be so nervous.

I look down at my phone and bite my lip.

Me: *how you doin', rockstar?*

Rockstar: *shitting a brick, turn around, Sunshine.*

I look up and turn my head. Carter is behind the bar. Without a word, he leans across it and kisses me deeply, taking my breath away.

"I needed that," he whispers into my lips. "Now I can get on with this shit show. Stay here, okay? I need you." His eyes are stormy as he moves away then turns and walks into the back area. For fuck's sake. I really am in trouble.

"Ah, young love," an older woman sitting next to me says with a twinkle in her eye. "My husband used to look at me the same way when we met. He still does."

"We are not a couple," I smile politely.

"Oh, honey, we weren't either," she laughs. "I was in love with the lead singer of my band when I met Rico. It took him two days to convince me he was the love of my life and that I should marry him, so I did. Haven't looked back since."

For What It's Worth

"You must be Lola," I look at her with interest.

"My daughter does love to tell the story," she giggles. "You'd think she was the one whisked away to Vegas at twenty-one."

"Your story is amazing. I can only hope I'll find my true love one day."

"Oh, sweetness,"—she pats my hand and winks—"I think, soon enough, you will."

PART II

Worth It

When I look into your eyes
I can't justify the thoughts I had of you
When you speak my name
I can't explain the days I wanted you
And when you dance
All that romance was such a waste of time
Cause baby you ain't worth it
You ain't worth the pain
And as I stand in this pouring rain
Of the tears I should have never cried
I know
Baby you ain't worth it
You ain't worth the pain
Shit I can't explain
You ain't worth it

Chapter 11

I Can Make You British

Carter

"One, two, three, four," the drummer behind me shouts the beat, and the first song of the night starts. My eyes don't leave Sydney's form as I strum my guitar and sing the lyrics to one of my originals. There won't be any covers tonight. That's the deal with Lola's. You get a gig, but you put your heart out on a chopping block for everyone to have a look and decide if it's worth saving. My legs are shaking, but my fingers move confidently and my voice is steady as Sydney grins from behind her phone, broadcasting the gig to the world. Even if I wanted to, I can't take my eyes off her. She's mesmerizing. The pull she has on me is unreal. The lyrics of the songs I wrote, the heartache I felt, they don't feel right anymore. Not compared to how desperate I am to be around Sydney. Her pale blue eyes stir up feelings in me I don't understand.

She rocks from side to side as the music picks up, matching the beat. I go through songs in a daze, barely noticing the reaction the audience has to them until I get to 'Worth It'. Although this song originally was about heartbreak, earlier it felt off. For the first time, I struggled with my own stuff until Sydney pointed out that with upping the tempo, a key change, and by replacing some lyrics, this song is completely different. Who knew swapping *'can'* for *'can't'* and *'are'* for *'ain't'* can make so much difference. Now it feels like an anthem rather than another ode from a broken heart. Sydney is jumping around to the beat, surely giving those watching on Instagram whiplash. Her lips move along with mine as I repeat the chorus, *'Baby, you ain't worth it, you ain't worth the pain'.*

Everything comes into focus as I watch her enjoy herself, entranced by the music I wrote. In this moment, no one else matters in the whole place but her. When I told her today that she was my anchor, that she kept me focused, I didn't lie. Sydney has got this power over me. I can't explain it, but with her near me, my stage fright disappears.

All I see is her.

All I want is her.

All I want is for her to enjoy herself. So I play, I sing, right into her hand. The same place my stupid heart seems to be heading.

By the time the gig is finished, I'm sweating like a nun in a dildo factory and am happier than a pimp in the Red Light District. Adrenaline is still pumping through my veins as I hop off the stage and zero in on my target. Sydney is sitting on a barstool, swinging from side to side with a huge grin on her face.

I saunter toward her, smirking. I've got an idea how I'd like to release the adrenaline, and by the look on Sydney's face, she is on the same page. Ten feet. Nine. She's closer, almost within reach. I'm five feet away from her when someone steps in my way. Irritated, I look up and...freeze.

I know him.

The guy in front of me is wearing a pair of faded blue jeans, a black t-shirt, and Vans. The casual look suits him but doesn't deceive me. He belongs in a tailored suit and leather loafers. I know this because that's his usual look, at least the one that's portrayed on the internet and in magazines.

"Hey mate, I was hoping we could have a chat," the man in question speaks. From behind him, I can see Sydney cock her head with interest.

I swallow. "Sure, let's find somewhere quiet." I walk toward Sydney and grab her hand. "I need your confidence in me, Sunshine," I whisper.

She squeezes my hand tight and turns to the guy next to me.

"Hi, I'm Sydney," she introduces herself as we go through the bar and to LolaJeans' office.

"Nice to meet you, Sydney." He looks her up and down with definite interest in his eyes. My blood starts to boil. "I'm Josh Coda." Sydney stops in her tracks and gapes. He laughs. "From Coda Records," he finishes smugly. "How do you do?"

"Are you shitting me? A fellow Brit!" Sydney exclaims. "You have no clue how amazing it is to hear your accent!"

He blinks. And as irritated as I was two seconds ago at the thought of Sydney being impressed by this asshole who could potentially be my golden ticket, I'm now fighting the laugh that's trying to escape me. Sydney has no clue who he is.

"You wouldn't believe how refreshing it is to talk to someone who knows the true meaning of football and knows what an aubergine is," she huffs, and I raise my eyebrow, taking a seat in one of the empty chairs. What the fuck is an aubergine?

A smile plays on his lips. "Don't even get me started on coriander," he agrees. Sydney throws her hands up.

"Thank you!" They laugh. "Finally, someone I can be British with."

"You can be British with me," I scoff, annoyed at the camaraderie between them.

"Aww, rockstar." She walks over to me, leans down, and kisses my cheek. It's not as good as her kissing me senseless in front of Josh, but it's good enough for him to see she's mine. "It just means we like to moan about everything."

"In that case, Sunshine," I whisper in her ear. "I can make you British all night long."

Ladies and gentlemen, Sydney Buyer blushes. She fucking blushes. My thoughts immediately go to how far down that blush spreads.

Sydney straightens and smiles, her eyes lingering on my lips. "Let me go get us some drinks." I nod. It might be best if she leaves for a bit. Carter Junior has been feeling a bit blue lately, and one look from Sydney has him standing to attention. Who knows what will happen if she keeps blushing like that. He might stop giving a shit that we have company.

"Use my tab, love." If it wasn't for Aiden, I'd have punched the guy for calling my girl 'love'. But having a bro who's a Brit comes in handy in situations like this, where you might potentially hit the CEO of a record label, who is interested in talking with you, for using a term that's commonplace in the UK. Thank fuck for small graces. Sydney nods and walks out of the office. The loud music and chatter of the bar's patrons seep in through the door as it slowly closes behind her.

"She's very beautiful," soon to be ex-CEO of Coda Records and a future corpse of Six Feet Underground Inc. says. I growl, not able to stop myself. "Objectively speaking," he laughs. "Don't worry mate, it's clear as day you guys are together."

Is it though? Because technically, we aren't together. I want her, and she clearly wants me. But does she want anything more? Do I? I can't deny the attraction. I don't want to, in fact. I want to take full advantage of the chemistry between us. The fact that Sydney has a sense of humour, great taste in music, and is easy to be around is an added bonus.

"So, Carter, I don't want to beat around the bush," Josh pulls me out of my thoughts. "I have been following you on YouTube and Instagram for a while, seen some of your live gigs broadcasted, and frankly, after tonight's performance, I'm disappointed." My heart drops at his words and my shoulders sag. "Ah! I'm messing with you, mate! Just doing the Simon Cowell bit. I'm disappointed in myself that it took me so long to come out and see you in person. I fucking loved it!"

Motherfucker. I can't help but grin as he slaps my shoulder. The door to the office opens, and Sydney walks in carrying a tray with beer on it.

"So I was thinking," Josh continues, swiping two beers off the tray and handing one of them to me. "We should record some of your stuff together."

Bang!

The tray Sydney was holding crashes to the floor as she stares between Josh and I, the last beer thankfully in her hand. She bites her bottom lip, trying to contain her excitement. Josh slowly walks over to the tray on the floor and picks it up, handing it back to Sydney with a wink. If this fucker doesn't stop flirting with her, I don't think I'll be able to work with him. I won't be able to stand more than a few hours of him acting around her like that, so forget about trying to make it however long the contract would be.

Whoooaaa!

Where did that come from? No one said Sydney would be around after our trip was over. But...it would be nice if she stuck around, even if just as a friend. If she wanted, that is. I wonder what she wants? *Except for a piece of me.* I smirk to myself.

"I'd love to hear what you have in mind," I say as Josh turns to face me while Sydney loses her shit behind his back, silently jumping and screaming with glee.

"Great," he says, sitting down in a chair opposite me. Sydney calms down and goes to sit on a small love seat in the corner of the room. My eyes follow her as Josh continues talking. She gives me a thumbs up and takes a sip of her beer, making herself comfortable.

She's asleep when Josh and I finally stop chatting. I covered her with a blanket about an hour ago while Josh was making calls to his team, scheduling a formal meeting for me to come down to his office in LA. It's surreal to think that a few hours ago I was just another dude with a guitar hoping that people would like his stuff. And now? Well, I'm still just another dude with a guitar hoping that people would like his stuff, but hopefully with a record label behind him. We'll see. Nothing has been signed yet.

I walk over to Sydney and slide my arms under her, picking her up and cradling her to my chest. It's been a long day and she must be exhausted after all the snowboarding we've done and the excitement of the gig. She doesn't even stir until I slide into the car idling in front of the bar.

"Shhh, baby, I've got you. Keep sleeping," I whisper into her ear, stroking her hair. She buries her face into the crook of my neck, moaning softly. The ride doesn't take long and, before I know it, we're in front of the apartment.

Getting out of the car with a five-ten model in your arms is not as easy as getting into it. Trying to protect Sydney from banging her head on the car door basically means contorting myself like a pro acrobat. Don't even get me started on pulling my keys out of the back pocket of my jeans and trying to unlock the apartment door. Somehow, I win the battle of key versus man and victoriously stroll into the apartment, Sydney intact in my arms.

I gently place her on the bed and start removing her shoes and clothes. She's down to her shirt and panties when I stop myself. She still hasn't woken up, although she's made a couple of grunts of protest when I shook her too hard. If this girl was in Pompeii when Vesuvius erupted, she would have slept through the whole thing.

I'm nowhere near tired, too keyed up from talking with Josh and the buzz of the gig. Things are happening, falling into place, and I can't help but think about the woman in the bed. Is she my lucky charm, or is this whole thing a coincidence? Will this whole thing lose its appeal once we fuck?

I start packing up our things into bags. There aren't many, leaving space for toiletries and essentials. I get our snowboards loaded onto Jeepak's roof rack and smile to myself. Sydney thinks that they're just rented, but she's wrong. That first morning on a whim, I snuck out and went to my buddy's shop. Got her clothes to snowboard in and arranged for shoes and board to be fitted. It's strange, as I never was the lavish sort of guy. Not with women, in any case. The most I'd treat them to would be a few drinks before we'd go to either mine or their place. With Sydney, I'm finding myself wanting to do anything to see her smile, be it making a stupid joke or buying her a whole set of snowboarding gear and then pretending it's all rented. She'll have one hell of a shock when I drop her off at the end of this trip and give her all the stuff to take in. I can't wait to see her face.

The end of the trip.

I don't really want to think about it. We've got more time ahead of us and I know just the place to take her next.

Somewhere it'll only be the two of us. For as long as we want.

Finally.

Chapter 12

Soon

Sydney

Can you get blue balls if you're a woman? Or blue ovaries or something? Asking for a friend.

But seriously. Can you?

Because I'm pretty sure I've got them. This gorgeous specimen in the seat next to me, this embodiment of tall, dark, and handsome, has been honestly messing with my libido. Libido, which I was pretty sure, lay dormant in the dark caverns somewhere deep inside my brain.

But, nooo.

Apparently, Carter and my libido are besties and want to be together all the time because ever since we left South Lake Tahoe this morning—sexless, might I add—I have been sitting in his Jeep trying not to pant and squirm at every look he gives me or every brush of his skin against mine. I'm so beyond turned on that a freaking speed bump might bring me to climax, I swear.

We set off as soon as we got up this morning, Carter having packed all of our stuff into the Jeep the night before while I was sleeping, and we've been driving close to four hours. It's absolute torture even though Carter is a great and considerate driver, asking if I'm okay with the music or if I want to stop and stretch my legs. The roads are covered in snow, and as pretty as I thought that looked for the first twenty minutes, the longer we are driving through it, the scarier it gets, especially for someone who's never driven in these conditions. Thankfully, Carter seems to know what he is doing.

It's also a huge plus that I seem to have been upgraded to playlist controller. A small give considering the rockstar next to me is yet to tell me where our next stop is. Weirder still is the fact that I'm not pressing for the information. For the first time in my life, I'm letting someone else take control and I'm just tagging along. The feeling is new and scary, but also exhilarating. I trust Carter, at least not to take me to the deep, dark woods and kill me then dispose of my body.

It seems as soon as I think that, Carter gets off the highway and drives into the fucking woods. I covertly pat my pockets to look for my phone and send an SOS to someone when I realise my phone is currently plugged into the stereo. I tentatively reach for it when Carter's warm hand stops mine. He squeezes it, eyes focused on the road as we make turn after turn and drive onto smaller and smaller roads until I can't see a road at all. He seems to know where we're going, and after about fifteen minutes, we arrive at our destination.

Once again, Carter Kennedy takes my breath away. Well, the place he brought me to does.

We're in a small, snow-covered meadow, surrounded by pine trees and shrubberies all blanketed in white. Right by where we're parked, there's a wooden cabin with a brick chimney coming out of its side and a wrap around porch. It looks like something out of a fairy tale with icicles hanging off its slanted, snow-covered roof.

For What It's Worth

Carter opens his door and walks to the cabin like he owns the place. It only registers that we might be staying here once his hand, the one holding the key, aims for the lock and is not immediately rejected when it comes into contact. In fact, the key seems to turn, and the door opens. I'm still stunned, motionless inside the car when Carter turns and winks at me then saunters inside. I look around like a buffoon, making sure there's no one else around before I open the door and make my way toward the cabin.

Tentatively, I step through the doorway. Carter is taking white sheets off the furniture, revealing a sofa and two armchairs set around the fireplace. There's a small dining table with wooden chairs around it, right next to a cozy kitchen with a wood-burning stove.

"I'll go grab some wood," Carter says as my eyes immediately go to his crotch. He lifts my face up with his fingers and places a small kiss on my nose. "Soon."

I wink at him, playing him at his own game, then shrug away and go explore further. There are two bedrooms. I frown at the possibility of us not sleeping in the same bed. They're both fairly large, at least by my mediocre London standards. A shoebox is bigger than the first studio flat I ever rented on my own in London.

I'm not going to assume that just because there's an attraction between us, Carter will want to sleep in the same bed as I do; plus, it might be nice to have my own space after being forced to spend every moment with him, not that I'm complaining. I like his company. But no one needs a clinger. I head back to the car to grab our stuff and spot Carter fighting with a lock on the side of the cabin. I walk over to him, enjoying the moment. Carter looks flustered, swearing at the padlock.

"Fucktard, lock, fucking, rusted shit motherfu—"

"You okay, rockstar?" I interrupt his litany.

He turns in one swift motion. His cheeks are flushed as he looks from me to the key in his hand to the rusted lock.

"The key," he moans. "The rotten key is broken, Sunshine." Sure enough, the key in his hand is missing a part. "We're doomed. No wood—no fire. No fire—no warmth, no hot water. We'll freeze. Although I see some positives as I'm talking. Skin on skin is advisable in situations like that. Go inside and undress. I'll be right behind you. I'll save you if it's the last thing I do on this Earth."

"As tempting as that sounds, move over." I walk past him and examine the lock. It doesn't look too bad. The core is clean and free of rust. "Let Sydney take care of you," I say and pull two hairpins out of my ponytail, bending one in the middle and creating an L shape with the other, then bending the edge. You see, earlier, when I thought I was going to jail and was disappointed it wasn't for something a bit more high profile than trespassing, I should have elaborated. I know how to pick locks. I kneel in front of the lock, insert one hairpin at the bottom, and then fiddle with the second, listening for clicks.

It's not exciting—the story of how I learned to pick locks. My mum used to lock me out of the house. If I didn't want to sleep on the street, I had to come up with better options. So I taught myself how to pick locks. Then, I'd sneak into our flat once she was passed out on the sofa. Not as glamorous as you thought, I bet. But at least it created a habit of always having hairpins on you, which, in turn, definitely just made me into the coolest chick Carter has ever known. As the last weight clicks into position and I turn the lock, his jaw hits the floor.

"Sydney... Sydney, Sydney, Sydney..." He shakes his head. "I have never been this turned on by a criminal in my entire life. You naughty, naughty girl." He opens the door to what seems to be an insulated storage area. Chopped wood neatly stacked inside. I bite my lip and shrug my shoulder. He shakes his head, looking at me hungrily. "Soon," he repeats his earlier words then grabs a few logs of wood in his arms. "Stack 'em up." He motions with his head to the logs.

Carter lights the fire in the living room and under the kitchen stove, and the place instantly heats up. I shrug off my jacket, hang it on the hook near the door, and then grab my bag to take it into one of the rooms. Earlier, Carter and I brought all our luggage and food supplies in. I hesitate in front of the two bedrooms, not sure if I should bring up the subject of sleeping arrangements, when hands sneak around my waist and woodsy smelling Carter nuzzles my neck.

"Let's sleep in this one." He pushes me into the slightly larger bedroom then takes the bag from my hand and sets it on a chair behind us. He turns me around to face him. Even though I'm tall, he towers over me, and I find myself looking up to meet his gaze. "Soon, Sydney. So fucking soon." He licks his lips, brushing mine with the pad of his thumb. My stomach growls, reminding me that I'm hungry. "Eating food first, eating Sydney second. But, Sunshine, this is the first and only time eating you out will ever take second place."

His voice alone can turn my insides into jelly, but his words spoken in his raspy tone, with his gaze on my lips. That's something a girl can't just be expected to be exposed to and survive. My underwear is soaked, and he hasn't even touched me yet.

Carter takes a step back, then turns and heads for the small kitchen. Like a puppy wanting a treat, I follow. And like a puppy, I'm ready to eat out of his strong hand if he is so inclined. He silently hands me a bottle of red wine and a corkscrew then grabs a large pot of water and places it on the stove. There's fresh basil on the counter, cherry tomatoes, spaghetti, and a jar of vegan pesto. And now I'm salivating, not only because of the food he's preparing, not only because of his words, but also because this man is out of this world. How is he so considerate, so kind, so talented and so fucking sexy all at the same time? Shouldn't he be at least a little imperfect?

I look down at the bottle of wine and start the process of opening it. It should be noted, for future references, that I have never opened a bottle of wine before, so I have no clue what I'm doing. By the time I figured out how to take off the wrapper, there was a little knife hidden in the corkscrew. Thank you very much. Carter has put the pasta in the salted water and chopped the tomatoes and basil. My slowness had nothing to do with me watching his every move like a sex-deprived maniac and drooling all over the place. Nothing.

I stab the cork like I've seen it done countless times in movies and restaurants and start the motion of screwing it in. For someone with the delicate skills of lock picking, I instantly know I'm butchering the job, but hey-ho. He wanted me to open the bottle—he won't complain if there's cork pieces swimming in his Pinot Noir. The man in question comes up to me and, thankfully, takes the bottle from my hands, fixing the poor start I've made and uncorking the bottle in one swift movement. He then pulls out a nifty little device and pours the wine through it into a decanter. My mind is blown. I'm not a big wine drinker, and the wine I usually drink certainly does not need airing or decanting. I wonder how a musician trying to make it in the industry can afford a wine like that. He must really want to impress me. Ha! Jokes on him, cause your girl needs very little to be impressed. Like forearms. Give me good, strong, muscly, veiny forearms and colour me impressed for life.

"Sydney," Carter growls, and I pull my eyes from his forearms and innocently look up at him.

"Yes, Carter?"

"You know exactly what. Stop it or you'll go hungry for the next twenty four hours. Because once I start.." I swallow and walk to the decanter, pouring two glasses of wine then taking one of them. I gulp its contents. The arsehole chuckles. I give him the middle finger then pour some more wine into my glass and go sit on the plush rug in front of the fire, where it's nice and cozy and there's a lack of over-confident dickwads around. I still covertly sneak glances at him, because this dickwad is also hilarious, and patient, and kind, and seems to have me ensnared in his sex-god grip.

When he comes over and sits next to me, handing me a plate of pasta, I'm thoroughly impressed.

"Thank you, it looks delicious," I mutter as we clink our glasses, his eyes on mine.

"It sure does." He doesn't look away. In fact, his face grows closer. I'm not sure if it's because I'm leaning toward him or he is into me. But we're almost at a kissing distance, food be damned, when my traitorous stomach growls again. To be fair, the food smells incredible. "Eat," he orders before looking away and taking a sip of his wine.

I look down at my dish and get to work. It's amazing, but at this stage I'm not surprised. Everything this guy does seems to be amazing. Just another thing I can add to the list of his talents. I still can't help the moan that escapes me, surely fuelling his already inflated ego.

"You like?" His voice is unsure, and I realise maybe his ego is not as inflated as I initially thought.

"It's so yummy," I say through a mouthful of pasta. It really is. Carter smiles excitedly and, with more confidence, picks up his fork and starts eating.

"I wasn't sure what to feed a vegan, you know? But it's actually quite fun thinking of what to make and how to make it work without meat."

"Mhmmm," I agree, chewing my food. He smiles and takes a sip of his wine. I must have been starving because, within minutes, I polish off my plate and consider licking it clean.

"Next time I'll make the pesto from scratch," Carter says, taking the empty plates to the kitchen and refilling our wine glasses. "It'll be so much better."

"I didn't know you could cook," I muse.

He shrugs. "I live on my own, so it was a 'learn how to cook or eat toast and takeout' situation. And as much as I love bread and pizza, I love home cooked food more, so I decided to learn."

"That's impressive," I say as he hands me my glass of wine back and sits next to me.

"Just a necessity," he smiles.

"I get it. I had to learn early or I'd go without food..." I trail off.

"Don't," Carter says.

"Don't what?"

"Don't stop yourself from talking to me, Sydney. You can tell me anything. You should know that."

I pause, searching his face. I suppose a struggling musician will understand how it feels going without food. "I—

uh. You might have gathered, I didn't have the best childhood growing up." He nods. "My mother was...rarely there, and, when she was, I wasn't exactly on her priority list. I guess I had to grow up fast and learn to take care of myself. It's not all bad; it made me the delightful person I am today." I try to brush off the pain, thinking about my childhood with a joke. Carter doesn't buy it, though, and takes my hand.

"What about your dad?"

"What about him? Maybe he'd have done something, maybe he'd be father of the year? Maybe he is...somewhere. I wouldn't know. I don't even know if he knows about me."

"Your mum, she—"

"Never talked about him, except—guess why my name is Sydney. Bonus points if you can tell me how long they were together." I shake my head.

"City they fell in love in?"

"Fucked more like it. Once. They fucked once, and I was the result of that happy union."

"A happy result," he interjects. "Sydney, you are no one's mistake. You're a fucking prize. Someone that should be cherished and worshipped. For all the shit that happened in your life, you grew up to be an incredible woman."

I smile, playfully waving my hand in dismissal and rolling my eyes, pretending like his words didn't affect me. Inside, my stomach is churning. His words, as amazing as they are, can't erase the pain talking about my childhood brings.

"What about you?" I turn the tables and sip on the delicious wine.

"Nothing to report really," Carter takes the change in stride. "Parents are still married, and still very much in love. I had a good childhood and have a younger sister who is crazy and whom I'd do anything for. Also, I plan on taking over the world by hypnotising everyone with my music and sexy hip moves." I laugh out loud, instantly in a better mood. I don't know how he does it, but each time I'm on the verge of a breakdown, he pulls me out and lifts me up. I have never met anyone like him. So happy, carefree, and genuine. I can't help the butterflies that take flight in my stomach each time he looks at me. There's just one thing...

"Are you still in love with your best friend?" I blurt out.

"What?" He blinks at me. "What brought that on?"

Deflection, not a good sign. Instantly, the walls he's consistently been taking down brick by brick go back up. "Never mind," I blurt. "Forget I asked."

"Sydney, I... It's a tough question." Yeah, right. "Because I love her." My heart breaks. "As a best friend," he continues. "I...honestly, I'm starting to think I never have been *in* love with her. More like the *idea* of love itself." I look up, desperate to see the truth in his eyes. "What I ever felt for her is not even in the same stratosphere as what I'm starting—" I stop his words with my mouth. He tastes like red wine and Carter, a taste that's become so distinct I can't get enough of it. I want him. I need him. I crave him.

I try to stop myself, I really do, but with each stroke of his skilled tongue, with each slide of his hand against my ribs, I fall.

He breaks the kiss.

"Now, Sydney. Now," he growls.

Chapter 13

It's Been A Year

Carter

"Now, Sydney. Now," I growl, not able to wait any longer.

I've had a permanent hard on for the last forty-eight hours, but I could have easily held off for longer had it not been for Sydney's reaction. Reaction to words I didn't think would slip out. But I can't deny it. This woman has me in all kinds of knots. I can't seem to shake her off, and I'm starting to see that this feral need for her goes much deeper than skin. Yes, she's beautiful, but that's nothing compared to the beauty inside her. And she makes me feel. She makes me feel like a teenager, insecure but high on her at the same time.

I can't think clearly when I'm around her, all I'm able to focus on is how much I need to feel her skin against mine. How much I need to hear her voice, her soft moans. This time, I'll be damned if I let her fall asleep.

I pull the sweater she is wearing over her head. She's wearing a tank with no bra underneath, and my hand instantly goes to her nipple, pinching it through the thin cotton. Sydney moans into my mouth and pulls at my shirt, trying to rip or stretch it. Which, I'm not sure. I chuckle and move away from her lips, taking it off in one swift motion. Sydney doesn't need an invitation. She straddles me, pushing me down onto the rug and attacking my neck, kissing it, then sucking, then licking the sting away. All the while, her hands are roaming up and down my chest. Her kisses trace down my chest until she comes to my nipple then bites it. My hips drive up, searching for the friction my cock so desperately needs.

"Baby," I groan, flipping us over. "It's been a year. If you want this to last longer we better focus on you."

"A year?" she whispers then sucks in her lip. "Don't want me to take the edge off?" She smiles playfully, and I rock against her, showing her just how much I want that.

"What. I. Want," I punctuate each word with a drive against her pussy. "Is to taste you. I've been thinking about it since yesterday when I licked your come off my fingers." She moans. And I move my hand down, unbuttoning her jeans and pushing them down. She helps kick them off then looks at me intently.

"Yours too. Off," she demands as I pull her tank top up, exposing her breasts.

"I'm not wearing any boxers," I warn.

"All the better."

I pull the tank over her head. She's wearing nothing but her soaked white, lacey panties. As I drag my lips from her neck down to her belly button, inhaling deeply, I can smell her arousal. Her breathing is fast as I grip the edge of her panties with my teeth and pull them down. She lifts her toned ass up, helping me take them down.

She's in all her naked glory in front of me, letting me drink in my fill. She doesn't squirm away from my exploration; instead, she watches me.

She's a vision. All milky white skin, flushed with desire, her chest rising up and down with shallow breaths. The memory of her body I had from a year ago not doing justice to what's in front of me now.

She lifts herself up then reaches out to unbutton my jeans. My cock springs out the moment it can. I push my jeans down and kick them off as Sydney licks her lips, focused on my dick.

"I want to taste you so badly. Lick you all the way from the bottom to the top," she says, making my dick jerk. "I think you want that too." She reaches out with her hand, but I move it away, pushing her gently back down to the floor then leaning down to kiss her. My dick brushes against her belly, and just that simple skin contact has me on edge.

"There'll be time for this yet, Sunshine. But, first things first," I say, breaking away from her lips and kissing her jaw before moving down her neck to her pert nipples, which are demanding my attention. I suck one in while pinching the other with my fingers then blow cool air on it. Sydney arches into me, gasping. I bite the other nipple then flick it with my tongue, making her yelp.

"Fuck, Carter," she moans.

"All in due time," I smile then suck her nipple, giving it extra attention. My hand roams down from her breast and cups her ass, squeezing it. She lifts it up and rubs against me. I can feel her wet heat against my thigh. Fuck this nipple foreplay. I need to taste her so badly. I bite her other nipple and flick it with my tongue, so that it doesn't feel left out, then move down between her thighs. Kissing around her pussy, teasing her. Finally, when she writhes underneath me, begging for more, I lick her slit. She moans at the contact then moans with frustration when I stop just shy of her clit and remove my tongue. But I'm here to savor my dessert. I lick again, this time pushing my tongue into her wet pussy. The guttural sound that escapes her has me so hard and turned on, precome drips down my leg. I fuck her with my tongue like the starved man that I am, consumed with the absolute need to devour her. I dive in, licking and sucking, nibbling at her clit, before going back down to her slit. This is heaven. I could do this forever. But, within seconds, Sydney's thighs clench around me and she explodes, slick and loud. I lick every last drop, enjoying the taste of her on my lips, my mouth. The smell of her around me is intoxicating and, rather than stopping, I just continue licking.

"You taste so good, baby. So fucking good," I growl into her pussy as her thighs start shaking again and her moans get louder.

"Fuck, just like that, Carter," she moans as I flick her clit. "Now suck it," I oblige my demanding girl. "Harder, harder!" I suck and slide two fingers into her, curling them up and stroking her g-spot. I have never met a woman this in tune with me, this responsive to my touch. It's like she's made for me. "Oh fuck, Carter, how?" she breathes. "How are you doing this to me?" she gasps as her pussy clenches around my fingers and she comes again. I lick her sensitive clit as she comes down and wonder if I should make her come again before I fuck her. My dick says no, but, in my chest, something makes me keep going, so I keep stroking inside her pussy, gently at first, then harder as I lick at her clit. This woman is going to kill me because, within minutes, she's moaning again, her hands digging into my hair as she rubs herself against my face. A guy could get used to this. Going down on Sydney is like a religious experience. I feel like a god between her thighs. I add another finger and start really fucking her. She moans so loudly I nearly stop to puff up my chest and give myself a high five. Making her orgasm this hard is an achievement, but I don't stop. Instead, I keep going, letting her ride the wave.

"Your dick next." She gasps. "I need your dick, rockstar, or I'm going to strap you to the chair and straddle you until I get what I want."

I lick her clit one last time before moving back up, meeting her at eye level, my dick leaking precome on her thigh. She grabs my face and kisses me desperately, spreading her legs and wrapping them around me. I move, pushing away to grab a condom when she whispers into my ear.

"I'm on the pill." I nearly black out. She wants me bare? I've never done it without a condom, never trusted anyone to, but I can't imagine doing it any other way with Sydney. I want to feel her; I don't want anything between us.

"I'm clean," I say.

"I know. I mean, I figured since you haven't had sex in a year," she smiles. I smile back at her and position my dick at her entrance. She nods, assuring me that this is what she wants.

And, as I slide into her, my eyes don't leave hers. Her eyelids flutter with pleasure, but her gaze is firm on mine as I sink into her. The feeling like nothing I've ever felt before. It's like the first taste of water when you've been dying for a drink. It's like the moment you sit down after running a marathon. It's like heaven. Like home. I start moving.

In and out, in and out. Not taking my eyes off her. It feels different. Maybe it's because I haven't had sex in so long, maybe it's because I actually care for Sydney. Or maybe... It's because it's Sydney. *It's her*, my heart says as I pump faster and faster. Sydney's arms snake around my neck as she brings my face closer and drags her tongue around my lips. I lean into the kiss, savoring the feel of her around me. I want to be deeper inside her. I want to feel all of her. I want to feel her wrapped around my dick, milking me as she comes, but the need to make her feel good takes first place.

Without breaking the contact, I sit us up. Sydney's legs wrap around me as she clings to me tightly. This position brings a whole new level of sensations. I can feel her clit against me as she takes over and starts to rock. I push my dick up each time she moves in, hitting a spot deep inside her, holding her close as she rides me, her forehead against mine. Her eyes close in pleasure and her mouth opens as she starts shaking. I swoop in, claiming her lips, sneaking my tongue in and kissing her deeply. I hold her face in my hands as she fucks me. The feeling of her against me is everything and, as she speeds up, I can feel myself getting close to the edge.

She breaks away from the kiss, her face still in my palms as she looks into my eyes. Her aqua-blue eyes turn dark, and, without breaking eye contact, she falls apart around me. Moaning my name as she comes around my dick. I pump harder into her, the feeling of her pussy clenching around me bringing me over the edge, and, as I come, her eyes are still on mine. Staring into my soul.

And for the first time in my life, I'm not afraid.

We stay connected like that for a while, just looking at each other and kissing. My dick goes soft then starts growing harder again. I have never felt like this about anyone I've been with. I can't put my finger on it, but Sydney is just right. With everything.

Her sense of humor, her sarcastic nature, her brain, the way she moves, the way she holds my hand, the way she looks into my eyes, the way she makes me feel. She's just right.

I start moving inside her again, unhurried until she twists and drags us both down onto our side, facing one another. Slowly, we begin rocking back and forth in unison. Each movement is like the rhythm of a dance, which sparks a million new sensations inside me. My chest constricts as I get lost in her eyes, warring with the emotions swirling inside me. I've never fucked sideways, usually preferring doggy so I can look at their ass, but having Sydney like this, close, our mouths only inches apart, I can't imagine doing it any other way. Is this what making love feels like?

I speed up as she fuses her mouth with mine, biting my lip then licking the sting away.

"Carter," she gasps between kisses, my name on her lips sounding like a prayer. I want to hear her say it over and over again, like gospel. I'll be her church if she wants me to. "I-I, fuck, that feels so good." I swirl my hips around.

"It never feels like this," I groan as sensation ripples through me.

"Never," she moans in agreement as I pump into her. "Never." Her leg wraps around me, and I pull it up, hooking my arm under her knee, giving me access to a whole new angle. "Fuck, Carter! Yes," Sydney cries. "Harder, harder!"

I move into her, fast and hard, no longer making love but fucking her right into an orgasm. Once again, when she climaxes, she milks me so hard I come right with her. I bury my face in the crook of her neck. Even though I'm spent, I can't get enough. There's this insatiable hunger in me that is not getting satisfied. The more I have her, the more I want her. The feeling is unfamiliar and strange. I thought that I could fuck her out of my system, but so far, this has been the exact opposite.

I pull out of her and kiss a mole above her left breast before standing to go to the bathroom and grabbing a wet cloth. When I get back to her, she's lying naked, her eyes closed in front of the warm fire, the flames dancing in the background. I kneel beside her and kiss a trail from her shoulder to her hip. She sighs and shivers as my fingers trail the curve of her bum. Gently rolling her onto her back, I spread her legs and clean her up with the warm washcloth. I don't know where all this gentleness is coming from, but Sydney does not deserve anything less.

"Do you want to stay here or shall we move to the bed?" I ask. She lifts her eyebrow and looks at me questioningly.

"More?"

"Oh baby, I'm just getting started."

Chapter 14

Take The Leap

Sydney

I don't remember the last time I had sex. It's been *that* long. What I *do* remember is that it left a lot to be desired. I don't even think I came if I'm being honest. It was a rushed, drunken fumble. Back from the day before, I was assaulted and didn't care who I slept with as long as it scratched my itch. Oh, how times have changed. Since then, I found it difficult to trust guys, and the only time I even remotely felt the want to do anything was last year with Carter, and we all know how that turned out. So the fact that, in the end, it's Carter again is like going full circle. Finally finishing something that was started a while ago.

It doesn't hurt that sleeping with Carter was an experience on a whole different level. It's like his mission in life is to make me feel good. He knows exactly which buttons to press, how fast and how hard. It's weird. I have never been with anyone this in tune with my body. I still can't believe I fell asleep on him the first time we tried it. What a cop out. I could have been having amazing sex all this time. Except... neither one of us wanted a relationship. *Wants*, I mean wants! Because surely an afternoon of incredible sex doesn't mean we want anything more from each other. That would be silly, wouldn't it?

After we moved to the bedroom, Carter, the insatiable beast that he is, was true to his word. He, indeed, was just getting started. Because, as soon as we hit the soft covers, he was inside me again. Then again...and again. I'm not complaining. In fact, I'm shocked. I'm not a prude. I've had sex more than once in a night, but never, ever, *ever* have I come every single time and so many times in a row. If things continue this way, Carter will have to go to jail for first-degree pussy murder, because, as much as I'm loving it, he's not small, and my girl needs a little rest.

"How are you feeling, baby?" He kisses my shoulder and pulls me into him, my butt against his already hardening dick. What did I tell you? Insatiable! His hand strokes down my ribs to the curve of my hip, then back up again, grazing the side of my breast. I inhale sharply, my back instinctively arching into him as wetness pools between my legs. There've been many 'nevers' I've already mentioned that Carter claimed and destroyed, and I swear this is the last one. But I have never before been this turned on this quickly, and over and over again, by one man. Never. One touch from him and I'm wet. One kiss has me begging for more. One nibble has me moaning and ready to climax. In his hands, I'm an instrument, a guitar he knows exactly how to handle, how to touch in order to make my body sing.

His hand sneaks down from my ribs to my belly then down between my legs as he starts rubbing circles around my clit. I didn't think I could take it again, but he has me ready for him in seconds. I moan for him as his movements get faster, and he takes the cue, easily sliding into me from behind. Pleasure ripples through me as he buries himself right to the hilt. He starts moving, the angle perfect, and I push my arse into him, eager for more. His fingers don't stop their assault at my clit as he pumps faster and faster. I get lost in him, in the feeling of him inside me. The rhythm is feverish as I'm getting closer to the edge.

"Sydney, baby, can you feel this?" He moans into my ear. I squeeze my eyes shut, wishing the emotions away, but it doesn't work.

I feel it. I feel a hell of a lot.

And it scares the living shit out of me.

Hours later, we come up for air. Naked, thirsty, and hungry, we trudge into the living area. The fire is slowly dying, but the cabin is still nice and cozy enough for us not to feel the chill. Carter walks over to the rug where we first had sex and picks up our empty wine glasses before walking over to the kitchen counter and refilling them. It's a nice gesture, but I'm so thirsty after all the exercise that wine is the last thing on my mind. At my expression, Carter bursts out laughing then hands me a bottle of water, unscrewing the cap. As I gulp it down, he opens the little cubbyhole that doubles for a fridge—ingenious if you ask me—pulls out a bunch of things, and sets them on the counter.

"Hungry?" he asks, rummaging through the drawers and pulling out a large chopping board.

"Starving," I nod as he starts taking food out of paper bags. Carrots, cucumbers, hummus. He turns to the sink to wash grapes, and I take the time to admire his backside. If Michelangelo was alive, he'd be inspired for years just by watching this man washing bloody grapes in the sink. The man in question turns and winks at me then walks, grabs a loaf of bread from the counter, and starts slicing it. I have to admit, it's nice letting someone take care of me for a change. Someone who does so willingly and of their own accord.

As Carter gets the food ready, I grab a blanket off the sofa and wrap it around me, a bit because I'm starting to feel the chill from outside and a bit because Carter's gaze on me has me all sorts of flustered. He pouts as he sees me wrap up and mutters, "Bye boobies." He's such a dork. He can be the most amazing, kind, and caring person one minute, then have me in stitches, laughing, the next. I love it. And the sex. The sex is incredible.

I add a log onto the fire and sit down on the rug, the feeling of happiness, contentment, and satisfaction making my heart beat faster. It's a first for me, these feelings. There's always something at the back of my head, niggling, spoiling, putting a damper on my thoughts. Carter puts the chopping board loaded with food on the floor and settles himself behind my back, wrapping his legs and arms around me.

"I like you Sydney Buyer," he mumbles, nuzzling my neck. My heart does a flip flop at his words. Does he really? We're so different. But there's never any awkward silence, never a dull moment. And with his arms around me, he fits, moulds into me and makes me feel safe. My heart flip flops again as I open my mouth.

"I..." I'm not one to show emotions, and I struggle with even this small term of affection, but I take the leap, nonetheless. "I like you too, Carter Kennedy," I blurt out in a single breath. But once the words are out, I don't feel scared, I feel liberated. I feel like it's okay to trust someone else. Somehow, Carter drilled a hole in my armour and managed to sneak in, making me feel things I've never felt before.

"I wish we could stay here forever," he whispers, his

chin on my shoulder as he gazes at the fire. My stomach drops. Because, for a minute there, I forgot that we have an expiration date. That nagging thought, the damper on things I thought wasn't there? Well, it's full force settled in my brain. It even brought an armchair, a lamp, and a book to read and arranged itself comfortably, wrapped up snuggly in a blanket, with a glass of wine in hand. That fucker is here to stay, I realise, and my walls instantly try to rebuild themselves. But the problem with walls that have been slowly taken down brick by brick is that building them up again is not as easy. Not when the person who took them down is still holding on to the bloody bricks.

Carter reaches for an oat cracker and pops it in my mouth. My jaw moves as I chew, but all I taste is saw dust. How did it happen? How did I let him in? And how on earth will I take it when this trip is over? Being with Carter is easy when we're all alone and there's no outside world to get in the way, but Carter is going places and I'm...running away from them. This could never work.

With a heavy heart, I snuggle deeper into him. It may not work in the long run, but I'm not going to sabotage the time we have left together.

"How long are we staying here?" I ask, popping a grape into my mouth.

"Two days. We leave on Christmas Eve," he says.

"I forgot it was Christmas," I trail off. Carter chuckles and starts singing a Christmas song: 'Jingle Bells' by Frank Sinatra. The song that played on repeat that cold, dark night a year ago when I was determined to break my dry spell. As his raspy voice sings the chorus, I close my eyes, lost in this new feeling. I never cared for Christmas, never really got to care for it as my mum liked to celebrate Christmas by getting so drunk she'd pass out for two days straight. I didn't mind. Those were the only two days in the year I was guaranteed peace and quiet.

"I was such a grinch last year," he says, and I laugh. I've been a grinch for the past twenty-one years.

"And this year?"

"Hmmm, I'm the grinch from the end of the movie. Adorable." That he is. Sexy and adorable.

"I suppose with having a road trip, we can't exactly do the whole Christmas spirit thing," I muse.

"Oh, Sydney," he shakes his head. "Sydney, Sydney, Sydney. Must you always doubt me?" He gets up and, in all his naked glory, walks over to a wooden chest in the corner of the room. With a glance over his shoulder, he smirks at me then opens the chest. I can barely contain the curiosity, but I stay still, cool as a cucumber, letting this all play out. Carter pulls out a small, mangled Christmas tree and starts straightening its branches. The thing looks pretty pathetic, but he perseveres, and soon enough, there's a fairly presentable, two foot high Christmas tree with small ornaments stuck to its branches. He flips the tree upside down and flicks a switch on its base. Nothing happens. He flicks it again and again, without a result. "Motherfu—" He bashes the base of the tree against the chest, and it instantly illuminates. "Aaah, there it is. Christmas spirit can fix anything." He grins at me. "Now, onto decorations." He hands me a pair of scissors and white sheets of paper. I blink at him then shrug and start folding the paper like I remember doing in school. I start cutting out little chunks, hoping it won't look too awful, and when I'm done, I slowly unravel a fairly decent looking snowflake.

When I look over at Carter, he's holding a chain of wonky looking snowmen.

"It's good." I take the chain from him and place it next to my snowflake.

He shakes his head. "Arts and crafts aren't really in my wheelhouse."

"And what is in your wheelhouse?" I walk right into his trap.

"Music, food, naps...you." On the last word, he launches at me, tickling my side then kissing my face all over. I'm laughing so hard my stomach starts hurting.

"Please, Carter, please!" I beg him through laughter.

"If I must," he stops, hovering over me, his hand on my hip, the blanket that was covering me strewn across the floor. He moves his hand from my hip to my cheek, cupping it, then leans down and pries my lips open with his tongue before kissing me. I pull him in, savouring the kiss, wrapping my arms around him as he settles himself between my legs. It's weird how quickly we became comfortable with each other.

It takes us over two hours to make a few decorations, and, as wonky and childlike as they look, I couldn't love them more.

Chapter 15

Gizmo

Carter

I have never felt this way in my entire life. Last night after Sydney fell asleep I was so keyed up I went into the living room, unsure what it was I wanted, until my eyes fell on my guitar case propped up against a wall in the corner. Naked, I sat down in front of the fireplace and let my fingers take over. I kept playing for an hour until a melody formed. It wasn't sad or haunting. It was slow and melancholy, and as I played it, arranging it into a song, one word kept at the forefront of my mind. *Sydney*.

The lyrics floated in and out of me until, without thinking, I sang the first verse then the chorus. I always thought songs came from your soul. They're the truest form of what you're feeling and they're hard to write because they make you face your emotions, accept them, and then share them for everyone to judge. I have never written a song so easily. Music and lyrics just flowing out of me. I guess my soul was ready to shout from the rooftops at what my heart started to feel. I don't want to let her go. I don't want this trip to end. And, if I could, I'd have her stay in this cabin with me forever.

Is it because we're all alone? Away from other people and life's worries? Or is it because Sydney makes me feel like I can be anyone, do anything. But it won't matter unless she's with me. What will it be like when we're back in LA and real life comes crashing back? Will she even want to give it a chance? I can't help but hope that she will.

I tie the shoelaces on my boots and grab a pair of gloves, handing them to Sydney. We've interrupted our itinerary filled with sexy times to go for a walk. The snow stopped falling, and the sun came out, making it sparkle. I could see Sydney's longing stare as she gazed out the window while we cuddled on the small sofa, and I decided I should really take my girl out and show her where I spent most of my winters with my family. The excitement on her face when I asked if she wanted to go for a walk told me I was on the right path.

"It's so beautiful," Sydney says, zipping her jacket up, one of my sister's discarded items of clothing. As much as I like seeing Sydney wearing my stuff, or not wearing anything, Rey's jacket fits her better and will keep her warmer. A guy has to compromise in order to keep his woman happy and warm. Taking her gloved hand in mine, I bring her to a trail that will lead us to a small waterfall. As we walk, breathing in the crisp air, an eerie feeling comes over me. Like someone is watching us.

Sydney doesn't seem to notice my discomfort and keeps walking, looking around in awe, stopping every now and then to pick up a pine cone or a small branch that broke off a tree. The further from the cabin we are, the more uneasy I get, looking around as we walk, trying to spot the murderer who's clearly out for us.

"Are you okay?" Sydney asks when, once again, I whip my head to the side, ready to exclaim 'Aha!' the moment I spot the creeper.

"Fine," I brush her off and continue on our walk. If I'm going to be a hero, I should act a bit more covertly.

"You sure?" She clearly doesn't believe me, so to distract her, I spin her around and push her against the trunk of a nearby tree, pressing myself against her and kissing her deeply.

"So fine," I growl into her lips as she kisses me back, nipping at my bottom lip. The way she kisses should have poetry written about it, songs sang, books written... Wait. I can write the songs. In fact, a lyric comes into my head as she grabs my hair with her gloved hand and moans against my lips.

'On this winter day, you are all I see. All my fears go away, cause you make me so happy. And I am falling... just like your snowflake kisses'.

I pull away, the thoughts of whoever is following us all but forgotten as Sydney smiles lazily and puts her head on my chest. My heart thumps in my chest as I hug her. Thump. Thump-thump. *No, Carter. No. Don't do this. She'll break you!* my brain says, but my heart has other ideas and starts beating just for her. Fuck. Fucketyfuck with a fuckaduck on top!

I kiss the top of her head, getting a mouthful of pink pompom, and sigh, stepping away from her warm embrace.

"C'mon, Sunshine," I say. We walk hand in hand for a few minutes until we get to a bend in the road. Once we pass it, the trees thin out and we're met with a spectacular view of a waterfall frozen over. It looks like something out of a fantasy book. Untouched mounds of snow and sheets of ice glistening in the midafternoon sun, looking like a work of art. Unhurriedly, I pull out my phone and take a picture of Sydney staring at the masterpiece in front of us. If I wasn't desperate to be a musician, I'd be a photographer and Sydney would be my muse. She already is. And now that she's more comfortable with me taking photos of her, I take every opportunity I get to do so.

I spent an hour this morning photographing her. The mole above her right breast, her hand holding a mug of coffee, her feet in my lap, her lips. As I look through my album, it's clear that I'm besotted with her. There's a photo of her sitting in nothing but my shirt, looking out the window into the winter wonderland beyond. Her hair is up in a messy bun. All you can see is her neck and part of her profile. I post that picture onto Instagram with a caption 'Australia', and tag our general location.

I walk over to Sydney and snap another photo of us. This time, a selfie. She's grinning, clearly happy and at ease. My heart soars at the sight of it.

"Did you know this was here?" she asks.

I nod. "We usually go swimming there during summer." I point at the frozen body of water beneath the waterfall.

"You've been here before?" She turns to face me.

"My family likes to come to the cabin at least once a year; although, now that Rey and I are grown up, we don't do it nearly often enough. So it sits empty most of the year."

"Your family owns it?" Sydney gawks.

"Yeah, it used to be my grandpa's. He loved spending time here when he was still alive. He'd live here for months, all by himself, and we'd come to visit. Bring him food, not that he needed it. He was a master forager."

She looks into the distance. "I'm trying to imagine you and your family out here."

"You should come next time we're all here," I blurt out and nearly smack myself in the face for the outburst. Sydney's eyes search mine. "I mean, if you want. We're all a bit crazy, so I get it if you'd rather stay away..." I trail off. Turning my back to her I walk back down the way we came, but she quickly catches up to me and without a word, grabs my hand. We walk in silence for a little while, my stomach in my throat.

Of course. Why would she want anything to do with me after this trip is over? It's not like we made any plans for the future. So the fact that my heart wants her means nothing. If I could, I'd keep her here with me forever, away from the world. Live off the land, just like my grandpa did. The possibility of skipping Christmas and any other gigs I have planned makes my heart race. We could just stay here until she demands to be taken back to LA.

"I'd love to," she says in a small voice. My head whips to her as I stop in my tracks.

"What did you say?"

"I'd love to come back here. With you. And maybe your family. If the offer still stands?" My heart soars at her words and I pick her up, twirling us around.

"Fuck, yeah, Sunshine! You're always welcome here." She giggles as I put her down. A creepy squeal sounds to my right, and I whip my head around, knowing full well that whoever was watching us earlier is back, and this time he's here to stay. Not today, amigo! I grab Sydney's hand and start running back towards the cabin, aware of the skittering sound right on our heels. What the hell is this? 'Children of Corn' in the snow? I look back, but I can't see anything.

"Carter, what are you doing?" The crazy woman next to

me clearly doesn't value her life as she digs her heels in and stops us from running.

"Danger, Sydney. Danger!" I whisper loudly, still looking around. Jesus Christ, what if it's a grizzly bear? Sydney's eyes go large. As the throaty sound starts up again. "Fucking grizzly on our heels! C'mon, babe!" She starts walking as I drag her forward. It's better than standing still when there's a grizzly about.

"Grizzly?" she asks. "Don't bears hibernate in winter? Also, aren't grizzly bears extinct in California?" Well, color me surprised. Who knew Sydney likes to moonlight as Sir David fucking Attenborough while a bear is hot on our heels.

"Sydney!" My voice goes up an octave or two while she stops again. The angry growls are coming from way too close for my liking. A screech sounds to my left then something scampers above us. A thought crosses my mind. *Since when are grizzlies light on their paws moving from one branch to another?* I look up just as something furry parachutes right into my face.

I scream, or maybe the gremlin-like thing screams. Quite possibly, we are both screaming at the same time as I try to shake the thing off of my head.

"It's okay, rockstar. Shhhh. It's as scared as you are." Sydney grabs my shoulders to steady me. Scared? I'm not scared? I'm fucking terrified!

I'm about to be scalped by a gremlin. And my hair is my best asset! Well, one of my best assets. Top five. Ten maybe. Still, I like my hair! "Shhh," she soothes. "Are you okay, little guy?" I'm not little, but whatever.

"I think so. Is it still on me?" I'm hoping the gremlin claws I think I'm feeling on my head are just phantom.

Sydney chokes, and for a second, I think the gremlin

must have attacked her before I realize she's trying to hold back laughter. I narrow my eyes at her. "Don't move, okay?" I'm about to nod but think better of it, the weight of the bloodthirsty creature heavy on my head.

She reaches up and takes off my beanie, cradling the feral thing to her chest before digging in her jacket pocket and pulling out a couple of almonds. Why the fuck does she have almonds in her jacket and what is she planning to do with them?

As she brings her hand up to the furry thing, dread seeps into me. "Be careful. It's probably feral and riddled with rabies!" I want to smack the thing out of her hand when two huge black eyes poke out of the beanie hammock. They're black as night. As black as Lucifer's hellhounds. Come to think of it, it's probably a hellhound that's transmuted into the ugly thing. I take a step back, remembering the last encounter I had with a creature of the same species. I had to go to a hospital, get stitches, and a rabies shot. I still swear by the fact that it attacked me. The thing came out of nowhere, sauntering in my direction like a furry pimp, so naturally, I ran in the opposite direction. Not my fault. I tripped and cut my leg in the process. I wasn't going to be its next meal.

"It's just a squirrel," Sydney baby-talks to the disgusting thing. Its nose is moving and its eyes are fixed on me. "I think it likes you." I take another step back. Sydney sighs and gives in, placing my beanie, gremlin inside, on the snow then dropping the almonds next to it. "Bye little buddy." She waves at the thing. "Be careful, all right?" Ha! Like *it* needs to be careful. It's clear world domination is its end goal.

We walk away, but not trusting the thing, I keep looking back every so often, making sure it's not following us.

Maybe it doesn't know where we live. The gremlin just keeps holding onto the beanie like a trophy, smirking at me.

"It looks so sad," Sydney says, making me scoff. *Yeah, it's sad because it didn't get to eat me!*

"I'm sorry, what?" I look at her sideways, her lips in a thin line, eyes full of mirth. Shit, did I say that last thing out loud?

"I don't like squirrels. They're like bad gremlins and they're out to get me." I mumble, crossing my arms in front of me.

"You don't say," she starts laughing, but, seeing my expression, she stops herself. "Awww, I'm sorry, rockstar. If it makes you feel any better, this one was a baby gremlin, so it probably didn't have super sinister plans just yet. Plus, he's gone now." I look back and, sure enough, the thing is no longer there. I exhale, tension leaving my body.

When we finally get back into the cabin, I push Sydney against the door then slowly undress her, reclaiming some of my lost manhood when she starts screaming my name over and over as I bury myself deep inside her.

I wake up in the middle of the night again and, naked, walk into the living room. Picking up my guitar, I walk over to the fireplace and add a couple of logs to keep it going through the night. It's dark, the only light coming from the fire dancing in the corner. I pull on my jeans then sit on the sofa and start strumming a melody I think would go with the lyrics I came up with earlier.

When I pause, uncertain where to take the song next, a chirrup comes from behind the window. The hell? I gently lay my guitar down on the sofa and walk towards the door, peeping through the small window next to it and straining to see anything in the dark of the night. The chirrup sounds again; it's familiar. It takes it one more try before I realise it's the last few notes I played. I peel the door open and—I kid you not—nearly scream when, outside, I find the squirrel from earlier wrapped in my beanie. Its black eyes shining in the night, looking up at me.

"The fuck you doing here?" It makes the same sound again. It must be a coincidence. Without turning around, I take a few steps back to the sofa and feel for my guitar. I walk back while strumming a couple of notes. The squirrel looks at me intently then chirrups again, this time parroting the notes I just played. My mouth opens.

I kneel down by the door, not caring that I'm letting the cold in, and play three more notes. It cocks its head to the side then repeats the sound. Are. You. Shitting. Me?

"All right, Gizmo," I mutter and narrow my eyes then play the sequence all together. The little gremlin just looks at me, squeals an unrecognizable sound, then starts coughing. Hell, no. The thing is laughing! I crack up. "Okay, okay, I was being too ambitious, wasn't I?" I tentatively reach my hand out for it to sniff me. That's what dogs do, so why not try it with the squirrel? It sniffles my fingers then starts licking and gently nibbling at them. Unlike the feral creature I first thought it was, this guy seems to be fairly civilized. "You hungry, eh?" I stand up and start closing the door to go get some nuts and veggies. What do squirrels eat? But the look on his furry face made me stop at the last minute. "Fuck it, come in then." I open the door a bit wider. "But if you eat me in my sleep, I swear to God, I'll skin you alive." It cocks his head as if trying to compute what I just said. I sigh. "C'mon, Gizmo! It's getting cold in here. Soon enough, I'll be able to cut glass with my nipples."

Finally, upon hearing the name I've given him, Gizmo stands up and takes a few steps toward the door. "What now?" I mutter just as he looks back at the beanie discarded behind him. "I'll get it, just get inside." I lean over and pick up the black scrap of wool. It dawns on me that I must be a little bit crazy, because—correct me if I'm wrong—I'm having a conversation with a squirrel...

Chapter 16

No Shitting In The House

Sydney

"Carter," I mumble, still half asleep, grappling for him in the dark. But the space next to me is empty and cold. I sit up and look around, letting my eyes adjust, and when I don't find him on the floor, I swing my legs out and get up. Carter's t-shirt hangs off the side of the bed and I grab it, pulling it on before making my way out into the living room area.

The lights are off and the fire is low, casting a dim, orange glow across the room. There's food on the kitchen counter, a weird mish-mash of carrots, lettuce, bananas, and nuts. I walk over to the sofa, where I can see Carter's feet hanging off the side, his guitar leaning on the armchair beside. I walk around and try to decide whether I should wake him or cover him with a blanket. He looks delicious in nothing but his jeans hanging low on his hips. I take my time just drinking him in, my gaze moving slowly from his toes, up, up, up, until I notice something weird on his upper chest and in the crook of his neck. His arm is cradling something. I walk up tentatively and kneel beside him, trying to see better. There are crumbs on the floor beside him. Cookies, maybe? I wipe off a few that stuck to my foot, realising it's nuts. Weird. I lean closer to Carter, examining the thing on his chest. It looks like a little teddy bear, except it's got feathery fur. I come a bit closer and the thing moves, making me jump. What the hell? I get up and turn on the lights then go back to where Carter is groaning, arm covering his eyes. The squirrel, the same one that was enemy number one earlier today but seems to have been upgraded to a cuddly, stretches then rearranges itself into a ball, putting its fluffy tail over its eyes.

"Carter," I whisper. "Baby, I don't want you to freak out."

He instantly tenses. "What happened?"

"There's a squirrel on your chest." I decide to just rip off the bandaid, consequences be damned. Carter pats his chest then moves his hand up to where the squirrel is snuggling into him. He lifts his arm up and looks down at it.

"Gizmo!" he bellows like a parent reprimanding a child. "I told you, if this is going to work out you sleep on the floor in the beanie, didn't I?" The squirrel, apparently named Gizmo, lifts its head and sits up on Carter's chest. "Giiiz-moooo," Carter grits through his teeth, and the squirrel jumps off him, settling on the beanie that's lying on the floor.

"So you made a new friend." I raise my brows as Carter sits up and rubs his eyes, yawning.

"More like got forced into a friendship," he huffs and looks down at the squirrel. "He better not get in the way or it's back to living in the snow for the little guy."

A corner of my mouth lifts. "He?"

"Yeah, he's clearly a dude."

"You checked?" I'm trying hard to hold back the smile.

"Well, no. But he's definitely a dude. Aren't you, Giz?"

For What It's Worth

A growly squeal sounds from the floor. "See?"

"Oh, so what you are saying is that you guys talked, and he told you he's a 'he'?"

"Don't insult his intelligence. Of course he can't talk. He communicates." Carter is as serious as a heart attack.

"That's nice," I say to appease him. "Is he staying here for the night?"

"Well, yeah, do you know how cold it is outside? He'd freeze out there. Plus, he was hungry." I nod, just going with the flow.

"And you're fine with it?"

"We had a heart to heart, and he promised he would not eat me, so we're all good." Carter winks at me. I'm starting to doubt whether he's been pretending to be afraid of squirrels earlier on and orchestrated the whole ordeal with his pet circus-trained squirrel. I wouldn't be surprised, if I'm being honest.

"So..." I trail off. "He's sleeping here?"

Carter nods then leans over to the squirrel. "Gizmo." A little nose peeks out from under a tail. "No shitting in the house, dude. You need to go? You wait until you can go outside, comprende?" The squirrel just looks back at him blankly, but Carter must have seen something more in his eyes as he nods in approval. "Good boy," he says, then reaches out and pets the squirrel with his finger. My heart melts at the sight. To be honest, it already melted at the two of them snuggling on the couch, but I was too afraid Carter would freak out to truly appreciate the moment. "C'mon, Sunshine," he says as takes my hand. "Let's go snuggle in bed." A loud chirrup comes from where Gizmo is curled up. "Sorry bro, that's a party you're not invited to." He pulls me towards the bedroom door and flicks off the light.

Once inside the bedroom, he closes the door behind

him and saunters over to me. "Why so many clothes, Sydney?" he asks.

I swallow, knowing the look on his face already. He comes closer and lifts the hem of my t-shirt up until he exposes my breasts. He bites his lip then leans down and sucks a nipple into his mouth. My knees buckle as a throaty moan escapes me. Carter catches me and effortlessly lifts me up then walks, carrying me in his arms to the bed where he proceeds to kiss every inch of my body. His touch makes me feel alive and cherished, and I struggle internally with myself, trying desperately to separate the physical from the emotional. Because, surely, it's too soon to feel any type of emotions. Yes, we've spent all this time together and got to know each other. Yes, I've told him things I've never even spoken out loud, but that doesn't mean anything except the fact that I trust him.

So why did my heart stop when he asked me if I'd like to come back to this place with his family? Why did it feel like a thousand butterflies took flight in my stomach? Why is it that each time he looks at me, each time he touches me, all I can think of is getting wrapped up in him?

Christmas Eve will be here too soon, and then what? What happens after? The road trip won't be over for a few more days, but the days will be numbered, and after that, I can already feel the despair my heart will feel with his absence. Carter made himself at home there, and not having him around will break me if I let this continue.

I push him away, my whole body screaming in disapproval, my heart hammering in my chest.

"Can we go to sleep? I'm s-o tired." My traitorous voice breaks mid sentence.

"Of course, baby, anything you want." Carter doesn't question, he just pulls me into him and moulds his body around mine. I squeeze my eyes shut, dread filling my lungs, making it hard to breathe as my face presses against his chest. I relax a little with each rise and fall of his chest, but the dread is still there, at the back of my throat. Am I too late to stop this? Surely, if I put the brakes on, I can still get out of this unscathed.

Thank Heavens for small graces. Small squirrels in particular. Avoiding Carter's advances is a lot easier when he gets cockblocked by a little critter who is in love with the guy. Gizmo follows Carter everywhere, and by everywhere I mean *everywhere*.

"For fuck's sake, Gizmo," Carter's exasperated voice comes from the bathroom. "Can't I have a piss in peace?" I stifle a chuckle as Gizmo chirps happily in answer. It's been like that all morning, and each time Carter steps near me, Gizmo runs up and clings to him in protest. I'm beginning to think Gizmo is female. One that is feeling quite possessive and jealous of any attention that does not land on her. Typical woman, if you ask me. She is clearly laying claim to him and making sure everyone knows about it. I'm not going to share my thoughts with Carter, as he is still convinced that the squirrel is a boy. Even so, the guy who was afraid of squirrels not even twenty-four hours ago is doting on this one like it's his long lost child. Cutting up carrots into bite sized pieces, taking her outside every hour to make sure she is 'toilet trained'. How on earth does he think he can toilet train a wild animal? I have no clue, but he is trying. And it's adorable.

Carter walks back into the living room, Gizmo sitting on

his shoulder. The two of them together is quite the sight. My stomach flips, and once again, I'm wondering if maybe my initial thought of putting the brakes on things was a silly one. Maybe if I just talked to him, see where he stands, it would be easier to decide one way or another. If he says it's just a fling, then I can just shut off my heart and try to enjoy the time we have left together. Even though I don't think my heart will be capable of shutting out the emotions. But I could just be honest and break it off, clean, try to contain the mess I'll surely be in once our time is over.

On the other hand, what if he says he wants more? There is a small chance he might. He wouldn't invite me to come back here and meet his family if he didn't think that there might be a little bit more to us than just sex, would he? How would this work anyway? Carter is sure to have an amazing career, be in the limelight, have women throwing themselves at him. I, however, want to be a recluse. Hermit life is my ultimate goal. If I could write books and earn a living from them, I'd be a happy woman. I don't even have to earn much, just enough to live comfortably. Until that happens, I'll have to keep modeling.

I look at my phone and sigh. I keep getting emails from one of the agencies about amazing photoshoot opportunities. And the photographer requested me specifically. What's the catch, you ask? It's Darius, the dark cloud over my otherwise perfect time with Carter. Despite the restraining order and my clear dislike toward him, he has not stopped trying to get in touch with me. In fact, it seems like the only job offers I have are with him. My explicit directions for the agencies to not schedule anything with him have been completely forgotten. The last five job opportunities seem to be with him, making me wonder what the hell he has said that makes no one else want to hire me. I have money saved up, thank God. But if I want to think about my writing career seriously, paying bills until my books come out would be much easier if I could do shoots every now and then. I could always go back to waitressing, if Darius's games don't stop, but that wouldn't leave me much time for writing.

And, speaking of writing, I have been so wrapped up in Carter that since we set off on this road trip, I haven't written a single word. I look up. Carter is busy feeding Gizmo some lettuce, so I decide to open Google Docs on my phone. I've been working on a thriller, but it doesn't feel right anymore. I open up a new document and start typing, words pouring out of me at a speed my fingers find hard to catch up to. As I type, the story gets clearer and clearer in my mind. A young woman who's always been an introvert falls for a busker whose music she hears every day on her way to work. She never sees his face but is mesmerised by his voice and his music. She battles with herself, trying to figure out if she should take the next step and look at him, but she is worried that it would ruin it for her. What if he doesn't look back at her? What if he ignores her? She starts taking a different route to work, avoiding temptation, but then one day she finally breaks and—

Rockstar: *WHATCHA DOING SUNSHINE?*

I look up, a grin on my face as Carter kneels beside me, his phone in his hand. Gizmo is nowhere to be seen. He leans over and kisses me passionately, and I forget all about my resolve to keep him at arm's length.

"Writing," I murmur against his lips. Carter stops and pulls his face away from mine.

"Writing?"

"Yeah." I blush. Apart from my literary agent, no one really knows of this passion of mine, not even Hayley, and she's as close to a best friend as I've ever had. "I, uhm, I'm writing a book."

"You are?" Carter's eyes shine with excitement. And I truly forget why I never told anyone. "Sydney, that's amazing! Have you been writing long? What's your book about? Gah! Why are you so perfect, goddamnit?" At the last bit, he shuts his mouth, his eyes huge and a blush creeping up his neck.

"I'm not perfect, rockstar. You bloody are!" I defuse the situation, laughing. I'm not joking though, he truly is perfect. For this guy, I'd let all my walls down in a heartbeat if he said he wanted them down. "I've been writing for a few years now." I wring my hands, the topic bringing the awkward teenager out of me. "I've been writing psychological thrillers and suspense. I finally got an agent too, and my first novel is getting published."

"That's incredible," he says in awe.

"Yeah, it's pretty exciting"

"So who's murdering who? What are you working on right now?"

I bite my lip. "Uhm, this is not a thriller, it's a, uhm, romance, actually."

"It iiis?" he draws out the last word. "Got inspired, did ya?"

I roll my eyes, but can't deny the truth. The main love interest is a musician. "Maybe."

"I'm yo-ur mu-se," he sing-songs.

"Maybe," I sigh, my face getting hot.

"Don't be embarrassed, Sunshine." He leans forward, cupping my cheeks. "You're my muse too." His lips are inches from mine.

I look into his eyes. "For real?"

"For real, real," he says and puts his lips on mine.

Chapter 17

Road Trip Fun?

Carter

I break away and stroke her cheek with my thumb, new music and lyrics running through my head. Honestly, I have never been this inspired to write in my whole life. Not when I was a teenager getting my angst out, not when I thought my heart was broken by my best friend. With Sydney, the songs just flow through me effortlessly. They just do, and it's all because of her.

I just hope she doesn't hate them when she finally hears them. The look in her eyes coupled with the small smile on her lips relaxes me.

"I can play you some of the music you inspired." No lyrics, that would basically be like telling her I'm obsessed with her and asking her to please like me. She nods, swallowing. Anticipation is palpable in the air.

I grab my guitar and sit down, facing her. Taking a big breath, I strum a couple of chords to warm up, gaining courage to bare my soul to her. "It's a work in progress," I say then start playing.

It starts simple, melancholic, and, before I know it, I'm quietly singing the lyrics.

J. Preston

Never want to let you go
Stay with me, drive me crazy
Let's stay naked all day
Let's be lazy
Let's bury our souls
Under a blanket made of snowy dreams
You are my everything
Stay with me, drive me crazy
In my arms just be lazy
And if the world comes knockin'
We'll tell them we're snowed in
Let's bury ours souls
Under a blanket made of snowy dreams
You are my everything

I play the melody for a few more notes before looking up, afraid of what I'll see, terrified that she'll laugh at my infatuation with her, or worse, be offended or just hate it. I take a big breath and meet her eyes. They're brimming with unshed tears and, as she blinks at me, one spills over, running down her cheek.

"Baby," my voice cracks as I move the guitar aside and pull her into my lap. "Don't cry, please. It's not ready, just a rough idea. If you hate it, I can change it or just toss it," I mumble a million miles a minute.

"No!" she exclaims, startling me into silence. "Don't you dare change a thing," she sniffles. "It's perfect, Carter, so perfect." Her hand reaches my face, cupping my cheek as she searches my eyes. There are things there I want to uncover. Emotions I want to let free, but I also see the walls she built and know that task won't be easy. Her reaction, though, gives me courage, so I decide it's time to start operation 'get Sydney to fall in love with me and be in my life forever'. Because, as much as I might pretend I'm not, I'm falling for this girl, hard. Who am I kidding? In the space of the last four days, she's claimed my heart.

"You're perfect," I say, leaning into her hand. She bites her lips. "I wrote it the first night we got here."

"The first night, after..."

"Yes, after I thoroughly fucked you, Sydney. I woke up in the middle of the night and couldn't stop thinking about you even though you were right next to me, so I got my guitar and wrote this song."

"Surely you don't mean every word, there's... What is it called? An artistic licence to embellish?"

"What are we doing here, Sydney?" I ask. Maybe I'm pushing too hard, maybe she needs it, but what *I* need is some clarity of how she feels about me.

"Here?"

"You know exactly what I mean, Sydney," I growl.

She looks down at the floor. "I don't know... Road trip fun?"

The fuck? Road trip fun? Does she really think it's road trip fun? I'm ready to roar when I see her hand twitch. It's that tick again, the one she has when she's avoiding telling me something. My heart beats faster.

"Road trip fun?" I growl. She wants to deny what this is? Fine. "As you wish." I'll show her just how much fun this road trip can be until she finally admits she's fallen for me.

In one swift movement, I have her pinned under me, her arms above her head, wrists pinned under my hand. Her eyes are big and, as I grind my hips into her, a moan escapes her lips. I lean down and, at the last moment, swerve and hover my lips by her ear. I rock my dick into her as she moves against me, gasping. "You want a fun road trip fuck?" I ask, biting and then licking her earlobe. She moans, trying to get her hands free, but I hold them in a firm grip. "No, Sunshine, my rules. And if you're a good girl, I might even let you come."

With one hand, I unhook my guitar strap and wrap it around her wrists.

"Carter," she gasps.

"If at any point you want me to stop, just say so," I say, stroking her face.

She nods and bites her lip. "Do I need a safe word?"

"If you want. I do respond to 'stop', so it's up to you."

"*Stop* is good."

"Good, now shut your pretty little mouth or I'll shut it up with my cock." She's wearing one of my button up plaid shirts, so I don't waste a minute unbuttoning. Instead I rip it open, buttons flying everywhere. Sydney yelps then moans when I suck her nipple through her thin cotton bra. Not one for unnecessary garments, I push it up over her breasts, licking then nipping her rock hard nipples. She moans and gasps as I bask in the feeling of making her feel good.

"Fuck, Carter," she moans, and I grin.

"What did I say, Sunshine? No talking." I move away from her nipple, causing a groan of frustration. At an unhurried pace, I unzip her jeans and slide them down her legs. She squirms as I run my hands down her freshly exposed flesh. Just as she relaxes, I flip her over and spank her ass. "Keep. Quiet. Or. I. Will. Have. To. Punish. You." I punctuate each word with a slap, a red mark forming on her bum. "Do you understand?" She hums, her face pressed against the cushions. "You may answer if I ask you a question."

"Yes, Carter," she moans as I run my fingers down

between her thighs, feeling how soaked she is for me. I lean over, burying my face in her panty-clad ass and grazing at her slit through the flimsy material. I fucking love the taste of her. She moans loudly and I smack her ass once then stroke the sting away. I don't know if I can hold on much longer. I want to make this good for her, but she's got me so rock hard my cock is about to punch a hole through my jeans. I slide her underwear down her legs then move my shirt out of the way and lift her butt in the air, pushing her knees in. Once she is in the right position, I slide an extra cushion under her, grazing her nipples with my fingers then giving each a tweak for good measure. She wriggles her ass at me, and I can see her glistening pussy, ready, waiting, and so fucking inviting. I run my finger up and down, spreading her wetness around her then slide it inside, stretching her. She whimpers at my touch.

"You like that?" I ask, slowly pumping in and out.

"Yes, God. Yes." I smack her ass with my other hand.

"I'm the one fucking you with my fingers, not God."

"Yes," she purrs.

I smack her again. "That wasn't a question, Sunshine. We really need to work on your etiquette." She chuckles but doesn't say a thing, so I let it go. I add another finger into her pussy, rubbing her steadily, enjoying how wet and warm she feels. In. Out. In. Out. She starts whimpering and squirming, pushing her ass back into me, meeting me stroke for stroke. I have her right where I want her. I can't take the wait anymore, anticipating being inside her again, where I belong, eating all my resolve to make her beg. I remove my fingers from her pussy and unzip my jeans, pulling my cock out and stroking it, coating it in her juices. Sydney moans as she looks at what I'm doing. I smirk at her then position myself against her entrance and slide in. The feeling of her clenched around me will never get old. It's like coming home after a long day of hard labor. I groan with pleasure as I pull out almost to the tip then slam back in. It's not enough, it's never enough. I need to be deep inside her, feel her everywhere. I continue this assault until her pants, mixed with her moans, change into chanting my name. I'm not going to punish her for that. Instead, I rub my fingers around her opening, coating them in her wetness, then move them to her asshole. She stills and looks at me over her shoulder.

"Trust me, baby," I say. My finger right against her hole, I rub around it gently, making sure it's nice and slick. She nods almost imperceptibly and puts her head back down. "Relax, Sunshine." I start moving inside her again, and when I feel her relax a little, I move my fingers back to her hole. I pump faster and faster then slide my thumb into her ass. She tenses, so I wait a little until she's relaxed before moving it deeper. When she starts moaning again, pushing her ass into me, I nearly lose it. I'm so close, I'm going to explode. It feels like it's been forever since I was last inside her, when in reality it's been less than a day. I move my free hand to her clit and start tweaking and rubbing it as I gain speed.

Sydney whimpers, begging for more, faster, harder, so I oblige. It's funny how I used to love this position because it made me feel detached from whoever I was fucking at the time. Not with Sydney. I've never felt closer to anyone, as I do now, moving inside her, feeling her tighten against me. She feels so good, fits me so well. She feels like home. She needs to fucking understand that this is no road trip fun bullshit. She. Is. Mine.

"Mine," I growl.

Sydney cries out, coming, her walls clenching around me, milking my climax. I pump into her gently a few more times then lean over, untying her wrists and kissing her shoulder.

She smiles at me dazedly as my heart races. I pull out of her then gently turn her over and kiss her. Emotions are swirling inside me, making me want to say things I have never spoken out loud to anyone. I break the kiss and nuzzle her neck. My mouth opens, but no sound comes out.

"I'll go get a cloth," I finally say and move away from her, feeling the cold.

I clean us up and get a new shirt for Sydney to wear. As she buttons it up, she looks around.

"Where is Gizmo?" she says just as an angry meowl sounds from outside. I rub my neck sheepishly.

"I left him outside with a bowl of almonds," I say, walking over to the front door and opening it. I don't even feel sorry for that. He's been following me everywhere since last night, and I wasn't about to have an audience to my sex life. Don't want to scar the little guy.

Gizmo runs inside, going straight for the kitchen counter where he stands and looks between Sydney and I, sniffing every which way.

Sydney walks over to him. "I'm sorry, Gizmo," she whispers to him and gently picks him up, cradling him to her chest. He buries his face in the crook of her arm, making scoffing noises. "I know," Sydney whispers. "I tried to stop it, but I can't anymore. I'm sorry, girl. He still thinks you're the best." Who is she talking about? Gizmo is a boy. She looks at me and walks over with our squirrel still in her arms. "You need to apologise."

I roll my eyes, but I am starting to feel bad for the gremlin. Maybe he got chilly outside? I hope he doesn't actually catch a cold. Can squirrels even catch a cold? Next time, I'll just lock him in the bathroom. There, sorted. "Sorry, man." I wrap them both in a hug. One. Happy. Family.

Now, if only Sydney could get out of her head and admit that she wants me—life would be made.

Chapter 18

Good Luck, Corky

Sydney

Best. Sex. Of. My. Entire. Life.

I nearly died. The orgasm was sooooo good. I knew Carter was skilled in the bedroom department, but this was another level of good. Like, if someone asked me if I believe in God, I'd be like, 'Duh! Haven't you seen the moves Carter's got? Nothing short of a bloody miracle!'

The only catch? He agreed to the whole thing being just fun. I know, I know. I shouldn't have even mentioned that, but I was hoping he'd say I was being ridiculous and that he wants me before throwing me on that sofa and taking me. To be fair, he did throw me on that sofa, and delivered an 'A plus' performance, one I should still be clapping for, but sadly, he didn't disagree with my comment. So now I'm stuck between a rock and a hard place. On one hand, I for sure, one hundred percent, do not want to break things off with Carter. Not just because the sex is so good, and trust me, it's soooo good, but because it's kinda too late, which brings me to the other side of the coin. On the other, my heart, which I was so set on protecting, is already his. I don't know when it happened. I don't know how. I was always so sure I could never fall for anyone, so sure I was the only person I'd ever need to be happy, and that's when Carter snuck up on me. I did not expect him and, even though I fought, even though I tried so hard...I had no chance. He sauntered into my life with his huge grin; amber-brown eyes; dark, messy hair; and his huge heart.

He didn't ask, he didn't demand. He just came and claimed what was his...my heart.

And now I'm in a pickle. Because as much as I want to be with him, I know there's an expiration date on us.

We spent the last few hours packing our stuff into the car and avoiding looking at Gizmo. That little critter knew exactly what transpired and was in a huff with Carter. Finally, with our things loaded up in the car, the cabin all cleaned out and locked up, we were ready to set off. Just one small matter left.

We debated about what to do with Gizmo. She's a wild animal and she should stay in the wild. However, our decision was made when Carter opened the car door for me. I know, swoon, right? And Gizmo ran between us and launched herself into the car. No amount of carrots, nuts, or treats would convince her to come back outside. So it was settled. Gizmo was coming with us, wherever we were heading next. We found a small, empty basket, put a fluffy towel and Carter's beanie inside, then put it in the footwell behind my seat. Gizmo, straight away, settled herself inside like she was waiting for us to make a space for her all along. It's hard trying not to get attached to her as well, but I have to try.

I'll miss her when we have to part ways. My building doesn't allow pets, and I guess she'd rather stay with Carter anyway since she's head over heels for him. I can't blame her. It's just sad that, out of the two of us, the squirrel is going to get the guy... Huh. She is playing the long game, and I'm clearly getting beat. Classic Syd, losing to an animal.

"What are you thinking about?" Carter asks, one hand on the steering wheel, one on my thigh sending shivers up and down my leg as he drives us away from the cabin. His sleeves are rolled up, and I take a good, long moment, staring at his perfect forearm before looking out the window. It's been snowing hard, and you can barely see which way to drive. I guess it's good that we left when we did. We would have gotten snowed in if we stayed any longer. Not that I would have minded being stranded with Carter.

"I don't know how you drive in these conditions," I sigh.

"I like it. The crunch of the tires on fresh snow reminds me of some of my best times. Coming here with my family. Learning to snowboard. And now..." he trails off, looking ahead. He's silent for a long while. I'm about to ask him what he meant when he speaks again, his voice quiet. "This. Us. You."

I turn my head, watching his profile as he takes a breath. "You, Sydney, are part of my best memories now, and I don't want them to stop. I don't want us to stop. Fuck 'road trip fun' unless having fun is what you want—"

"No!" I interrupt him, my heart hammering in my chest. Is he serious? Is this really happening?

"No?" He smiles and glances my way. I try to contain my grin but fail. I want him to pull over. I want to climb on his lap and show him just how happy this makes me.

"No, I don't want this to st—" A loud ringing sounds through the speakers, interrupting me.

"Hold that thought." He squeezes my thigh then answers his phone.

"*Carter?*" a female voice shouts through the car speaker. Hmmm.

"Yeah?" His voice is steady and bored as his hand sneaks back to my thigh, stroking up and down. Is he crazy? Does he want me panting while he's on a phone with another woman?

"*Oh, thank God! I've been trying to reach you since yesterday,*" the woman says.

"I've been at the Cabin; you know the reception there," he brushes her panic off. So it's someone he knows. I place my hand over his, trying to stop his casual stroking, but he just grabs my hand, puts it on my other thigh, then continues his assault.

"*Ugh, yeah. Sketchy. Last time we were there I nearly died from internet withdrawal.*" I still. The fuck? Is this someone else he brought to the cabin? Am I truly just one of many?

Carter smirks. "That's because you are addicted to your phone, Rey." The sudden dread that took me over leaves my body, and I exhale, relaxing my muscles. What the hell is wrong with me? He's talking with his younger sister.

"*Not my fault you are bo-ooo-ring,*" she sing-songs. I see that lovely trait runs in the family.

"You know, Rey, what's really tragic is how you can't stand your own company for even two minutes. Who's boring again?" he quips.

"*Whatever,*" Reagan scoffs on the other side of the line. "*We can discuss who the boring sibling is later. There's a far more pressing matter at the moment. Which you would have known about had you bothered to check for a signal.*"

"I was," he coughs, "otherwise occupied." His hand squeezes my thigh then focuses on the road ahead.

"*Well, now you'll be occupied by trying to find a*

Christmas tree. Last minute. Aunt Bertie decided that the one we decorated was inadequate, and, uhm, she decided to dispose of it."

"She what?" Carter gapes. His hand leaves my thigh and goes to the steering wheel.

"*She said you always find the best trees and wouldn't listen when we tried to explain you were travelling and couldn't get one this year. So she snuck out in the middle of the night, dragged the tree outside, and set it on fire.*"

"She what?" His knuckles go white, gripping the steering wheel.

"*Do you have any other words in your repertoire?*" Reagan sighs. "*She set it on fire. Fiiiire. At least she had the decency to take the decorations off. Probably because most of them are handmade by you. I swear she thinks you hung the moon.*" Just another woman in the collection who does, then.

Carter shakes his head in disbelief. "So, what do you want me to do? I won't get there for another few hours." I straighten. Get where?

"*Well, from where I'm standing, it's simple. You need to find a tree, and you know how particular she is.*"

"Fuck." I place my hand on his thigh and start stroking gently, trying to calm him down.

"*Yup,*" she agrees.

"It's Christmas Eve, Rey. You're nuts if you think I can find anything."

"*Yup.*"

"Fuck." I squeeze his thigh. His hand comes off the steering wheel and he threads his fingers with mine.

"*All right then,*" Reagan chuckles. "*Good luck, Corky.*" She hangs up.

"Fuuuuuuuuuuuck!" Carter swears again. "Where are

we going to find a decent Christmas tree two minutes before Christmas?"

I don't answer, thoughts swirling in my head. What did he mean that he won't get there for a few hours? My face pales. Was he planning on bringing me with him, or was he going to drop me off in a hotel somewhere? And why the hell wouldn't he say something about it to me?

"Sunshine, you look pale. You feeling okay?" He squeezes my hand.

I don't know what to think. I'm assuming here that he's not just going to drop me off on a side of the road and tell me sayonara until after Christmas while he goes to visit his family. And if he wants me to come with him then that's a big deal. A huge deal, in fact. At least for me. I've never met anyone's family, at least not anyone I dated. It's funny because I just never wanted to. One person to deal with was always enough. Imagine getting a whole family as a package deal. Too many people to answer to, and since the guys I dated were never long-term boyfriend material—at least not in my eyes—I'd be breaking up with the whole family. I just wouldn't be able to deal with all that, disappointing people I barely knew.

What about now? I don't want Carter to be a fling, and from what he's been saying and the way he's been acting, I know he doesn't want that either. But to meet his family, already? What if they hate me? The only family I know is my mother, and I'm pretty sure she hates me, so why would a stranger's family like me if she doesn't? I look up and turn to face him.

"Can you pull over, please?" I whisper. He looks my way then quickly pulls onto the side of the road.

"Baby, what's wrong?" He switches off the engine and fully turns to me, taking both my hands in his.

"I just—I, I don't know." I take my hands out of his and put them on my face, covering it. Maybe that will help me organise my thoughts.

"Then talk to me, let's figure it out together." He pulls my hands away from my face.

I nod, slowly. How do I even start this conversation? "So, next stop is your family."

His face goes red. "About that." Oh shit, I guess it's the side of the road for me after all. "I'm sorry I didn't tell you earlier. I just wasn't sure how to invite you, and then you said it was just a bit of fun for you. I don't know, I didn't want you to feel like you had to come along…"

"It's not. A bit of fun, I mean."

"So you'll come?" His eyes are hopeful, and a small smile creeps up on his face. And, without thinking, I nod my head, the terror I felt earlier nowhere to be seen.

"I have to warn you, my family is a little bit crazy. Well, that is a bit of an understatement. But you already said yes, so no take backs!"

I laugh, "Okay, weirdo."

Carter grins and pulls me in, kissing me senseless before breaking the kiss and placing his forehead against mine, his eyes closed. When he moves away, he has this intense look in his eyes. I think he's about to tell me he wants to fuck me right here on the side of the road in this jeep, and I'm all for it, ready to unzip his pants, when he opens his mouth and says, "I like you so much, Sydney."

I blink once. Twice. Three times. My heart resuming its gallop. I want to say it back, but something stops me. It's not that I don't like him. I do. Hell, I'm pretty sure I'm falling for the guy, but I've never been one to show emotions of any kind. And I have already stripped down so many layers for him. It's like this is one of the last pieces of wall covering my heart, and I'm holding onto it tightly. Afraid to let go. "You don't have to say it back," he says. "I know deep down you love me. Who wouldn't, eh?" I smile. He truly is great, and he's right, it's hard not to fall for him. So hard.

"So about the Christmas tree."

Carter groans. "Fuck, why'd you have to go and spoil the mood, Sunshine?" I giggle. Gah! If anyone will get those words out of me, it will be him. I know it. "I don't know. We'll have to hit up every place we can find on the road. See if any tree will live up to my aunt's expectations," he sighs.

"We'll find it." I squeeze his hand. "We'll get the perfect tree one way or another, I promise."

"Ah, Sydney. Don't make promises two hours before everything closes on Christmas Eve."

"Watch me, Corky." I wink at him.

"I'm only letting you off for calling me anything other than 'handsome', 'rockstar', 'sexiest guy alive', or 'Carter'," he leans over and softly speaks into my ear. "Because I like you, but make that mistake one more time and I'll have to spank you."

"Corky," I breathe, knowing full well what I'm getting myself into.

"Mmmmm." He nips my earlobe, causing a gasp to escape my lips. "As much as I'd like to follow up with my threat right here in this car." He moves down to my neck and licks where my pulse is racing. "Gizmo decided to join in and jumped up on my shoulder." He pulls away, laughing, and sure enough, Gizmo is clutching onto his shirt. "Cock-blocked by a squirrel, again. We'll have to talk about this Giz, or you'll be getting a cage." Gizmo scoffs, outraged. "Exactly, dude. Anyway, we have a Christmas tree to procure, we better get going."

Chapter 19

Ride Or Die, Rockstar

Carter

"This is a joke!" I slam Jeepak's door as, yet another lot that's supposed to sell Christmas trees comes up empty, bar a couple of what can only be described as naked tree branches. Honestly, what was Aunt Berta even thinking? How on Earth am I supposed to magically conjure up the perfect Christmas tree, on Christmas Eve, in the middle of nowhere. I briefly considered pulling a *National Lampoon's Christmas Vacation*, but unlike Clark Griswold, I don't have an axe on hand.

"There's still time," Sydney says. She's right, there is still fifteen minutes before everything closes.

"I guess so." I try to be as positive as Sydney, but the sinking feeling that there's not a chance that we can find anything even remotely good enough starts in the pit of my stomach. I guess we'll be having a Christmas without a Christmas tree. I sigh and start the engine. It doesn't take us long to get to the next lot, but the place is empty as well. As is the next one. And the next. At this rate, we'll have to get a *Charlie Brown* Christmas tree and call it a day.

"Hey, don't worry," Sydney says, seeing my expression as yet another place has no trees to offer. It's two minutes to closing time, and it's not looking good for us. "If we need to, we'll steal the bloody thing," she laughs, but an idea starts forming in my head.

"Sydney, you clever beast!" I pull her back into Jeepak and drive us to the little market town right outside from where my aunt lives.

The place is deserted, not surprising as everyone is probably back home with their families and not panicking around trying to get a last minute Christmas tree. I run out of the jeep, Sydney hot on my heels as I navigate through the cobblestone streets. Any other time I'd casually stroll down, holding Sydney's hand in mine, pointing at the cutesy things a market town like that has in spades and trying to get her to fall in love with this place so that she'd want to come back with me every year. Not this time, though. This time, I'm a man on a mission. I pump my legs, lungs burning, dragging Sydney behind me until we get to my destination. My heart drops to the ground. Fuck. Fuuuuuck!

I walk up to the closed gate and kick it a couple of times. There's a notice on the metal fence next to it.

'Christmas Eve - the market will close at five o'clock'.

We're two hours late. I groan as Sydney walks up behind me and places her hand on my back, soothing me. I turn to her and pull her into a hug, inhaling her sweet scent.

"What was the plan, rockstar?" she asks.

"They usually don't close until seven on Christmas Eve," I mumble into her hair. "They have a lovely Christmas tree on display each year and they take it down the day the market reopens after New Year's. I was going to offer to buy it off them since, technically, no one will see it after today anyway."

Sydney pulls away from me. "But we're too late?" I nod sadly. "And no one is here?" I nod again. "And you are certain this tree is perfect?" I nod once more.

"It doesn't matter. Who needs a Christmas tree anyway?" I pout then pull her into my arms. "I just wanted to have one...for you. But really, what's important is that you're here. Nothing else matters. Fuck the Christmas tree." I kiss her gently then step away and turn my back on the market. It's true. As long as she's with me, I don't care what I have or don't have. It's weird how quickly she became one of the most important people in my life.

I take a few steps before realizing that Sydney is not walking with me. I turn back to call her. She's by the gate, looking at it intently.

"Sydney?" I ask, walking back to her. She keeps looking at the gate then looks up at me abruptly, her gaze intense.

"I don't want to go to jail, so we need to be really quick about this," she says. Confusion must be painted on my face as she adds, "I mean, if I *do* go to jail, I'm okay with it being for a heist. A Christmas tree heist." She smiles up at me and pulls two hairpins out of her loose bun. Her blonde hair cascades down her shoulders, making her look like an angel with the Christmas lights shining from a store window behind her.

"Sydney," I whisper.

"Thing is, Carter, I like you so much too." I grin as my heart speeds up. "And the only way I know how to say it is to show it. And if going to jail for stealing a tree is how I show you, then so be it. Because I do. I fucking like you."

"Baby," I take a step toward her. "You just said it. You don't need to—"

"Ride or die, rockstar." She grins.

"Ride or die," I reply and swoop her up. She wraps her legs around my waist and kisses me. I want to fuck—no—I want to make love to her so badly I can't think, so I groan in disapproval when she pulls away and unhooks her legs. I put her back down on the ground. "So what's the plan, Bonnie?"

"Well, Clyde, we're breaking in, taking the tree, and hightailing it outta here." She grins and starts doing the bendy thing with her hairpins again. The first time she did that at the cabin, I nearly took her right there and then in the snow. She's so fucking irresistible it's unreal. All sweet, blond angel with a naughty side to her. And the fact that she never fails to catch a reference I throw at her makes her even more appealing and perfect for me. "Light, please," she says, bending down, her face near the lock. I pull out my phone and snap a picture of her perfect ass before turning on the flashlight and illuminating the lock for her. She puts the hairpins in and starts the whole 'moving them around' thing. I'm so mesmerized it doesn't even register when the lock clicks and the gate opens.

She bites her bottom lip and stands up, shaking the snow off her jeans with her hands. "Is it wrong that I find you so hot right now, my little criminal?" She smirks and winks at me, pushing the gate open.

"Lead the way."

I walk past her but at the last minute reach out and grab her by the ass, pulling her in. "I'm going to fuck you so hard tonight, Sydney, you'll need a pillow to muffle your screams," I say, grinding into her. Although it's dark, I can tell a blush is creeping up her neck. But she quickly catches herself and puts her hand on my hard dick, cupping it.

"All that talk, Carter,"—she pouts—"and no action. You better back up all these pretty words."

I moan, frustrated, as she gently squeezes me through my jeans. "Fuck, Sydney, if we weren't in a public place and if we didn't just commit a crime, I'd fuck you right now just to prove a point. Let's go." I step away and walk through the gate. There's a little unlit alleyway that leads to the main area.

"Humph," Sydney huffs quietly. "A little exhibitionism never hurt anybody," she mumbles.

In one movement, I turn to her and push her against the alleyway wall. "Oh, Sydney. Sydney, Sydney, Sydney," I tsk. "When will you learn not to challenge me, huh, Sunshine? It's like waving a red cape at a bull."

"Noted," she gulps as I reach down and push her yoga pants down, pressing her back against the wall.

"Can you be quiet, Sunshine?" I rub her panties, which are already soaked. I moan at the feel of her need for me.

"Yes," she gasps as I push them aside and unzip my jeans, pulling my cock out.

I'm inside her before she can say 'please', pumping fast as she buries her head in the crook of my neck stifling a moan.

"Do you like this, Sydney?" I say as I speed up, feeling her legs start to shake. "Do you like that at any moment someone could walk by and see us? See how I'm fucking you? See how you like it?" She moans and pulls her head away, throwing it back as I pound into her. "You like that, don't you? You wouldn't mind someone watching how I make you feel?" She moans again, much louder this time, so I cover her mouth with my hand. "Thing is, Sunshine, I don't share. You are mine and only I can watch you come. Understood?" Her muffled moans are so loud, I'm ready to burst. "Come for me, Sydney," I growl, and my girl listens. With a cry, she comes around me, making my orgasm so strong I can barely keep us upright. I search harder for her lips, kissing her, still trying to catch my breath as I try to come down from the high that is Sydney Buyer, but I don't think I can.

I pull out of her and move her panties back into place. "I'm sorry, baby, I've got nothing to clean you up with," I say, pulling her yoga pants back on and stuffing my dick back into my jeans.

"That's okay," she smiles. "I kinda asked for it, didn't I?"

I place a gentle kiss on her nose. "You did, but I love making your wishes come true. So no hardship there." I wink then take her hand. "Now, let's go steal us a Christmas tree."

The market is as empty as the shopping district around it. The stalls are empty, the booths boarded up. And in the middle of the place, in all its Christmasy glory, stands the perfect Christmas tree. It's about ten feet tall with green branches full of pine needles. Someone already started work on taking off the decorations. There's a box filled with baubles and garlands.

"Huh," Sydney says. "It really does look good, but how exactly are we supposed to get it out of here unnoticed?"

I start unwinding the lights and put them on the side next to the box. I might be stealing a tree, but I'm not about to steal someone's possessions.

"There's a place at the back where I can drive up, so we can take the tree through there." I motion to the back, handing Sydney a stray bauble. She takes it from me and stills.

"What?"

I smile. "There's a break in the fence at the back of the market where it backs out onto the forest."

Sydney crosses her arms and starts tapping her foot. "So what you're saying is that I broke in for no reason?"

"Do you regret it?" I cock my head. "Do you regret saying that you like me, breaking in, and the alley?" She bites her lip and shakes her head.

"There's a reason for everything, Sydney. And this time, it was for you to come to terms with how wonderful I am and how much you like me." She rolls her eyes and continues taking the rest of the decorations. When the tree is bare, I examine the bottom of it: it's screwed into a metallic looking stand. I start to unscrew it when Sydney stops me.

"It looks like it might take a while. Why don't you go get the car in place and I'll try to take it off the stand."

"Are you sure?" I hate to leave her by herself in here, but she's got a point. The sooner we get out of here, the better, and we've already been taking our time. She nods and kneels next to me.

"I've got it, now go, go, go! No time to waste." She pecks me on the cheek and pushes me away. I don't argue; instead, I turn and run back to the car.

Gizmo is inside, looking pissed as hell for being left alone.

"Sorry, dude," I mutter, startling the engine. "When the crime calls, the crime calls." He makes a noise at me. "You'd just have been in the way. Trees are like catnip to you." He chirps again, this time louder. I turn onto the dirt road behind the market and drive to where I remember the hole in the fence being, hoping they didn't fix it. "I promise once the tree is up at Bertie's you can go to town on it, okay?" He huffs at me just as I spot the break in the fence. Awesome.

I park, pulling pen and paper out of the glove compartment and scribbling a quick note.

To whom it may concern,

Sorry I took your tree. I'm hoping it saved you from having to dispose of it while we were in dire need. You've probably heard of Alberta Kennedy. She burned ours just before Christmas, and you see, my girlfriend is spending Christmas with us... I had to get a tree. Anyway, I'm leaving you some cash to compensate for the inconvenience. You'll also see that all the lights and decorations are in the box, the only thing I took is the tree itself.

I hope this is okay, but if not, I'm really sorry.

Merry Christmas,
 Carter Kennedy

PS. You'll notice I signed my name, this is just in case you want to press charges. I hope you won't, though.

I take three hundred dollars from my wallet and wrap the note around the cash then run back inside the market through the opening. Sydney is holding onto the tree trunk with one hand, beaming at me.

"You did it." I beam back and stuff my note with the cash into the box.

I help her pull the tree out of the stand and, together,

we drag the tree through the stalls to where the car is parked.

It's heavy, sticky, and very, very prickly. I'm starting to regret my idea about stealing a tree that's not wrapped up in a net. How did Griswold do it again?

Chapter 20

You Brought a Pet

Sydney

By the time we get to the car, I'm sweating, and my hands are covered in sap and tiny needle marks that are starting to itch. How the hell are we supposed to heave the prickly monstrosity up on the roof of the jeep that's currently looming over us in all its tall car glory?

"You can put your end down here," he says, waiting until I do so before unceremoniously dropping his side to the ground and walking over to the boot. He's there for about a minute before, with a triumphant 'aha', he comes up for air holding a rope-like looking thing with a hook at each end.

Seems like rockstar has got a plan, and who am I to get in a way of that? A frail damsel, that's who. No, seriously, my upper body strength is non-existent. Carrying the tree a hundred meters to the car nearly broke me.

As I examine the roof rack with the big black box on top housing our snowboards, Carter gets to work on wrapping the rope around the trunk of the tree. The feasibility of it fitting on the top of the car and staying in place is low, but stranger things have happened; plus, we need to haul it up top in the first place. Carter stands up, dusting his hands off in a satisfied manner, then looks at me expectantly.

"I'm going to need you to turn around, Sunshine. This ain't going to be pretty." I laugh and stay still, crossing my arms in front of me. "Fine, have it your way. But if, by the end, you don't want to rip my clothes off, I'll be devastated."

He turns around in a huff as the right corner of my mouth lifts a little. He's dreaming if he thinks there's a chance I won't find him attractive. Carter is pure sex on long, muscly legs. My mouth starts watering as he lifts one side of the tree and props it against the back of the car. When he squats, lifting the trunk and sliding the tree up into place with a bit of grunting, I'm positively salivating. In fact, I'm ready to jump him. He's strong and masculine, and if he wanted to throw me over his shoulder and take me on the hood of the car right next to that freaking tree, I wouldn't complain. Not even a little bit.

Gizmo shows her face through the window, looking at me pointedly as if she could sense where my thoughts went. I shrug my shoulders at her, stick my tongue out, making a face and walking over to where the fine male specimen is currently attaching the hooks onto the rack. I help by holding the thing in place as he tightens, adjusts, and readjusts the rope until finally, in less than fifteen minutes, we have a Christmas tree secured to the roof. The term 'secured' being used loosely here, but the tree is there, and it'll hopefully stay in place until we reach our destination. Carter brushes the pine needles off himself and walks over to me.

"Still want to make out?" I don't respond. Instead, in a few short steps, I close the distance between us and attack his mouth. His arms wrap around my middle as he hums into my mouth the moment our tongues tangle. A hum that reverberates right down to my toes. My fingers dig into his thick, shaggy hair, pulling it gently and coming up with a pine cone. I laugh, breaking the kiss. He exhales happily while Gizmo scratches at the window, clearly pissed off. Sorry, not sorry Gizmo, a girl's gotta pull all the tricks out if she likes a guy like Carter. "Well, we better be going," he sighs.

I nod and turn back to the car, the tree completely dwarfing it. Seriously, it's massive, and a large chunk of it covers the windscreen. I'm not sure how on earth he is going to drive with it mostly obscured by green pine needles. But I'm confident he'll surprise me with his skills yet again. I tap my chin in thought, wondering if it's even wise to drive while not being able to see, especially since it's dark now, when the telltale sound of a phone camera shutter makes me smile to myself. Carter thinks he's so covert, but he's been taking pictures of me when I'm not looking and posting them on Instagram with enigmatic captions. They're sweet, thoughtful, and sexy. I'm secretly starting to love it, even though it's inevitable for someone to put two and two together and recognise me.

I turn to him just as he types something into his phone then looks up at me and smiles, walking over and opening the car door. As I slide into the seat, he leans over and whispers into my ear, "Thank you, Sydney." He brushes my cheek with his thumb, lingering for a bit too long, then pulls away, his usual amber-brown eyes almost black in the dark of the evening.

"Ride or die," I smile, but inside my stomach releases a thousand butterflies. I'm not quite sure what he's thanking me for, but I have a feeling it's not just for the Christmas tree heist.

J. Preston

While driving to our destination, I rediscovered God, reciting prayers in my head and promising whatever I can think of if we just make it out of this trip alive. The tree covers most of the windscreen except for a small part on the driver's side, so it feels like we're driving blind and from sheer memory. Not something you want to experience, ever. And, once again, I find myself thanking God for looking down on me and making sure my stomach is empty, because your girl would have barfed from the stress at least ten times in the short drive.

But I didn't.

Carter parks and turns off the engine, giving me a toothy smile. I open the door and step outside, taking in my surroundings. Despite the fact that it's dark, I can see that the place, although not big, is the fillet mignon type of crowd, whereas I grew up in the chicken burger crowd. Where my housing estate was littered with food wrappers, dead trees, and plastic toys, here, snow covers beautiful landscaping crisscrossed throughout. The end effect is so stunning it would make Santa Claus envious.

"Where are we?" I whisper as Carter stands next to me with Gizmo on his shoulder. He puts his arm around me just as Gizmo spots the tree on the car and launches herself at it.

"My aunt's house," he explains. Clearly, his aunt is Mrs. Claus because the view in front of me is like Winter Wonderland. Candy Cane lights illuminate the pathway to the two story house. All smaller trees and shrubs surrounding us glow with twinkling lights. In front of the window, there's a real-size, wooden sleigh painted red with a freaking reindeer in a small stable beside it. I gape, looking around, trying to take it all in. "She's big on Christmas."

"You don't say," I mutter.

The front door opens and an old, feeble looking lady steps out dressed in a red jacket with a white collar and a red skirt, clearly channeling Mrs. Claus.

"Carter, my boy, is that you?" she asks weakly. "Do you have the tree?" she demands, her voice a bit more stern with the question.

"Hi, Aunt Bertie," he says loudly, walking up to her and dragging me behind him. Here we go. Faint music comes from inside the house, an old Christmas song I vaguely recognise.

"Hello," I say, waving my hand. "The tree is on the car roof," I state the obvious.

She looks at me inquisitively, a glint in her eye. "The flea learned to whoof?" I crack a smile.

"No, Aunt Bertie." Carter shakes his head and corrects her loudly, "Sydney said that the Christmas tree is on the roof of the car." She nods, eyeing me up and down. I must look bedraggled, not surprising with all the scrapes from the Christmas tree and the sap stuck to my hair and hands. I fidget with my fingers at her scrutiny. For some reason, I feel like I need her approval, like she is the deciding vote on whether I'm good enough for Carter or not.

Her eyes move slowly from me to the car and the tree on top of it. As beautiful as the tree looked when we first saw it, I'm sure, by now, it looks as sorry as I do—or at least it will by the time we take it down. Her eyes widen, and her hand covers her mouth.

"That's not a flea," she gasps. "What is that thing?" Both Carter and I turn our heads in unison, seeing Gizmo having the time of her life, jumping from branch to branch, squealing and chirping. Disappearing inside them, poking her little head out and back in again. Her antics make me want to giggle, but I stifle the urge. I don't want to appear ditzy in front of Carter's distinguished, albeit a bit Christmas crazy, aunt.

"Oh, that's Gizmo, our squirrel." Awwww, he said 'our'. A warm feeling spreads around my tummy. I want to squeeze him and kiss him and do naughty things to him. But, we've got company, so I don't.

Aunt Berta takes a tentative step forward. "A squirrel, you say?" Curiously, this time, she didn't have an issue with hearing exactly what Carter said. Carter doesn't seem to notice that his aunt can suddenly hear perfectly, but I've got my eyes on her. I smirk and watch her take a few more steps forward. Carter rushes to her and helps her walk towards the car.

"Gizmo?" Carter shouts. A little head pops out from between the branches. "Come here, boy," Carter whistles at her like she's a dog. But it seems to be working because Gizmo fully exits the tree, jumps on the ground, and starts running toward him. I swear she'd do anything for that boy. Well, get in the line, sister! She climbs up his trouser leg, over his jacket, and settles herself on his shoulder. "Say hi to Aunt Berta, Gizmo." Gizmo's little nose starts moving side to side, sniffing the air until she decides that Aunt Berta is not an enemy and tentatively chirps at her. The sound is very quiet, yet it still makes Carter's aunt squeal in delight. Curiouser and curiouser.

"You brought a pet." She claps her hands. "What a wonderful surprise! I did miss that shaggy dog this Thanksgiving. How is Jason, by the way?"

Carter snorts then mutters, "He's safe at home."

"Shacked up with a gnome? How strange. Oh well, they

can't all be perfect." She shrugs her arms. I briefly wonder who the hell Jason is, but Carter's aunt starts shuffling us into the house. "I'll get your dad to help you with the tree." She pushes us through the doorway. "Rooobeeert!" My eardrums nearly burst from the decibel of her shout. I guess her lungs work just fine.

"Coming!" A voice comes from one of the rooms nearby, followed by the sound of footsteps, then a tall looking man walks into the hallway. My heart stops. I have a clear view of what Carter will look like in the future. And let me just tell you, I'm not disappointed. Carter's dad is hot. In an 'I dress weird but I don't care and still can rock it' kind of way. Actually, his clothes remind me of the really posh countryside boys from England I used to crush on when I was a teenager. I take him in, head to toe. His hair is thick and shaggy like Carter's but differs in colour. Where Carter's hair is dark brown, his dad has got grey strands peppered throughout it. He's wearing thick-rimmed glasses that cover eyes strikingly similar to Carter's, and when he smiles, spotting us, it's the same smile that Carter has when he's genuinely excited. He's wearing a Fairisle knitted sweater over a light blue shirt with a collar, the bottom sticking out from underneath, covering the top of his brown corduroy trousers, which have stitched-on Christmas trees and are rolled up at the calf. In his hand is a tumbler with a brown liquid in it, ice cubes clinking to the sound of the Christmas song playing in the background, and on his feet he's got the most ridiculous looking elf slippers I have ever seen. If this is what Carter will look like in years to come, where do I sign?

"You made it!" his dad exclaims, pulling us into a big hug. "And you've got the tree. Brilliant! Let's go get it, son," he says, peering over our shoulders and through the open doors.

"Good to see you, dad. I've missed you."

"You French-kissed poo?" his back to being hard-of-hearing aunt says. "Well, that's just not very sanitary." She says it with a straight face, looking at her nails with interest, and I can't stop myself. I burst out laughing. Is no one else seeing this? This woman is hilarious, and I want to *be* her when I grow up. I bite my lip as she narrows her eyes at me, trying to gauge my reaction. I wink at her. For a moment, I think I made a huge mistake when her features don't move and her eyes continue boring into mine. But then a small smirk appears on her face, and she nods at me almost imperceptibly. I think I just made a new friend, and this one is a keeper.

Chapter 21

So, So Hard

Carter

"So, Sydney seems nice." My hands still as my dad's words reach me. I'm in the middle of unhooking the Christmas tree on my side of Jeepak.

Trying to see him through the thick branches, I reply, "She *is* nice. She's amazing, really." There's silence between us, and since I can't see shit, I get back to unhooking the rope.

"What about your soul searching?" he asks after a while. "I thought that was your priority. Are you sure bringing a girl along is a good idea?" Sighing, I drop the rope and round the car to where he's standing, facing him.

"Plans change." Crossing my arms over my chest, I lean against the car and wait for him to say something. He doesn't, so I keep going. "And Sydney is exactly what I needed to open my eyes. She's kind, caring, smart, and witty. She is everything I didn't realize I needed or wanted. So, if you're worried about my soul searching, don't be. I found my soul. Her name is Sydney." The words couldn't ring truer. Now that I've spoken them out loud, relief washes over me. Relief that I'm no longer holding all these feelings inside me, locked up in a cage, aching to get away. Setting them free feels right. Now if only I had the guts to say them to Sydney. But I don't. It's too soon, and I don't want to scare her.

His face lights up as his lips stretch into a huge grin. "You *finally* fell in love!"

"So hard." I place my head in my hands, shaking it. So, so hard. Not sure when exactly this happened, but it had, and it was blatantly obvious that it was coming.

"Aaah, why the long face? You're a Kennedy boy, and when it hits us, it hits us hard." Dad pats my shoulder.

"I thought I was in love before." I peek through my hands at him. "I really did, but the feelings I'm having for Sydney are like mountains compared to molehills."

He chuckles. "Ah, yes. Thinking you're in love and being in love are two completely different things. At least it taught you to open your heart to the possibility. And look where it brought you." Right to Sydney. The thought makes me warm inside as I look up.

But as quickly as it showed up on my face, the smile falters. "Dad, if she doesn't feel the same way..." my voice cracks. "It'll break me." I know it will. If the way I feel for her is any indication of the hurt she could cause should she decide my feelings weren't reciprocated, I'd be devastated. Like a tsunami, she'd rip apart my soul, scattering all its broken pieces under her feet as she walked all over them on her way out. Just the thought makes my heart clench in pain.

"I don't think you have to worry about it, son." He pulls me into a side hug. "I'm pretty sure she feels the same way." My head whips up, looking back at the house, trying to spot her silhouette through the frosted-over windows.

"God, I hope so. But,"—I search for the right words—

"she's not like...us." His eyebrow lifts in question. "She didn't have a good childhood, or life, to be honest. I think she's always had to rely only on herself. And she's guarded, closed off. But, Dad, when she lets her guard down, even just for a moment, it's iridescent. She shines so bright, everything else pales in comparison."

Dad laughs. I know I'm being soppy as shit, but it's how I feel. I shrug and turn to unhook the rope on his side. He hasn't even started on it. "I can't wait to get to know her better." He ruffles my hair. Not the hair! I duck and take a moment to appreciate the warm feeling in my chest. My family seems to have accepted Sydney with open arms. At least, the two crazy members she's met already. Two more to go. The two *really* crazy ones. Both Mom and Rey are a force to be reckoned with, scaring off any potential girlfriends since I was ten. Rey with her buggers and Mom with her inquisition. My junior high study partner probably still has nightmares and talks about the two Kennedy women at each of her weekly therapy sessions.

As sure as I am that Sydney can survive the absolute carnage that my mom and sister have in store for her, I speed up in untangling the rope. The sooner I get back inside, the better.

Getting the damned tree down is definitely easier than getting it up there, and, within minutes, Dad and I are carrying it through the front door and into the living room where everyone is sitting. I still when I spot Reagan sitting right next to Sydney, her hands clasping Sydneys as she whispers something into her ear. They both burst out laughing. Mom walks up and hands them each a glass of wine, kneeling beside them, looking excited. A lump forms in my throat, and I'm finding it hard to swallow. This picture perfect image is everything I could have hoped for. They're chatting in hushed voices, bursting into giggles every now and then. Sydney is looking comfortable with Gizmo settled in her lap as my sister kept gesticulating, clasping her hand still. Aunt Bertie is on her rocking chair by the fireplace, eyes half closed and a smirk on her face. Her eyes fly open and she stares at me.

"Carter?" Dad says, pulling me out of my thoughts. I shake my head and resume walking. Together, we secure the tree in its stand. It's not awful. I mean, some branches are broken, there are bald spots all around, but if we turn it just 'so', it's passable. Mom gets up and puts her arm around Dad, cocking her head to the side while examining the mangled tree. He pulls her in and kisses the top of her head. My eyes instantly go to Sydney. She's looking at my parents, biting her bottom lip and absentmindedly stroking Gizmo, who is lying on his back, paws up in the air, enjoying her caresses. My mind goes straight to the future. Ten years from now, sitting in this living room, possibly a baby in her lap. Will she look at me the same way? Like I'm the answer to all her questions. Will our eyes always be drawn to each other? As if on cue, Sydney's gaze locks onto mine. I give her my best grin, hoping she can't decipher the tornado of emotions I have in me.

In my peripheral vision, I see Rey's head swing from me to Sydney, then back to me. She whispers something to Sydney then tickles Gizmo on his tummy and walks over to me. "Good job, Corky."

I look back at the tree.

"I'm sure it's nowhere near as nice as what Aunt Berta burned, but it's a tree." I shrug. I can feel the absence of Sydney's gaze deep inside my bones as cold seeps in. It takes a lot not to look back at her straight away.

"I meant Sydney, you buffoon." She playfully punches

my shoulder. I lose the war and find Sydney again, her expression unsure as she takes in the tree. "And yes, I do believe our tree was better, but, hey, no-one here plays favorites, right?" She shakes her head. It's a long-standing joke that Aunt Berta would let me get away with murder. I nod absentmindedly, taking in every twitch on Sydney's face, every minuscule tick. "Go on then, go to her. Jeez, I've never seen anyone look as love sick as the pair of you," Rey sighs. I don't wait for anything else my sister might have to say; instead, my feet start moving and, in just a few short strides, I'm in front of Sydney.

Feeling nervous and all out of sorts, I sit next to her, placing my hand on her lap, desperate for contact. As usual, electricity courses through me at the touch of her skin as her aqua eyes slowly leave the tree and settle on me.

"Sydney." My voice comes up gruff, as if I walked the Sahara with an empty flask. I try to clear my throat, but even that doesn't seem to help the scorching.

"Carter." She presses her lips together.

I lick my lips, trying to figure out where to start; there are so many things I want to say to her. How she's the sunshine in the moonless dark of my life. How she lifts me up and makes me believe anything is possible. How I can't imagine a future without her. How all I want is to make her happy. "You okay? I'm sorry I left you."

"I'm fine," she says just as the first notes of *'Driving Home For Christmas'* play through the speakers. My mom squeals with delight as my dad pulls her into his arms and guides her, slow-dancing around the tree. My body cools the instant Sydney's eyes leave mine and trace the path my mom and dad take.

I move closer to Sydney, seeking her warmth once again as Rey starts jumping around the laughing couple, making gagging noises until they pull her in and she dances with them, thrilled. From the corner of my eye, I see something glisten and turn just as Sydney wipes away a tear.

"They're so happy," she says quietly. My heart breaks at the thought that Sydney has never experienced a Christmas like this before.

"It's *their* song," I reply. Sydney looks at me, waiting for me to elaborate. "They met at Christmas, this song was playing in a bar..." I trail off, realizing the similarities.

"I love that," Sydney mutters.

"I guess our song would be 'Jingle Bells'," I laugh, rubbing the back of my neck, hoping she doesn't think I'm a sentimental idiot.

"Our song," Sydney repeats, tasting the word on her tongue. "I've never had *a* song. And it makes it more special that it can only be played once a year." As if on cue, the next song starts up, and it's *'Jingle Bells'* by Frank Sinatra. I stand up, brushing my jeans off, and hold my hand out.

"Mademoiselle?" She looks up at me, her eyes huge. I smile encouragingly. "C'mon, Sunshine, you know you want to," I say as she bites her lip. Rey pops over my shoulder.

"Sydney you've got to dance, we're all being dancing fools! Join us!"

"It's *our* song," I nod.

"Shut the front door!" Rey exclaims, waking Aunt Berta and the dead.

"You want to go to the store? Everything is shut, child," she interjects loudly, making Sydney crack a smile. Rey just rolls her eyes and nudges Gizmo off Sydney's lap. He reluctantly comes off and settles himself on a sofa cushion. Sydney looks from me to Rey to Bertie then nods and gets up.

"What the hell," she smiles and shrugs one shoulder. "Let's do this, Kennedy."

"Ooooh! We've got ourselves a Christmas dance off!" Rey shouts. The girl needs volume control. I ignore her and pull Sydney into my arms then lead her around the leaving room, holding her close. I twirl her a couple of times then dip her, making her laugh. Too soon, the song ends, but my sister, the Angel, is by the speaker, fiddling with her phone and the first keys of 'Say all you want for Christmas is me' starts playing. I keep Sydney in my arms, swaying us side to side, quietly singing along. I don't falter when Shania and Nick sing *'I'm gonna love you like it's always Christmas Eve'*. Instead, I sing the words along, looking straight into Sydney's eyes, deciding to let her draw her own conclusions.

We keep slow dancing as Rey plays the DJ with every sentimental Christmas song she can find until Aunt Berta starts snoring loudly, at which point Rey can't take it anymore and bursts out into a huge fit of laughter.

"Well, I guess we should start decorating the Christmas tree anyway," Mom says. I reluctantly let go of Sydney and take her hand into mine, not ready to lose the touch of her skin yet. We all crowd around the big box near to where the tree is standing filled with Christmas lights and ornaments. Dad takes out the lights and hands one end to my sister. They then proceed with their annual Christmas tree maypole dancing. No, seriously, it's exactly what it looks like.

Sydney giggles. "Your family is incredible," she whispers, shaking her head. It's on the tip of my tongue to say that they are just all right or dismiss her statement in another way, but I stop myself.

"It seems to me," I say, "that they think the exact same

thing about you." Just as the words leave my mouth, my mom turns around and grins at us, motioning for us to join them. "I hope you've got Christmas tree decorating skills, because if there's one thing that the Kennedy family lacks, it's that."

"Well then, you should probably call for help, cause this girl,"—Sydney points two thumbs at herself, laughing—"ain't it." My mom wraps an arm around Sydney and hands her the first ornament: a gingerbread man I made when I was four.

"You do the honors." Sydney looks from her to me, then back to her, making sure she isn't joking. I gently nudge her towards the tree, and she tentatively places the decoration right in the middle. I never thought of my family as weird, but as they clap and woot at Sydney, I can't help but consider what we must seem like to an outsider. A family that gets excited by the hanging of the first ornament on the Christmas tree, one that has Christmas dance offs and a crazy, half-deaf aunt. Yup, we're a bunch of lovable weirdos.

Sydney blushes and steps back to me just as my sister shouts, "Daddy, bring on the eggnog! Let the tree decorating commence!" She boogies over to the box and starts picking out decorations before hanging them haphazardly on the tree. As my dad shuffles away to the kitchen, Rey grabs Sydney's hand and pulls her closer. "Come on, Sydney, I need your help."

I turn and make my way to the kitchen to help Dad with the drinks. My mum is already there, opening and closing cabinets in panic. This doesn't bode well. Panic in the kitchen is something I'm well accustomed to. Mom always insists on making all the food from scratch, and it always ends in a disaster.

"Oh, Wilson. What are we going to do?" She throws her hands up.

"You haven't lost the ham again, have you?" I ask, coming up behind her. She turns around and barrels toward me, enveloping me in a huge hug.

"My baby, you've grown. Have you grown? You seem taller, broader...happier." She says all that straight into my chest, not letting me go. You would think it's been a year since the last time we saw each other, but it's only been two weeks.

"I am happier," I smile, wrapping my arms around her.

"It's Sydney, isn't it? She seems wonderful," she mumbles and pushes me away. "How could you not tell me that you are bringing a girl over?"

"I wasn't sure she'd agreed to come."

"It's not that, Corky. She's vegan. I'm afraid we don't have anything to eat for her for tomorrow."

I smile. "Don't worry, mama. On our way here, we stopped at Whole Foods and picked up a nut roast." I placed a kiss on my mom's hand and untangled myself. I use the kitchen door to go outside and bring in all the food I bought earlier then return for our bags and the gift I picked up for Sydney. Once the bags are in our room and the present is stowed away safely, I make my way back to the living room. The tree is decorated, mum and dad cuddling on the loveseat; Rey is feeding nuts to Gizmo, and Sydney, my beautiful Sydney, is sitting right next to my aunt. I should probably go and rescue her.

Chapter 22

Bridesmaid

Sydney

It's not often a family you don't know from Adam takes you in and treats you as one of their own. In fact, most people I've met in my life are quite averse to taking in strays. Stray dogs, cats, humans. You name it. In London, everyone always looked out for themselves. Doors always closed to those in need. And intruders were rarely welcome. Especially when barging in on precious family time. In fact, invading someone's 'me' time could downright make you feel like a Jehovah's witness knocking on doors. If you're lucky enough to get a smile, it's usually to shut the door in your face as soon as humanly possible without seeming too abrasive.

Carter's family is not like that. They welcomed me with open arms, sharing stories, asking questions and genuinely seeming interested in what I had to say. It's...well, different. From what I'm used to, I mean. I've been on my own for so long I forgot that spending time with other people can actually be fun. And I've never experienced the warmth and happiness of spending time with a loving family. Their effort to make me feel included as we dressed the tree was admirable, although did little to suppress the nagging feeling I had in the pit of my stomach. I'm just an outsider. A passerby. Someone looking in on a picture perfect family through a frosted window as they walk by in the cold winter night.

When the tree was dressed and the vegan eggnog was served, courtesy of Carter, the 'I sneak things into the shopping cart when you're not looking' magician, we all sat down on the floor to play a few games. I don't know how or when he managed to sneak in all the vegan treats, probably when I snuck off to get him something resembling a Christmas gift. Carter constantly kept surprising me with his attentiveness and caring side. Aren't guys our age supposed to be dickheads who only care about when they're getting laid next? How has this gem of a guy managed to slip through the cracks and set his eyes on…me out of all people? Not that I'm complaining, but I can't help feeling like maybe I don't deserve all of this. I've never been a girl scout. I helped an old lady just once with her shopping bags, and I jay walked. Surely someone up there made a mistake. Carter also insists that he will only eat vegan food when I'm around, to support my decisions. Rey joined in straight away, claiming that she's been meaning to be healthier anyway and animals are too cute to eat, especially now that Gizmo has imprinted herself in her heart. I couldn't believe how easily his family adjusted to having me around, how easily they showed affection to each other. I've never experienced anything like it. And, secretly, I loved it. I had no clue how I'd ever go back to the lonely existence I led pre Carter Kennedy and his amazing family.

As the evening went on, it quickly transpired that Carter's family, although kind and loving, has a mean competitive streak, one that had me in a state of shock. No longer will I look at Pictionary as anything other than the competitive sport it seems to be. A referee was in place, notes were being taken, cheating accusations thrown about, and curse words uttered at inabilities to guess the scribbles correctly. And let me just tell you, those were some scribbles. Needless to say, although lovely, Carter and his family did not have drawing in their DNA.

Don't believe me? Picture this, a balloon crucified on a skewed cross. Any guesses? You sure? Imagine it circled ten times. Still no guesses? Well, according to Wilson, Carter's dad, that was *Babe in the Big City*. When, once again, patience was lost and a screaming match ensued between daughter and son, I slinked off to sit right next to my new favourite old person.

"Are they always like that?" I whisper.

Aunt Berta turns her head towards me and smirks. "Every damn chance they get," she confirmed in a hush just as Carter stands up and saunters over to the easel. That guy could not walk awkwardly if he was given a hundred dollars to do so. His eyes focused on his mum. He points at her, mouthing 'we've got this' at her. She nods eagerly and claps her hands. "Bella and Carter never win," Aunt Berta murmurs. "You must be their lucky charm."

"Forrest Gump," Bella shouts excitedly at Carter's doodles. How the hell did she guess that from the scraggly looking sitting bench Carter was attempting? Beats me.

"Oh, for Pete's sake!" Wilson exclaims as Carter jumps up in glee. 'Cake', I mouth to Aunt Berta as she sniggers.

"You want a piece of cake?" she bellows. Tapping her finger on her thigh once. Wilson looks over to her, confused. "It's late, darling, and you know what they say. A moment on the lips, a lifetime in the hips." I bite my lower lip in an attempt to stop the giggle trying to escape.

"Sorry, Bertie, not what I was saying," Wilson says distractedly as I lean over and whisper 'praying'.

"I don't think praying will help you win this time, my boy," she replies. "Seems Carter and Bella are running circles around you tonight."

"Oh, Bertie, I don't know why you refuse to wear your hearing aid," Wilson shakes his head.

I'm about to say 'masquerade', fully engaged into this game Great Aunt Berta has devised when, with a devilish look on her face, she rearranges her face into one of confusion then excitement and says, "Carter, is this true? You want me to be Sydney's bridesmaid? I do think it's soon, but who am I to stand in the way of true love?" She nods her head as my jaw drops to the floor. "I accept!"

Awkward silence is what follows.

Carter walks over from where he was standing and kneels by his aunt as I pick my jaw off the floor, narrowing my eyes at the sly woman. It's all fun and games until it's all fun and games at my cost. He takes her hands in his and says. "We're not getting married yet, Aunt Bertie." He shakes his head. "But when we do, you'll be a beautiful bridesmaid." My jaw hits the floor again as Aunt Berta looks at me pointedly, challenging. I've got nothing to say. The thought scares and thrills me at the same time. *'Yet'*, he said. I stand up, eyes huge like a deer caught in the headlight.

"I'm tired. I think I'll go to sleep," I mutter.

"The rooms are soundproofed," Aunt Bertie says from the corner of her mouth, winking at me.

My face turns beet red and, like an adult, I flee the room.

It doesn't take me long to find the room Carter and I are staying in. I stumble in and fall on the bed face flat, groaning. Was my reaction extreme? Maybe. It's not like the words spoken meant anything, did they? Surely not.

'*But when we do*', Carter said. Not '*don't be silly*' or '*that ain't happening, weirdo*'. Instead, he alluded to the fact that he, maybe, possibly wants a future with me. A future involving marriage, not just the next couple of months while he figures out how to be a rockstar. My chest warms at the thought as my racing heart tries to figure out how to deal with the fact that it doesn't want to run for the hills. In fact, it wants to run back to that living room, grab Carter by the roots of his gorgeous hair, and kiss him senseless, screaming '*yes, yes, I want that too!*'. I groan again, pounding my fists onto the mattress, mumbling, "Shut up! Stupid, stupid, stupid!" Because, undoubtedly, my heart is being a big fat muppet right now.

"Sunshine?" A voice stops me mid punch. My hand stops, suspended in mid air. I grimace and let it fall to the mattress, burying my face as deep into the covers as I can, channelling my inner ostrich. Nice, I love it when the guy you like walks in on you while you're having a good old breakdown. The bed dips beside me as Carter sits down. A hand reaches for my head and brushes my hair behind my ears, exposing the side of my face. "I'm sorry," he says as I blink. "I didn't mean to scare you. It's just, you know." His hand rubs the back of his neck as it gets red. "My aunt is old, and I wanted her to feel like she'd been included. I meant nothing by it, I swear." My heart sinks. Of course. It was just a figure of speech. I should blame the atmosphere and the alcohol for making me believe that this could be more, that there's a future for Carter and I, but I can't. It's all on me and my stupid, stupid heart. I sit up in bed, pretending like he didn't just deliver a punch straight to my gut.

"Of course," I nod. "I knew that. I really am just tired." I add a yawn for good measure. "And your family, they're just so—"

"Crazy?" he interrupts me. "Weird? Over the top?"

I smile. "I was going to say nice. They're lovely, Carter." Come to think of it, it makes absolute sense that Carter is so caring and loving.

"Ha!" he laughs. "Wait until you get to know them better. You'll start seeing the crazy." I can see the crazy already, but it's the good kind of crazy. One that makes me want to be a part of all their family gatherings. "So we're good?" He pulls me into his lap. I nod into his neck. I still can't look at him, humiliated that my thoughts went *there* when we barely know each other. I'm acting like a teenager, smitten with a boy, writing his name in hearts all over my notebook. Something I've never done before. Well, not counting Justin Bieber. We can't all be perfect, and Biebs had me ensnared with his whiskey-brown eyes for a good few years. I'm happy to report I no longer write Sydney Bieber on all available surfaces. Although my love for brown eyes stayed.

And the pang in my heart when Carter mentioned marriage? It's stupid, isn't it? We've known each other for what? I do the mental math in my head. It's been just over five days... It's definitely impossible, isn't it? There's no chance you can feel for someone so deeply, so quickly. It's the hormones. Genetically modified corn or something. I nuzzle his neck some more, inhaling his delicious cologne. Just his scent has me aroused.

That's what it is. Sexual attraction, nothing more.

Chapter 23

Ours

Carter

I nearly lost her. I know it. I saw the fear in her eyes when I mentioned that Bertie could be our bridesmaid in the future. The speed at which Sydney fled the room had my heart cracking into a million pieces. *She's not ready*, I remind myself. I know it's probably too soon to discuss things like that. Sydney hasn't been back in my life long, but God help me, I want to keep her. Forever. Am I crazy? Probably. But my dad always says 'when you know, you know'. And damn it. I know!

She's the one. And only.

Now if only she could stop being so skittish and give into the feelings I know she feels inside. I see the emotion swirling behind her eyes and see the battle she wages against them. Considering how long we've been together, I understand her apprehension, but I can't help the go-getter inside me. In the wise words of Queen, '*I want it all and I want it now*'.

Lying to her last night, telling her I didn't mean what I said, was hard. But she soothed the ache with kisses, warm, wet, and needy. I undressed her slowly, worshipping every inch of her body, and when I finally entered her...it was different. We didn't have sex, we didn't fuck. We made love. I know she felt it too. Her eyes never left mine as I slowly moved in and out. The words were at the tip of my tongue. Almost there, ready to break free, and just as I was going to whisper them in her ear, she climaxed hard, her tight walls clenching around me, making me feel invincible. It only took a couple of more strokes before I was coming inside her. We slept spooning all night, dead arm be damned. I needed to feel her skin on mine; I needed to feel her. We made love once more in the middle of the night, lazily and quietly as the house slept. I can never get enough of her.

It's still dark when I wake up in the morning. Sydney's ass pressed against me, making the morning wood that much more prominent. I gently kiss her shoulder, stroking her arm up and down with my fingertips. She mumbles in her sleep and slowly turns around to face me, her eyes still closed. I kiss the tip of her nose then each of her eyelids. She sighs and opens her eyes, bathing me in blue as soon as her gaze lands on me.

"Merry Christmas," I say, making a wish for all days to start like this, with Sydney snuggled into me. I'm becoming a soppy bastard. I can't even think back to a time before her, a time where I was with different women every night. Just the thought makes me sick.

Her eyes crinkle at the corners. "Merry Christmas." I lean in and kiss her, ignoring her protests about morning breath. I don't give two shits about that when Sydney is naked, pressed against me. We fit perfectly and, as my dick presses between her thighs, I rock back and forth, sliding it against her wetness, deepening the kiss.

"You're insatiable," she mumbles as I move my lips to her neck.

"Where you're concerned? Always, Sydney. I will always feel this carnal need to be inside you." I nip her neck, coaxing out a moan.

Bang! Bang! The fuck?

I stop moving. My lips against Sydney's collar bone as her shallow breaths lift her chest up and down.

Bang! Bang!

I remove my lips, my hand steady on Sydney's hip as my head turns to look at the door.

"Guuuuuys."

Oh, for fuck's sake. Why? Why did God burden me with an excitable sister? Why?

"Guuuuuuuuys. Are you awake?" Rey whispers loudly through the door. I groan, moving away from Sydney's warmth. Sydney reaches to the side of the bed and pulls on my t-shirt. My hard-on is gone, so I slip on my boxer shorts and make my way to the door.

"Guuuu-" I swing the door open, rearranging my features so that the cock blocker of the century knows I'm annoyed. "Oh, hey, Corky! You're awake. Good!" She grins, oblivious. In my head, I come up with a hundred ways to get rid of her. "It's Christmas!" she squeaks and jumps in place excitedly. "Where is Sydney?" She tries to look over my shoulder as I start closing the door on her.

"Merry Christmas!" Sydney's head pops from behind me.

"Merry Christmas," Rey squeaks.

I take the time to take her in. She's wearing a pair of pyjamas with elves and candy canes all over it. It looks like Christmas threw her up. "Oh, great. Relf is back..." I shake my head at the crazy we've got to look forward to.

"Relf?" Sydney asks as Relf rolls her eyes.

"This genius likes to call me Relf at Christmas. Like

Rey and elf. I get excited about the holidays." She lifts her shoulder as Sydney giggles. "Speaking of! I've got something for you!" She thrusts a package at me.

"Aren't we opening presents together?"

"Yes, yes, but this is for the present opening. It's a pre-present. Without it, Christmas doesn't count!" She pushes me aside and barges into our room. "I've got one for you too, Sydney. Thankfully, I bought two for myself! You never know when you'll be in need of an extra pair! Accidents happen!" I'm so confused it's unreal. What the hell is she talking about?

Sydney takes away the bag Rey hands her and looks inside then straight back at Rey, excited.

"Oh my God." Her hand reaches in as she takes out the exact same pj's my sister is wearing.

"Put them on!" Rey urges, pushing Sydney into the bathroom. I reluctantly look at the package in my hands, already knowing what's inside, and sigh. Alright then, I guess we're doing Christmas Relf-style this year.

Everyone is wearing the same set of pj's, including Aunt Berta, like we're on a set of 'The Goldbergs', except it's the Christmas edition. Relf is ordering everyone around, telling us where and how to sit. I'm considering putting her in a headlock until she admits she's being ridiculous, but Sydney seems to be enjoying this brand of crazy, so I let it go.

"Alright, we're gathered here, on this special and magical day, to celebrate the birth of one extraordinary baby." I groan. Here we go. "One that was actually born sometime in summer, according to astronomers and gospels that have clearly been disregarded, but hey, no one's nitpicking here."

"What's a bummer? The lingo these days, I swear!" Aunt B interjects.

"So, on this special day," Relf disregards the interruption and picks up a remote lying on the side using it as a makeshift microphone, swinging her arm around as if painting the scene. "A baby boy was born. His mummy and daddy had nowhere to stay—"

"They took in a stray? How is Jason, by the way?" Rey blushes but continues.

"With no AirBnB, the only place they could find was a stable. And there, amongst the sheep, horses, and cattle, the baby boy took his first breath. And to this day, each year we celebrate his birth, because he performed the miracle of all miracles." She gazes into the distance, holding a finger up to Aunt Berta, who opens her mouth. "It was years after his birth when one scorching day he turned water into wine, something we shall never forget, and something many have tried yet no one since has replicated." She shakes her head in dismay.

"All right, Reagan, that's enough of that," my mom laughs.

"Just saying!" Rey shrugs, making Sydney snort. Pleased with herself, Rey bounces over to us and sits beside Sydney. "Did you like my speech?" She leans over to her.

"It was...enlightening."

"I love to educate. I think I may have been a teacher in my previous life." Relf nods. Riiiight.

"Has anyone seen Gizmo?" I look around, looking for my little sidekick, suddenly aware I haven't seen him all morning. I'm a bad squirrel dad. Hearing his name, Gizmo pops out of the Christmas tree, yawning. My heart leaves my throat and settles back in my chest, and I mentally promise myself to take better care of him. "C'mon Giz, let's go potty," I say.

Rey sniggers just as Mom says, "He's already been. In Bertie's plants."

Aunt B narrows her eyes. "You lost your pants?"

Chaos ensues as Relf calls for present distribution time, using the remote as a gavel. We're one of those weird families. Since we like to buy each other gifts throughout the year, Christmas is a special affair. We each only get and give one present. A present that has to be handmade and doesn't cost more than fifty bucks to make. I explain this to Sydney as we start unpacking our gifts. They're more sentimental gifts. A jar full of seashells from the last holiday we all took together for Mom. A handmade brooch for Aunt Berta. A tie dye guitar strap for me that takes me back to that night in the cabin. A hand-knitted sweater for Dad, which he puts on immediately. As my family unwraps their gifts, I pull Sydney's from its hiding place and hand it to her. She looks at me, her eyes wide.

"Open it," I nudge her. She bites her bottom lip and carefully unwraps the paper. "It's a notebook," I say as she stares at the faux leather cover. "It's for all your story ideas, so you have somewhere to keep them." She flips it open and her gaze lands on the first page, filled with my handwriting.

"Carter," she gasps.

"Empty pages are the worst."

"It's the—"

"The song I wrote in the cabin. I thought you'd like it, but you can always tear off the page."

"No." She looks up at me, emotion in her eyes. "It's... everything. Thank you." I smile. "I've got something for you too," she says and searches her pockets before lifting up a small object and handing it to me. Carefully, I unwrap it, trying to hold in the excitement. She thought about me. Enough to want to get me a gift. "It's not much," she says. But I don't let her finish. I pull her onto my lap and kiss her, the guitar pick with scratched letters spelling 'ROCK-STAR' on it firmly in my hand.

"It's perfect, Sunshine. Just like you."

"Next year, I pick Sydney to get a gift for!" Relf shouts.

"You hear that?" I say. "No getting out now, you're ours."

Chapter 24

Shhhhhhhh!

Sydney

That guitar pick, the stupid guitar pick I painstakingly scratched out 'ROCKSTAR' on with my key, is staring at me from Carter's bedside table. It was a spur of the moment purchase. A 'just in case' sort of thing. And good thing too, since I'd be the only one who didn't bring a present! Speaking of those, how amazing is Carter's family? How down to earth and completely incredible are they to have this tradition of only having one present each? And made with love, not whatever money can buy? I was shocked and impressed at the same time. I couldn't believe that anyone would choose that over PS5's and watches and general shit you can buy all year long. But they do, and they act like it's not a big deal either. It made my dumb guitar pick that much less pathetic. Although, as pathetic and tiny as it was, Carter treated it like a prized possession. That's the sort of guy he is. Rey pouted that it's not fair he got two presents this year until Carter promised her two next year.

After exchanging the gifts, everyone retreated back to their rooms to get ready for the day's festivities, though not before Carter took a million photos of us wearing matching outfits and posted them on Insta. I'm slowly coming to terms that social media is part of his career and, as much as I shy away from it on a day to day basis, I know that if I want to make this thing between us work that I need to be more accepting of it and just roll with it. And the hate comments I got? Well, they're mostly nothing new. Mostly. This time they're just aimed at me because I 'stepped in the way of true love' and am a 'whoring, man-eating slut'. Very creative, the last one. I suppose they're something I should have expected ever since Carter tagged me in one of his posts.

By the time we emerge from the room, it's midday, and I'm starving. There's a distinct burnt smell coming from the kitchen, so I stop by the hallway to grab one of the sweets sitting in the bowl by the door and pop one in my mouth then hand Carter another one. Hopefully, this will settle my ravenous stomach, at least for a few minutes. Otherwise, I'll have to start eating the Christmas themed curtains or the fifteen year old Christmas tree ornaments, and no one wants to see that. We're the first ones to arrive back in the living room, and now that it's just us here, I take the time to appreciate how utterly festive it looks. Imagine the pictures in children's Christmas books. Yup, that's exactly it. There're mistletoe garlands hanging all around the room, Aunt Berta's favourite pastime seems to be pointing out every single time Carter is under one and then pointing at me in a 'go get him tiger' gesture. I don't know why, but she fancies herself a matchmaker, not that there's any hard work she needs to put into that. Carter puckers up every opportunity he gets, calling out "Oh, Sydney, my Sydney" way too often for my liking. I've only just met his family and wouldn't mind pretending I've got some class and decorum.

The two sofas are covered in tartan green blankets with red cushions scattered around. On the fireplace, there is a creepy looking display of nutcrackers, teeth and all. Fake snow is everywhere. There's a lit up Hanukkah candelabra on the windowsill and a little nativity scene right next to it. There are mismatched stockings hanging off the mantel, Gizmo poking his head from one of them, her fur a bit black from coals that were inside. She doesn't seem to mind and, instead, jumps straight for the clementine and nut ball, making herself at home in between the walnuts. The windows have cut out snowflakes and other decorations glued on, and right next to the Christmas tree, with light focused straight on it and tinsel hanging around it, there's a cardboard cutout of Will Farrell dressed as an elf.

Feeling a bit dizzy from all the Christmas accessories, I sit down on one of the sofas. There's not a single spot in the room where my eyes can rest. Everything is red, green, or sparkly gold. Carter throws himself at the seat next to me, making me bounce in place, and leans his head on my shoulder.

"Your hair is so pretty." He picks up a strand and sniffs it. "And it always smells so nice. How does it always smell so nice?"

"Shampoo?" I question, trying to focus my gaze on something that doesn't spin.

"Shampooooo," he sighs. "Why did they name it after poo?"

I look up at the ceiling, pondering the answer. There's a colourful cloud above me, and it's smiling. "I dunno," I say. "Hello, cloud."

"Alexa," Carter says dreamily. "Why is shampoo called shampoo?" Nothing happens. I look around then focus on Carter, the strand of my hair currently pretending to be his moustache. I giggle. "Aaaaaleeexaaa," Carter sings as his eyes find mine. "Sydney, why is Alexa shunning me?"

"Have you been a bad boy?" I wonder. "Maybe she's like Santa. You get on the naughty list and all you'll get is a stick and a piece of coal."

"You are so fucking clever." He shakes his head in astonishment, losing the blonde moustache in the process. I nod in agreement, because hell yes, I am! The swirly, colourful cloud floats above Carter's head.

"It likes you," I say in awe, trying to see into it. Maybe there'll be a Christmas unicorn hiding? Wouldn't that be nice?

"It does," he agrees. "Wait, what does?"

"The cloud!" I reply, exasperated, lifting my arm up, trying to catch the unicorn.

"Ah yeah, it sure does... I'm hungry."

"Me too," I say sadly just as my stomach rumbles.

"I'm so hungry, I could eat a steamed vegetable medley."

I giggle. "That's very specific."

"It is. It's the worst." Carter's stomach gurgles just as mine makes another noise. "Hey, they're talking to each other! What do you think they're saying?"

"Feeeeed meeee," I growl then burst out laughing. I'm so hilarious. Carter seems to think so too because he joins in, and we fall off the sofa, barely able to breathe.

"Eeerm, you guys okay?" Rey comes into the room.

"Raaaay!" we say in unison. She's so pretty. Their whole family is.

"You're so pretty," I say, reaching out my hand. She's standing a good distance away, so I come up with air.

"Rey, come hug us," Carter demands, closing his eyes and opening his arms.

"Yes!" I do the same thing, but also pucker up for good measure.

"What is going on here?" I hear her mutter before she comes over and stops right in front of us. "What the hell is this?" There's a small rustling sound, and I reluctantly open my eyes, watching her as she holds the candy wrappers up. Rey's lips are tight, and I'm not sure if she's angry or trying not to laugh as she shakes her head, looking from her hand down to the Sydney-Carter sandwich still on the floor. Oooooh, a sandwich. I could really eat a sandwich.

Just in case, I say, "Oh, this? Wasn't us. They were here when we sat down." Carter cracks an eye open, nodding at my blatant lie. He's so dreamy.

"The floor is lava," he whispers loudly as Rey covers her mouth.

"Carter!" I exclaim, pressing my hand against his chest. "If the floor is lava, how is Santa going to get here?"

"Reindeers, Sunshine. Reindeers. They can fly."

"You guys *are* on the floor. It's not lava. You just had some of Aunt Berta's edibles. You're not the only ones to ever make that mistake," she mutters the last part.

"You're so hard," I rub Carter's chest up and down, marvelling at how sculpted it is.

He growls and rolls over, landing on top of me.

"Always," he nuzzles my neck, inhaling.

"No! Nope! Not having that. Get off her!"

Carter doesn't move; instead, he rubs his scruff against my jaw, making me all tingly. "I like you, I'm going to eat you."

"Oh my god, I'm going to puke! Mooooom! Daaaaad!" Reagan cries.

"Shhhhhhhhhh!" I giggle as Carter licks the side of my face.

"Carter, get off her or I swear to god, pot candy or not, you'll be paying for my therapy years to come!" Rey exclaims, pulling the hanky panky monkey off me. I'm about to complain when she grabs my hand and stands me up. "Let's get the two of you something to eat." She turns around and starts walking toward the door like a pair of scorned teenagers. Carter and I nod our heads in unison then follow in her footsteps. But when we get to the hallway, Carter stops me abruptly.

"You hear that?" he whispers. I stop and listen, but, except for the wind howling outside and the Christmas music coming from the kitchen, I can't hear a thing, so I shake my head. He grabs my hand and pulls me toward the front door. "I think it must have been the hunger; it's making me delirious." He reaches his hand out and dips it in the candy bowl. Yaaay, more candy!

"Take your hand out of that bowl now," a very serious Reagan booms from behind us. Carter slowly lifts his hand, clutching a bunch of candy. "Drop em!" The knuckles on his hand go white, but he's not letting go. I'm frozen in place, like a gazelle who's heard a rustle but is not sure if it's a lion or just wind. "Carter, drop the damned Candy or else!" Nothing happens. Reagan sighs, and her voice changes from stern to soft. "I have snacks for you," she singsongs. My gazelle-like instincts have my ears twitching as I sniff the air. Something is burning not too far away. I slowly turn my head to Rey, who's holding a plate of bread rolls. I instantly start salivating and take a step away from Carter and towards the plate of doughy gloriousness. "That's it, come this way, there's some dairy-free spread too." Music to my ears. As I take another step forward, I hear a clink behind me then a shuffle. Carter must have dropped the candy. I straighten and pick up the pace as Reagan backs away with the plate. Carter is breathing down my neck, but the rolls are mine goddamnit! Mine! "Oh, shit," Reagan swears and takes off towards the kitchen. Not with my rolls, lady. This gazelle is hungry. We run after her, growling like feral animals but not caring one bit.

We come to a screeching halt when we reach the dining room, the large dining table between us and Reagan the bread roll thief. As she places the plate down and slowly slides it toward us, I pause for a second to take in the table laden with piles and piles of food. In normal circumstances, I'd probably think it's too much; no one in their right mind can eat this much. But this ain't normal circumstances, compadres. I walk over to the plate with bread rolls and pick one up, ripping a chunk out with my teeth, and, as I chew, Carter stands next to me, picking one for himself and taking a bite.

"All the veggies are dairy free," he says with his mouth full. "You're good to eat everything except the turkey, even the roast potatoes." My mouth is salivating at the prospect, so I try to mop it up with some of the roll. I fail, but the effort seems to be appreciated by Carter, who is looking at me with awe in his eyes. I shrug and look back at the table just as my stomach makes a large growling sound, but I'm not the least bit embarrassed. Nope, not even a little. This is my personal man vs food. Bring. It. On.

Chapter 25

Going Soft On Me, Relfie?

Carter

It took two hours for the weed to wear off. Best Christmas ever? In the grand scheme of things, maybe not. But it was pretty great nonetheless. Surrounded by family, and with Sydney next to me, I couldn't ask for more. And no one seemed to care too much about the fact that we were stoned out of our minds. Probably because, according to Reagan, they had all been victims of my aunt, the drug dealer, the first night they arrived. I wish I could have been a fly on the wall when that happened and experienced what surely had to be a spectacle. Just imagine my parents and sister high. And high they apparently were. All because of the unassuming bowl of candy. And who in their right mind keeps a bowl of edibles by the front door? Aunt Bertie, that's who. Where did she get them from in the first place and what does she do with them anyway? Pops one in each time she goes out shopping? Also, why by the front door? Does she prey on visitors hoping to roofie them for her own entertainment? No, surely not Aunt Bertie. It'll just have to remain one of those unsolved mysteries. Like Edward, who is still looking fresh as a day old loaf should.

As it stands, everyone had the front row seat to the Sydney and Carter show during the Christmas dinner. Dinner that we both took upon ourselves to eat every last bit of. Thankfully, it was delicious, even though the turkey was burnt to a crisp. No one minded though; instead, we had a vegan feast, with the main dish being Sydney's nut roast. It was the first vegan Christmas we've ever had, and it was a roaring success. Especially when Aunt B brought out her famous cherry pie on the table. My whole family jumped on the vegan bandwagon with cat-like reflexes, claiming that, just like me, they'd rather not eat animal products in Sydney's presence. A bunch of fibbers, if you asked me. But Sydney was happy, so I kept quiet, watching her as she got seconds, then thirds. We were both set on ensuring that there shall be no leftovers. We failed, but we came damn close.

Now in a post-food coma and finally sober again, we are lying on top of the blankets in the family room, fire on and Love Actually playing on the TV while a cardboard cutout of Will Farrell quietly judges us from the corner. Nothing against you, dude, Dad and I just got outnumbered by all the estrogen; otherwise, we'd be watching the story of a small orphan boy who climbed into Santa's sack one Christmas Eve.

We have a lazy afternoon, chatting and watching movies. That something that's always been missing is finally there. With that last piece found, finally, our puzzle is complete. The feeling of content washes over me as I realize that this is it. That thing I've been looking for. The part of me that always felt off, always cold, is now warm and happy. Because the missing piece is right here cuddled up against me, making my heart speed up each time her eyes land on mine, each time she smiles or giggles, each time her fingers graze my skin.

I lose focus of what's on the screen and spend my time watching her snuggled in our blanket cocoon as her eyes grow heavier and heavier until they close. When she falls asleep, I keep watching her, motionless, fearful of waking her up. Instead, I count every little lift of her chest, every twitch of her lips, every noise that she makes. It feels surreal, being so wrapped up in someone else, but also just right. She looks so comfortable, her palm against my chest as her head rests beside it. I pull her closer, my heart ready to burst with all the emotions I feel. They're too much, overwhelming almost, and I find myself having to rip my eyes away from her. I blink slowly as I take in my surroundings. The room is quiet and dark, the TV off, and Mom and Dad are getting up off the sofa. Everyone else has gone to bed. I don't know how long I was lost in Sydney, but it must have been a lot longer than what it felt like.

"Goodnight, darling." My mom kisses me on the forehead and brushes my hair to the side, a habit she's never let go of.

"Night, Mom, Dad," I whisper as they leave the room.

I scoop Sydney up and carry her back to our room. She doesn't protest and stirs only when I start undressing her, sleepily helping me take off her clothes, then again when I slide her in under the covers. She's back asleep in seconds and, when I slide in beside her, once again pulling her into my arms, she sighs, happy. This. This is all I need. Feeling her against me, the scent of her shampoo, the warmth of her body. It's everything. And as soppy as it sounds, I finally understand every single love song. I really do.

I try to fall asleep, but with my heart pumping a hundred times a minute, it's impossible. I can't stop it though, it beats for her now. So I spend the next few hours just enjoying the feel of her next to me. Then I feel it. The call. It's always like that. A little faint tug at first, then a few more. After a while they get stronger and more frequent until I can't take it anymore. So I listen. I slide my arm out from under Sydney's head and get up, sliding my sweatpants on before grabbing my guitar and quietly leaving.

The family room is bathed in the soft light coming from the Christmas Tree and the dying embers of the fireplace. At my approach, Gizmo wakes up and runs up to me. It's funny how quickly he's inserted himself into the family. No one even questioned why we'd bring a wild squirrel with us. In fact, they seemed overly excited about having a furry friend. But Gizmo is not a pet. He's still wild and belongs in the forest. Even if he seems domesticated, he still could be sick. I make a mental note to call the vet as soon as it opens and schedule an appointment. He stretches beside me and I scratch his tummy. Thankfully, upon our arrival, Gizmo has mellowed a little and stopped following my every move, taking a shine to Aunt B instead. He also decided to call the Christmas tree his new home, still with my beanie being dragged around the house, ending his cockblocking ways once and for all.

I pick up my guitar and start tuning the instruments, letting muscle memory guide my movements. Before long, I'm plucking the strings playing 'Yellow'. I haven't heard the song in years, but it's like riding a bike. Without a hitch, I sing the whole tune then keep playing different songs and chords until, finally, music takes over and starts pouring out of me.

The melody comes out first. Haunting yet hopeful. The tempo is slow as I string together the first few chords. Once I'm happy, the rest flows easily.

For What It's Worth

Where do we go from here?
What's next for us, I fear

I sing in a soft voice.

They don't know,
they don't have a clue
How my world would crumble without you

"That's really beautiful. Is it new?" Reagan sits down next to me, picking Gizmo up and setting him on her lap. My fingers keep playing the melody as I run through the lyrics in my head again. "Sooo... How's my big brother doing?"

I stop strumming the guitar and reach for my notebook, jotting down the words.

"How are you feeling? Sober?"

I smirk. "I sobered up a while back, thank you very much."

"Ah, tell that to the Scorcese wannabe who spent three minutes filming roast potatoes." I raise my eyebrows. "Check your phone, Corky. You'll be amazed at the amount of vegetable pictures on it. And the angles, God forbid I don't mention the angles."

I laugh. "All right, smarty pants, I get it, I was stoned and it was fun to watch."

"I missed you," she says softly.

"I'm here."

"You weren't, though. You know you weren't. After Jenny, you were different. Withdrawn, quieter, just not yourself," she trails off.

"Nah, I was still the old me," I deny, deny, deny.

She sighs. "You're getting there. You're laughing more,

making jokes again." She puts her hand on my forearm, squeezing it. "Sydney is good for you."

"But am I good enough for her?" I look at my sister, my worst fear coming to the surface. Who would want damaged goods like me, a guy who's just about to start his music career based mostly on songs about his heartbreak. It's a lot to ask of someone who barely even spent a week with me.

"You see, this is what I'm talking about! Last year, these words wouldn't even come out of your mouth! You'd be all like,"—she deepens her voice—"baby, you're so lucky to be in the presence of Kennedy awesomeness'." I crack a smile. "You're amazing and funny, and goddamnit, anyone would be lucky to be with you!"

"Awwww, going soft on me, Relfie?" She punches my arm playfully, but her candy cane pajamas speak the truth. She's Relf through and through. "You're right, though. I know deep down she feels the same way. I'm just worried, that's all."

She puts her head on my shoulder and wraps her arm around me the same way she used to when we were kids.

"Don't be," she says. "Sydney isn't stupid, and only an idiot wouldn't want to be with you. You're the best."

I pick my guitar back up and play an upbeat tune.

"Rey-Rey. You're my ray of sunshine," I sing. *"Little sister, when did you grow up? When did you get so wise? I remember when your face was full of snot, you were always a pain in my butt... Rey-Rey. My little ray of sunshine,"* I finish with a flourish, making Reagan giggle.

"I love you, you stupid jerk."

"I love you, pain in my butt," I reply and put my arm around her, kissing the top of her head.

Chapter 26

You Little Hussy!

Sydney

I pull on the warm socks Rey lent me and start lacing up my boots. We're heading out to the little village nearby. Yes, the one we stole the Christmas tree from. I'd be lying if I said that it's not causing me serious anxiety. I'm equally excited and terrified.

I want to see the picturesque place in daylight, the store fronts open with their Christmas decorations on display. Leisurely, we walk down the streets I had to run down before. Which brings me to the reason for my terror. What if someone saw us steal the tree? What if someone recognises us for the Christmas tree bandits that we are?

"Here, give me your phone," Carter says. "I'm going to do the 'Find my friends' thing in case we get separated or lost."

"What if they recognise us?" I voice my concern as Carter taps away on my phone.

"They will," he shrugs, making my heart stop. He looks up and must see the fear on my face as he walks over and sits next to me. "They will because they know us in town. Don't worry. The market is still closed. Most likely, no one has even noticed that the tree is gone and, if they have, they're probably counting it as a Christmas miracle." I nod, trying to believe him. "Besides, we're too pretty to go to jail. But if they decide we need to be punished, I'll take the full responsibility. I'll take the burden for the both of us," he sighs. "I'll go to jail, make a shiv out of a toothbrush, find myself a bitch called Steve or Dave or Skull Crusher. Each week I'll be eagerly waiting for visitation time, when you'll come to see how I'm doing and bring me cigarettes so I can trade them for liquid soap. Cause I ain't bending over in jail."

"You're crazy," I laugh, significantly less anxious.

"Crazy awesome? That I am, Sunshine. That I am." He smiles and gives me a kiss. "C'mon babe, they'll all be waiting for us."

I'm not exactly ecstatic at the prospect of facing his family. Not after they bore witness to the absolute carnage that is Sydney Buyer on weed. I'm pretty sure you could have mistaken me for a cookie monster last night, except I was eating everything, not just cookies. Everything! The only reason I'm not dying of embarrassment is because Bella, Carter's mum, assured me that not even two days before our arrival, they went through the exact same thing.

Whilst I was humiliating myself, stuffing myself like it was my last meal, Aunt Berta was having the time of her life. Why? Every single 'misheard' thing she repeated sent both Carter and I into fits of laughter that lasted at least ten minutes, and the lady was on form! Tears were streaming down our faces and snot most likely made an appearance. I haven't laughed like that in...well, never. By the end of the night, my stomach hurt like a motherfucker and I can only hope I didn't blow her cover, because at one point, I'm pretty sure I was shouting out rhymes to whatever anyone was saying. So excuse me if, after last night's performance, I'm reluctant to show my face around them.

The only thing getting me to move is the curiosity of why the hell Carter's aunt would even have pot candy in her hallway on display, in an ornamental bowl, within anyone's reach. I bet she knew exactly what she was doing.

"Alright, make sure to keep your phone on. That way I'll be able to find you if we get separated and you'll be able to see where I am." Carter pulls me out of my thoughts, handing me back my phone. I nod and let him guide me by my hand out of our room and straight towards his waiting family.

We bundle up and pack into two cars. Rey rides with us, in Jeepak, and Carter's parents and Aunt in another car, Gizmo in an old cat carrier with them. Aunt Berta called in a few favours and a veterinarian friend of hers, will check Gizmo over.

The drive takes less than fifteen minutes and is definitely less terror inducing than the last time we made it; probably because we can actually see where we're going.

In the light of day and busy with people milling about, the town looks completely different. The snow that has been falling consistently over the past few days with the fierceness of Destiny's Child's 'Survivor' has been shoveled off sidewalks, creating little white mounds on each side, the shop windows alight with flashing lights and Christmas decorations. There's a distinct smell of warm, spiced apple cider hanging in the air from the small stalls scattered around the streets, enticing shoppers with the opportunity to take a break and warm up while browsing. The air is crisp and filled with excitement at seeing your neighbours again after the short break. It's that small town charm I've heard so many times about but never experienced. London was never this open and inviting. Even in our small housing estate in Hackney, no one ever spoke to each other, apart from a curt nod 'hello' when passing. God forbid you knew more than your direct neighbour's name. Here, though, it's a different world. Streets are busy and full of chatter, and everyone seems to know everyone.

As we walk along, Rey's arm looped through mine, people do indeed stop us to chat, enquire about our Christmas and talk about their families. Thankfully, no one mentions the pot disaster. As Bella and Wilson catch up with friends they haven't seen in a while and Aunt Berta sneaks off to see her veterinarian friend, Rey and I treat ourselves to spiced cider. While ducking in and out of the stores that seem to carry everything from locally made pottery to artisan soaps and candles, we get a few more mugs of that spiced deliciousness and, by the time I've had my third, I'm feeling a nice, relaxed buzz. So when Rey walks into yet another boutique, I tell her I'll sit this one out and wait outside. As soon as she disappears inside, Carter grabs my hand and pulls me down the street. The cider making its way through my veins has me all loosey goosey cause I don't protest and think back to the alley from two nights ago instead.

But, to my dismay, we pass the turn off to the market and keep walking. The thought that we left Reagan and Carter's parents behind crosses my mind, and for a second I wonder if I should protest and turn back since this was supposed to be a 'family trip', but Carter's hand is warm, and besides, spiced cider knows best and spiced cider is telling me to keep going and follow this boy wherever he goes. Whoa! Where did that come from?

I don't have the time to think it through because Carter finally stops and turns to me. I look around, the place unassuming. There are no shops, no kids running around, no people milling about. We're in front of a church, and as I wonder why Carter would bring me here, he opens a little side gate and walks into the churchyard. I follow him, scouring my brain for any references of churchyards in pop culture, but the only thing I can think of is *Pet Sematary*.

We sit down on a bench shielded from the snow by a canopy of tree branches, and I am thankful for the long jacket I decided to wear as it shields my butt from the ice cold of the bench.

"Hey," Carter says, and it occurs to me he looks nervous. He's fidgeting, just like before each of his performances. I'm not sure what's got him all nervous, but I know a way I can help him. I slide closer to him and put my head on his shoulder.

"Hey yourself."

"So I've been thinking," he starts.

"Dangerous." I can feel the roll of his eyes without having to look at him. I giggle and sit up, angling my body so I can look at him. He slides one of his legs under mine and pulls them up on his lap so that my feet are dangling to the side. Warmth radiates from him even through the layers of clothing. My personal portable heater. "Sorry, go on."

"I've been thinking about what's next."

"Oh my gosh, yes! Tell me, where do we go from here?" I ask, and he blinks.

"What did you just say?" he whispers.

"What's next on the itinerary?" I cock my head to the side.

"Where do we go from here," he mutters then looks straight into my soul. "Sydney, I can't." My heart stops. What does he mean? He can't continue on the trip? He can't be with me? He can't...what? I don't take a single breath until he speaks again. "I can't hold it in any longer. Fuck. It hasn't been long, and I know this is crazy. But... Fuck. Look at you!" I blink, confused. "I'm saying this wrong. What I mean is you're so amazing inside and out, but especially inside. And well, I think it was inevitable."

"What was?" I'm seriously not sure what he's trying to say, even though the compliments are nice.

"Me falling for you." My jaw drops. Surely, I heard him wrong. He didn't just sa— "I love you, Sydney. In love with you. Crazy about you. All the '*It takes two*' stuff Mary-Kate talks about." He rattles on.

I-I can't think. My heart is hammering in my chest but my body is numb and my brain has decided it would be a great time to go on hiatus and hang up an 'out of office' sign. I'm up and running before I realise what's happening. Running through the churchyard, out the gate, down the street, and round the corner. I come to a stop in front of a cafe and go inside, taking an empty seat.

Pick up, pick up, pick up! I dial the only person I can think of.

"*Oh, so you are alive,*" she answers on the second ring.

"Hayley," I start, my voice cracking.

"*Everything okay, babe?*"

"Yes... No... I don't know!" I bury my face in my hand. The line is quiet for a minute.

"*Holy Shit!*" Hayley screams through the phone. "*You didn't, did you?*" I don't reply. "*Holy shit, you did! You slept with Carter, you little hussy!*" she squeals. I groan. "*I knew it! I fucking knew it! I knew it last year and I knew it now! The chemistry between you two was off the charts. So.... How was it? Oh my god, is that why you're calling me? Cause it was shit?*"

"Nooooo." I finally find my voice again and 'whine' is the setting.

"*So, it wasn't shit?*"

"No, it was good. Like life-changing good. Earth-shattering good."

"*Okay, so why are you on the phone with me and not currently screwing Carter's brains out?*"

"There might be a situation," I hesitate.

"*Aww, babe. Everyone farts. No need to feel ashamed if you let it loose in front of him.*"

"Hayley, I'm serious."

"*So what's the problem?*" She's way too cheery for the seriousness of the situation.

"You know, the best friend he was in love with? Do you really think he's over her? I mean, all his songs are about how much he loves her, and how he's hurting."

"*Ah,*" Hayley says. "*Jenny, my other sister from another mister.*" Jenny. Even her name is stupid. Why did she have to exist? "*Errr, it's a funny one. I know he was pining after her and wrote songs about that, but also, she's his best friend, so they hang out a lot, so unless he's into torture, I'd say he might be over her. Why?*"

I take a deep breath. "He told me he's in love with me."

I hear a snort and loud 'pffft' sound.

"*Sydney, are you trying to kill me? I nearly drowned on a drink of water just now. He said what? Carter said what? The most single guy on campus said WHAT?*"

"He said, and I quote 'I love you, Sydney'."

"*Babe, I'm sorry, but that's huge. He never said that to Jenny. Or anyone else, for that matter. When did this happen?*"

"Just now," I fidget with the zipper of my jacket.

"*And you are calling me mid-bang?*" she whispers,

aghast. *"Cause I sure hope you fucked like bunnies after he said that."*

"Not exactly... I kinda blanked then ran away."

A strained noise then coughing. *"When will I learn not to drink when talking to you?"* she mutters. *"You did what, now? Do you not like him?"*

"Ugh! I do! Too much. I don't know, Hayls. I just wasn't thinking. You know me, I don't show my emotions well, and he caught me off guard and fuck. I messed up, didn't I?"

"Yup," she pops the 'p'.

"This probably hurt him." I rub my temple.

"Yup."

"I should go and find him and explain that I'm just a weirdo who got spooked, shouldn't I?"

"Godspeed, my black empress. Godspeed."

Chapter 27

Bean Diggity

Carter

I sit on the bench for twenty minutes before I accept that Sydney is not coming back. I knew it was a gamble. I knew I could spook her. But honestly? I really couldn't stop myself. Those words were trying to burst out of me for the last twenty-four hours. I didn't expect Sydney to say them back. A small part of me hoped that she would, but I knew it was a long shot.

But I also didn't expect her to run off. Or for it to hurt as much as it did. And hurt, it does. I exhale, a white cloud of air forming in front of my face, and heave myself up. Dragging my feet, I make my way out of the churchyard through a snowy path then down the street and, as I turn the corner, I bump into something soft. It's a movie meet cute kinda situation, only the person is wrong.

"Hey, Carter," she smiles up at me. "Fancy seeing you here!" Here's the thing. I might have slept around. A lot. I might have been a bit of a player. But I never, never forgot a girl's name once I slept with her. Call it common courtesy, call it whatever you want. I just think every girl deserves not to have that awkward moment the morning after where she has to remind the guy what her name is. No. I draw the line at being a dick who used to live on one night stands. The least I could do is to remember their name.

"Hey, Callie." I look behind her, hoping to see a flash of blond hair.

"In town for the holidays?" Callie cocks her head to the side.

"Every year."

"You know..." she trails off. I really do hope she's not about to proposition me, because even though the night we spent together was awesome, just the thought of being with anyone but Sydney makes me physically sick. She bites her lip, her brows drawn. "I've been following you on Instagram. Your music, it's... It's really good."

I wince and grip the back of my neck. "Thanks, I guess?"

"Ugh. That came out wrong. I'm not a stalker or anything. Jeez, only a stalker would say something like that, wouldn't they? She laughs awkwardly. Her prattling somewhat relaxes me, and I find myself grinning at the flustered way she's swinging her arms around. "Please forget I said all of that. What I was trying to say is how would you want to do a small open mic night tonight? I know it's short notice and everything, but you remember Bean Diggity? Well, it's my parents' place and they've been meaning to do something like that for a while. It'd be smaller than you're used to..."

I now remembered the reason I slept with her. Probably to get her to stop talking.

"Sure thing. What time, and can my family come?" I interject before she talks my ear off.

We agree on the time and I make an excuse to leave. I wander the streets aimlessly, trying to figure out my next steps before I finally break and pull my phone out. It's 'spy on Sydney' time. Huh! And poor Callie thought she was a stalker! I open the app and wait until it refreshes. Sure enough, a round circle with Sydney's picture appears almost immediately. And wouldn't you know it? She's in fucking Bean Diggity. I walk towards it, trying to figure out what to say to her. Trying to ascertain whether searching her out is even remotely a good idea. But my need to go to her, to make sure she's alright, is stronger than any brain cells fighting for dignity. Sydney comes first.

I round the corner and walk down the street towards where Sydney should be, and, just as I notice the sign for the coffee shop, the door opens and she walks out.

Air rushes into my lungs as I take her in.

Is it even possible for her to get more beautiful than she was twenty minutes ago? She stops outside then looks left and right, a smile stretching on her lips as her eyes land on me. She lifts her hand up and waves. All the fear, all the uncertainty, wiped away with one little smile from her. My lungs start to burn and I have to remind myself to exhale. I take a step forward, then another, pulled in her direction by an invisible string. She grins and starts running toward me, not caring about how it looks. This girl. She laughs and skips, her hair floating up and down behind her. When she reaches me, she doesn't falter, just throws her hands up and around me, burying her face in my neck.

"I'm sorry," she murmurs just as my arms lock around her waist.

I inhale, breathing in the scent of her shampoo. "Don't be. I just sprung that on you. I don't want you to feel trapped or anything. I'm not taking it back, Sydney," I say as I feel her stiffen. "I'm just saying, I'm not expecting you to say it back."

She snuggles deeper into my neck, sniffling a bit, then slowly lifts her face, looking up at me. "Thank you," she says. And the gleam in her eyes says it all. Even if she's not ready, even if she's scared, even if she doesn't know it yet...I see it. She feels it too, and for now, that's more than enough.

It didn't take long to find my family. And, although Relfie was in a huff and pissed off that we abandoned her, as soon as I shared the news about the upcoming open mic, she squealed and threw herself at me. It seemed my whole family was excited to see me perform. I suppose they wanted to wipe the memory of the last time they witnessed me on stage where, after I walked out on wobbly legs; managed to kick over the mic stand; and finally looked at the audience, I generously threw up all over the first row then ran off. One can only hope this time will be less tragic. Even Aunt Berta, who appeared behind Dad out of nowhere mid-conversation, seemed excited. Gizmo sulked in the cat carrier, looking thoroughly violated. Poor guy got checked out, jabbed, and turned into a fucking girl. Because apparently I had it all wrong. My bud, Giz, did not have male reproductive organs according to the vet. Who knew?

After that, we headed back home. Giz made it clear he wanted to stick with Aunt B. It seems my bud has abandoned me for the time being and, to be fair, I don't blame the little critter. I haven't exactly been an attentive squirrel dad since we got here, what with being busy getting roofied by my aunt. Fortunately, she has really taken to the wild animal and seems extremely happy with the gremlin by her side. Gizmo also seems like he...she—this one will be hard to

For What It's Worth

get used to—seems like she is happier. It helps that Bertie's house is surrounded by forest, so Gizmo basically has all her play things right within her paws' reach. I can't help but think this might be better for her. Especially compared to LA or Starwood. Neither one of them is a good place for a cute little squirrel.

We decided to stay in town and grab a meal at a local restaurant before heading to the cafe. My whole family, including Aunt Berta, agreed on eating a vegan meal following the hit that was the Christmas dinner. Sydney's not complaining, so, once again, I sit quietly and stew that I'm no longer the only person who does that. It's silly, really, but I'm jealous that my family butted in on what was 'our' thing. Once we're fed and happy, my parents drop Gizmo back home then come back. Sydney and Aunt B are deep in a hushed conversation as we walk to the car to pick up my guitar.

I'm nervous, a little bit because of the usual stage fright but mostly because I haven't had my family watch me sing in front of an audience in forever, and what if they hate it? I know it's irrational, but I can't help it. There's something about having your whole family listen to your innermost thoughts that makes it just a little bit unsettling.

Thankfully, Sydney will be there, my anchor, ready to bring me peace while I have my inner freak out.

Before I know it, we're standing outside of Bean Diggity. It's already dark outside, the sun setting so much earlier this time of the year, and you can see the light coming through the fogged up glass. I take a deep breath and look around. Sydney, Mom, Dad, Reagan, and Aunt Berta are all standing still, waiting for my next move, as if feeling my hesitation.

No time like the present. The door opens, and a patron

walks outside, letting the warmth out. The quiet afternoon suddenly filled with the buzz of voices from the inside. The smell of coffee hits me next and, as I hold the door open for my family, I can see the place is packed, an unsettling sight that makes the usual stomach cramps start up. As if on cue, Sydney finds my hand and squeezes it.

"Go get 'em, rockstar."

With that, we walk in, hand in hand, letting the door close softly behind us. The only thing stopping me from shaking is Sydney's small hand in mine. We veer through the crowd of people, ducking between the small tables scattered around until we get to the coffee bar. From the corner of my eye, I can see the space they have set up for the open mic: a chair, mic, amp, and speakers in the corner of the room.

I squeeze Sydney's hand and let go just as Callie appears in front of us, shadowed by a middle aged couple who introduce themselves as Callie's parents and the owners of the establishment.

My hands are sweating as I nod at what they're saying, but most of their words don't register. It's like I'm watching my life through a camera. I still can't believe that I'm lucky enough to do this, lucky enough to have Coda Records interested in me. The only thing unnerving is the possibility of having to do this on my own. Without Sydney there.

My phone buzzes in my pocket, and I pull it out. Speak of the devil. I motion at my family and let them know I'm going outside to answer. I can feel more than one pair of eyes follow me as I step through the door and into the chilly air.

"Hi Josh," I put the phone to my ear.

"Carter, glad I caught you! Listen, mate, I could sit here and chat to you about Christmas and all this bullshit, but

let's be honest, you probably have other things you'd rather be doing and I sure do too." I hear a slap and a woman's giggle.

"What's up?" I say just as the front door opens and Sydney walks out. Without thinking, I put the phone on speaker mode and pull her in next to me, bracing her from the cold.

"I need you here in LA. Tomorrow or the day after at the latest," he says as Sydney sucks in a breath and stiffens. There goes my plan of spending more time on the road with her. *"Can you do that? I potentially have some big news but can't confirm until we meet in person."*

Sydney wraps her arms around me and squeezes me.

"Two days," I repeat. That's not enough time. I need more. I need more time with Sydney. She looks up at me and nods. "We can be there in two days," I sigh. I have a bad feeling about this.

"We? Is Sydney coming with you? Look mate, just don't let a pretty girl distract you from what is surely going to be a stellar career."

"Hi, Josh," Sydney says mechanically.

"No offence, love."

"None taken." But I can see the wheels in her mind spinning. Yeah, really bad feeling.

Chapter 28

I Waxed

Sydney

I'm here but not quite. There's this feeling of remoteness making its way through my subconscious. The conversation I bore witness to sobering. *'Don't let a pretty girl distract you from what is sure going to be a stellar career'*, Josh Coda, wanker extraordinaire, said. Is that what I am, a distraction? Or is this just some tactic from a music label owner? And if Carter's career is about to take off, can I really, with good conscience, continue this domestic charade with him? I know that right now things couldn't be better, we just work. But what happens once he's with a label and suddenly his stardom skyrockets?

As Carter sits down on the stool and starts tuning his guitar, I can see his hands shake. He lifts his gaze, searching for something against the spotlight that's focused on him. I take a few steps forward, positioning myself right next to the coffee bar, the perfect angle for doing a live video stream; plus, easy for him to spot me if it's me he's looking for. Rey stands next to me and puts her arm around me, squeezing my shoulder.

"I'm so excited," she whispers. I just nod and start the

stream. Carter's eyes land on me and a look of relief washes over his face, making my insides warm. As he starts strumming the chords, his eyes not leaving mine, he moves closer to the mic and starts singing in his husky voice. Shivers run up and down my spine as the lyrics of 'Breathing' by Anne-Marie fill the room. I don't think I move as Carter sings his mellowed version of the song. Every word, every note, seems like it's sung just for me. I briefly look at the screen on my phone, and the result is breathtaking. No wonder there are messages flooding my screen. As the song reaches the end, Carter seems more at ease and, when he speaks, his voice is steady.

"Good evening, Bean Diggity. I'm Carter Kennedy." People cheer and whistle. A group of girls giggle behind me and I smile to myself. "This next song is called 'Everything'," he says and starts playing the song he sang to me back in the cabin, the lyrics of which he wrote in my notebook. I blush as the lyrics entwine with my soul, squeezing my heart, making me want to run to him and tell me all my fears, all my worries, and all the amazing things he brings out in me. Reagan squeezes my arm, and I look at her from the corner of my eye. She's wearing a huge shit-eating grin.

"He's so in love with you, Sydney," she whispers. I bite my lip and keep looking at Carter, who is serenading me in front of the cafe patrons. As I gaze at the screen of my phone to make sure it's still streaming, a comment catches my eye. 'Did you guys hear that? Who the fuck is Sydney?', then the next one, 'bitch better back off, he's mine!'. I grimace and look away. Leave it to Carter's fans to spoil this magical moment for me. Thankfully, that's all that is, empty threats. Hopefully.

The girls behind me sigh. "Do you think that song is about you?" one of them says, making me stiffen. Reagan looks over at me as I strain my ears, trying to hear them better.

"Maybe, I mean, we did sleep with each other a few years ago, and it was magical," another girl says, her voice vaguely familiar. "His penis was amazing. Just thinking back to that perfection makes me salivate." I narrow my eyes, anger coursing through my veins.

"You're so lucky. I'd jump on him like a hot potato. Was he good?"

"So, so good, like honestly, best orgasm of my life. And tonight I waxed just in case... I'm going to get a repeat one way or another."

I feel physically sick, partially because they're objectifying a guy they barely know, partially because now I have a vision of Carter with someone else. The feelings from a few days ago come back, those thoughts that we're not going to work because, if Carter ever goes on tour, he'll have a swarm of waxed vagina girls just ready to service him, and I'll have a swarm of waxed vagina girls hating me on Instagram. Am I sure I can take the abuse, the slut shaming, and all the rage from people I don't even know? Am I sure I trust Carter, who, from what I've heard from Hayley, is a player? Does he truly mean what he said earlier today, and does it even change anything?

I don't know the answers to any of the questions, but what I do know is that I'm not going to let a bunch of hairless vaginas objectify my man. Whether this man is actually mine just for a couple more days or longer, no one deserves to be talked about like that.

I hand my phone to Reagan to continue streaming and turn around. Wouldn't you know it, the owners' daughter, Callie, is in the middle of the group.

"Does he have a say in that?" I ask. They all look at

me, dumbfounded. "Does he get a say in whether he wants your waxed vagina or are you just going to force yourself on a guy that's not even remotely interested in you?"

They all gasp, and Callie narrows her eyes. "Why wouldn't he be interested in me?" She smirks.

I smile sweetly. "For starters, maybe because he already has a girlfriend."

"Yeah," Reagan interjects, the phone pointed at me. Fuck. I try to angle away from the camera. I should not be the centre of attention when Carter is performing. I reach back for my phone. "Sydney is his girlfriend, so back off, Callie, and stop objectifying my brother."

"Hello, Reagan. Pleasure as always." Callie huffs but turns back to her friends and whispers something that makes them all giggle. I manage to get my phone back and point it back at Carter, who is still singing but has a look of confusion on his face.

My face must be pale since Reagan asks, "Are you okay?" I nod, mechanically, but inside I'm freaking out. I'm dreading looking at the comments on this live stream. Not only with one comment did Rey add fuel to the fire, but also admitted to whoever was watching that I, in fact, had stolen their chance at getting with Carter Kennedy. Pretty great going for someone who's been avoiding social media. To save my sanity and the shred of hope that Carter and I work on the outside world, I decide that, as soon as I finish streaming, I'll disable notifications on my social accounts. Some people have already worked out who I am and taken it upon themselves to troll me, but after tonight I can only imagine the amount of messages I'll get. At least he hasn't reached super stardom yet, so most messages are from keyboard warriors who have only ever seen his YouTube channel or watched him on Insta and are, hopefully, far, far away.

I suppose I'll have to deal with this shit sandwich when we get back to LA, which is in two days. My heart sinks. Two more days with Carter. And then we will figure out what's next for us. Because life without Carter seems less and less possible. No matter the consequences.

My mind is reeling for the rest of the show. I vaguely hear Carter dedicating a song to his family and another one to me, but I can't tell you what they are. Aunt Berta comes over to Rey and I and wolf whistles so loud my eardrums nearly explode. When Rey grabs my phone and moves around the room, streaming the gig from an 'artistic point of view' as she called it, I don't protest; instead, I let her walk around the room lifting the phone up then down and changing the angles. I hope whoever is watching it won't get seasick from her directing skills. Carter's aunt slides beside me and loops her arm through mine. I help her to the nearby chair, but she tsks at me.

"I may look old, but trust me, I've got stamina in me." She smirks, and, once again, I find myself trying to decipher the enigma that is Alberta Kennedy.

"Why do you pretend you can't hear?" I ask.

"Entertainment. I get bored." She shrugs, as if it's completely normal to dupe your family into thinking you're partially deaf.

"And the edibles?"

"Leftovers from a book club meeting." She smirks. "Let me just tell you, talking about Mr. Grey takes on a whole new meaning when you start hearing colors." I'm not sure what's more disturbing. The fact that Carter's elderly aunt likes to read smutty books or that she and her book club get stoned to discuss them.

"Carter said you write." It's a statement, not a question, so I just smile. "Any sex in your books?" I blush. "My nephew is giving you some inspiration, I hope?" Uhmm, hello floor. I am ready for you to open up and swallow me whole. Because she's right on point. Even since Carter, my book turned not only into a romance, but a romance with steam where I describe in detail what happens behind closed doors. "Good, good." She pats my arm. "I'll be happy to read it for you, if you want me to give you some pointers." I look at her, confused.

"Errm, sure?" I ask.

She chuckles. "He didn't tell you, did he? I'm B.J. Camming." I blink. She's what? Surely not. She must be pulling my leg. Just another one of Alberta Kennedy's famous pranks. Because B.J. Camming is a best-selling erotic romance author. Like worldwide best-selling. Books made into movies, best-selling. Translated into many languages, best-selling. My jaw is on the floor as Carter finishes the set and makes his way over to us.

"You sing lovely, my boy." She pats his cheek and places his hand on top of mine. My jaw is still hanging all the way by my shoes, so I shake myself out of my stupor and close my mouth. "Now, if you'll excuse me, this old bat needs to sit down. You may kiss your girl," she says, turning around but just as quickly turns back to us and with a wink says, "Don't think I forgot you promised I'll be Sydney's bridesmaid. I'm holding you to that or I'll start calling you a turd nugget."

Carter sighs as she walks away. "I don't know what's worse. When she doesn't wear her hearing aid or when she does." I almost smile but then swat him.

"Your aunt is B.J. Camming?" I exclaim.

He shushes me. "That's not something she shares

openly, so please don't say anything to anyone. She's very private about that part of her life, so if she told you she must consider you family." I blush. "Anyway, I came here for a reason."

"What?"

He licks his lips as anticipation coils in my belly. Stepping toward me, he cups my chin. "To kiss my girl," he says as his lips capture mine.

Fucking swoon.

Chapter 29

Couldn't Get Enough

Carter

After the gig, we drive back home and stay up a while with my family, who's genuinely so ecstatic after my set. You'd think they were almost sure I'd puke again. My mom can't stop giving me hugs, beaming with pride. Dad pulled out his celebratory red pipe and was walking around with it between his teeth telling everyone how amazing I was. They all nod in agreement. It's cute. But cute is not what I want right now. With the adrenaline from singing in front of the crowd still coursing through my veins, all I want is to expand the energy, and there's one perfect way I have in mind on how to do it.

After a reasonable amount of time spent with my family, I yawn loudly and stretch, saying how tired I am and wishing everyone goodnight. I grab Sydney's hand and drag her to our room, not caring if anyone bought my performance.

As soon as the door closes behind us, Sydney attacks my mouth. Fuck yeah, my girl needs me as much as I need her. Our bodies, our needs, are so in tune with each other, I find it hard to believe she hasn't been with me my whole life. I groan into her mouth as her hands trail down, down, down and undo my belt, skimming gently over the growing bulge in my jeans. She pushes my chest, and, taking the hint, I take a step back. Then a few more until the back of my knees hits the bed. My hands go to her sweater, pulling it up and over her head, leaving her chest covered in just a tank top. She slowly unbuttons my shirt, grazing my chest with the tips of her fingers, then gently traces her palms back up to my shoulders, pushing the shirt off. I'm so turned on by her unhurried yet seductive movements that it takes me a second to notice she unzipped my jeans and pushed them to the floor. I quickly walk out of them, pulling my socks off at the same time, and make a move to unzip her jeans, but she wags her finger at me and pushes me hard enough that I sit down on the bed. I'm not sure what she's planning, but fuck if I'm not all for it! My breaths are shallow as Sydney steps away from me, causing a jolt of longing. I want to reach out, touch her, and keep the connection between us. I'm addicted to her. And although the pull is strong, I stop myself from taking over and let my girl lead.

She pulls her phone out and taps a couple of times before the melodic beat 'Hold On We're Going Home' fills the room. She sets the phone down and moves her hips slowly, lifting her arms up, caressing her body as they make their trek up from her hips over her stomach, stopping for a second on her boobs to tease her perky nipples, and up to her neck where they disappear behind, lifting her blond hair up, fanning them out with her fingers. I can't tear my gaze away from her. She licks her lips and takes a small step forward, her hand finally landing on the button of her jeans. My cock is straining through my boxers, weeping for her as she slowly unbuttons her jeans and pulls them down, stepping out of them in a smooth motion. Her white, almost see-through tank top and white lacy underwear the only thing covering her body as she walks over to me to the beat of the song. Just as she's almost within my reach, she rocks her hips in a figure eight then drops down to her knees, arching her back and flinging her hair up. I have never seen anything as sexy as Sydney crawling towards me on all fours. When she gets within my reach, she gets to her knees and starts gyrating, stroking her body. I'm pretty sure I'm drooling right along with my dick. This is the sweetest kind of torture. Sydney, in front of me, offering herself up to me in this way. She gracefully gets up and, just as I'm about to grab her and lick her through her soaked panties, abruptly turns around and bends over, her perfect ass right in my face.

"Fuck, baby. Are you trying to kill me?" I groan.

She lifts up and, ever so slowly moving her hips to the music, lowers her ass onto my lap. As her cheeks connect with my dick, I grunt, unable to stop myself from rocking into her. She grinds against me. I'm unable to think. I'm seconds away from ripping her panties off and sinking myself into her. But Sydney, the mind reader, takes my hands and does something else to occupy them, moving them around her torso until I have a handful of boob to squeeze. I rock against Sydney's ass making figure eights in my lap and flick her nipples. She rewards my effort with a sexy moan. So I slide my palm down, cupping her soaked panties. I'm glad she's as turned on as I am. But it doesn't last long as Sydney pushes my hand away then stands up and turns around, bending down and dropping small kisses on my jaw line as her hands pull my boxers down. I lift up to help her, not one to stop whatever she's got in store for me. I'll take anything Sydney has planned, especially if it ends with my dick inside her. When my boxers are off and flung into the corner of the room, she takes off her t-shirt, finally giving me a view of her glorious breasts. I can't stop the utter need to taste her, so I reach out and pull her into me. My mouth instantly encloses around her nipple, sucking, then flicking it with my tongue as my hands knead her arse before pulling her panties down. Sydney's knees buckle as she whimpers, her hands pulling at my hair.

"Wait," she says in a hoarse voice, and reluctantly I stop, moving my mouth away. She takes a shaky breath then slips one of her legs between my knees and spreads them out. I'm about to grumble, but then she kneels in front of me, her palms on my thighs, rubbing them up and down. And I know. I have officially died and gone to heaven. "I've been wanting to do this for so long," she says, looking at my cock and licking her lips. It jolts at the prospect of Sydney's mouth around it.

Her head moves closer and her tongue darts up, licking it from the bottom all the way to the head in one slow, torturous motion before swirling the tip with her tongue. Her eyes lift up and she looks into mine as her mouth closes over the head of my cock. And I swear to God, I see stars as she sucks me in, swirling her tongue around. Her hand goes down to the base of my dick, wrapping around it and pumping it along with the movements of her head while her other hands start playing with my balls. She moans as she starts pumping her head up and down, and I realize she is as turned on as I am by this. The hand that was playing with my balls disappears, and Sydney moans again. When I look down, I can see her playing with herself. It is the sexiest fucking thing I have ever seen in my life. I can't help it as I start jerking my hips into her mouth when she takes more and more of my cock into her throat.

"Baby, I'm going to come," I tell her as the tingling

sensation starts up in my balls. I don't want to come in her mouth if it's not what she wants, but fuck, how I want to come in her mouth. As a reply, she moans again, the sound vibrating around my cock, and grabs my hand, putting it at the back of her head. Oh, Jesus Christ. She wants me to fuck her mouth. I nearly come at the thought, then I start pumping into her, fast and hard as her moans grow louder and closer together. When she starts shaking and groans around my cock, my balls tighten, and the orgasm that was threatening spills down her throat as I black out. "Fuuck," I exhale.

That's it. I'm going to marry this woman if I have to drag her down the aisle.

She swirls her tongue around my dick one more time, making the sensitive fucker jump in her mouth, forcing a not so manly whimper to come out of me. But I don't care. I just had the best fucking blow job of my life. I lift her up and pull her into my lap, kissing her deeply. I can taste myself on her tongue, but I honestly don't give a fuck. All I want is Sydney, all I need is Sydney. And if anything stands in my way, to hell with it.

Within a minute of kissing Sydney, her hands come around my neck, and she straddles my lap. I'm hard again and, as she starts rocking against me, I slip inside her. There's nothing like the feeling of her clenched pussy around my cock.

"Carter," she gasps as I move inside her. It's not fucking anymore. This makes me sound like a girl, but I make love to her as she gives herself to me.

"I love you," I whisper as she moves on top of me. Her eyes find mine, and in the depths of them I can see the feeling she's fighting. Even though she doesn't say it, I know she's there right along with me. I just need to give her time to jump off the ledge and not be scared. Because she doesn't need to be scared. I'll catch her. Every. Single. Time.

I woke up in the early hours again to a buzzing sound, Sydney tangled around me, sleeping soundly. I don't blame her for being knocked out. Last night, I couldn't get enough of her. We made love five times, and I still didn't feel sated. I just needed to be inside her. Feel her around me, feel connected to her in the most primal way. Exhausted, she fell asleep on my chest sometime around four in the morning. The buzzing sound starts again, and I feel my nightstand for my phone to check the time only to remember that it's probably still in the pocket of my jeans. I slide out from under Sydney and grab my jeans when they start vibrating in my hands, the buzzing explained. I lift my phone up to my face as Instagram notifications keep popping up. Confused, I scroll down, trying to figure out what happened. One word keeps being repeated in almost every message. Girlfriend. I unlock my phone and try to understand what prompted this when a message catches my eye.

Lazygirl2007: *OMG, your gf Sydney is so awesome!!! I'd totally fight for you just like she did!* 😍 🥊

Eh? What is she on about? I scroll some more, catching another message.

Rockinmyfrock69: *Loved your live gig last night, you were awesome as always. Loved finally seeing your girlfriend in action too!*

I go to my feed and press play on the live, lowering the volume so that I don't wake Sydney up. I stand up and go to the bathroom, cringing as I see myself shaking while tuning my guitar, then my eyes go straight to the camera and I visibly relax. Must have been when I found Sydney. The first song starts and I see the song I chose specifically for Sydney last night. *"He's so in love with you, Sydney."* My sisters' voice can be heard over the music. Ah. Is that why everyone is freaking out? I don't mind the whole world knowing that I love her. I'm just worried about how Sydney will react to having her name and face out there connected to me. Nothing else happens for a while until the camera starts shaking and a faint voice talks about my sexual prowess and how they want to have sex with me again. I groan. It's barely audible over the music, but it's there. For anyone to hear. Fantastic. The camera moves and changes an angle then swings to the side, no longer focused on me. *"Does he have a say in that?"* Sydney's angry voice can be heard clearly. *"Does he get a say in whether he wants your waxed vagina or are you just going to force yourself on a guy that's not even remotely interested in you?"* I guffaw then cover my mouth, trying to hold back the laughter. Kitty has claws. The camera moves to show the original speaker. It's Callie. I shake my head, of course. *"Why wouldn't he be interested in me?"* she asks, and I roll my eyes as the camera once again focuses on the girl I love. *"For starters, maybe because he already has a girlfriend,"* she says clearly and with confidence. Yeah, baby! Tell her! Tell her I'm yours and no one else's! *"Yeah,"* my sisters' voice comes from behind the camera as Sydney looks straight into the lense. Her face goes paper white as she tries to angle herself away and cover it with her hair. *"Sydney is his girlfriend, so back off Callie and stop objectifying my brother."* Callie says something inaudible as Sydney reaches for the camera and points it back at me.

So that's what was going down when Sydney turned

away. I was wondering what happened. I turn off the app and walk back into the bedroom. My girlfriend is sound asleep in our bed.

My girlfriend.

I'm going to miss this when we're back in LA. I could maybe convince her to move in with me?

Sliding under the covers, I pull her against my body and bury my face in her neck, inhaling her intoxicating scent. This is what happiness feels like.

PART III

It'll Never Be Me

Where do we go from here?
What's next for us, I fear
They don't know,
they don't have a clue
How my world would crumble without you
I could have the world at my feet
I could live a thousands lives
But without you by my side
It means nothing
It means nothing
So where do we go from here?
I gave you my heart
I gave you my soul
It's up to you now love if you take it or go
I can only ask so many times
Tell you that you make me complete
But is your heart beating for me
Not yet, is what I fear
So where do we go from here
What's next for us, my dear

Chapter 30

Baaaaabe!

Sydney

Carter's arm wraps around me tight as the sun dances on my face. I try to move, shield myself from it and fall back asleep, but it's too late. I'm awake, hungry, thirsty, and my bladder is screaming at me for some much needed relief. I wonder if my legs will even work after last night's vigorous activities. My bendiness has been tested to its limits and, if I'm honest, I'm pretty sure we invented some new positions. Although I'd need to reference the Kama Sutra first. Just the thought of what we got up to has my heart fluttering.

Carter's morning wood grinds against my butt, and that's when I draw the line. My vagina needs a rest for at least a couple more hours. I slide from under his grip, making him murmur in protest, and head to the bathroom to do my business and brush my teeth. When I walk back into the room, Carter is sitting up, his eyes on me, his phone cradled in his hands, the look on his face stricken as his gaze flutters down to his phone.

"What's wrong?" I walk over to his side of the bed and sit next to him.

He lifts his hand and flicks a nipple. "Morning, boobies," he says, then sighs. "Josh called. He needs me back in LA today."

"Today?" I repeat dumbly. He nods. "When?"

"He wants to have a meeting this evening." I look at his phone.

"But it's already midday..." I hope my voice doesn't come out whiney, but inside I'm a pissed off toddler who's just gotten their favourite toy taken away from them.

"Yeah, we need to leave in an hour or so." He tousles his hair, his eyes wandering around the room searching for something. What, I have no idea.

"Alright then," I say with a fake cheer. "I'll go grab a shower and then we pack." I stand up, resolved not to show my disappointment, and walk back into the bathroom.

I turn on the shower and walk in, not caring whether the water is hot or cold. The feeling of foreboding is unshakable. And as I let the water wash over me, tears start streaming down my face. I know I'm being irrational, but this feels like the end. The short trip we had together cut even shorter. I knew this was coming, and I was trying to get ready for it, but I wasn't ready for my heart to hurt this much. I know Carter said he loves me, I know he said he wants to be with me. But words are just words and, in the end, I'm a distraction he doesn't need when his career is just starting. Like a robot, I wash my hair and body then step outside and towel off. I take a minute to gather myself, splash some cold water on my red eyes in hopes that he doesn't notice, then take a deep breath and open the door.

Thankfully, the room is empty, so I walk over and start picking up clothes we so carelessly abandoned on the floor the night before, folding them and setting them on the dresser. I make the bed next and put our travel bags on top.

We managed to do a load of laundry when we got here, so most of our clothes are clean. Trying not to think about what's going to happen once we arrive in LA, I dress in blue jeans and an oversized sweater then grab my Timberlands and put them on. Next, I try to take control of my towel-dried hair, fingers combing the wet strands. In the end I give up and just pull them up into a wet, messy bun, not caring that they'll dry into a million kinks. My make up case is on the dresser, so I grab some concealer and dab it under my eyes, hoping that it'll cover the redness before adding some mascara for good measure.

Once I'm presentable, I get to work, folding our clothes and putting them into our respective bags. I sort them without thinking, Carter's t-shirt I slept in that first night, the shirt he wore the night I saw him perform for the first time. I put them all away into his bag until the jumper Carter wore the night we got stoned catches my eyes. I lift it up, burying my face in the soft material as Carter's scent envelops me. I inhale him in, unable to stop myself as millions of memories run through my head. When he carried me out of the cave then pulled me into his lap and stroked my face until I was calm again that first day. The time he held my hand as we walked down the streets of Bijou. The cabin, all of the cabin. On a whim, I fold it and stuff it deep into my bag.

Just then, the door opens, making me jump as Carters strolls in. He's wearing only a pair of jeans, his abs and V on full display. Jesus Christ, give a woman strength around all this ripped perfection. Said perfection saunters toward me and wraps his strong arms around my waist from behind, nuzzling my neck.

"Mmmm, I love the way you smell," he mumbles, nipping at my shoulder. A shiver runs through me, the effect Carter has on me instantaneous. I turn around and thread my fingers through his hair as his lips descend on mine. The kiss is slow, and deep, a little bit lazy. He nibbles my lower lip then licks it before diving his tongue back into my mouth, melting me from top to bottom. His hand sneaks under my sweater and trails up over my rib cage until it reaches my breast, giving it a squeeze. He groans into my mouth. "If we only had the time." That sobers me right up, and I move away. Because that's it. Our time is up. "I better go shower," he sighs, stroking my cheek before turning and walking into the bathroom.

I sit on the bed, my face buried in my hand, breathing calmly, trying to chase the sadness away while Carter has a quick shower. In less than five minutes, he walks out, his hair wet, chest glistening with droplets of water and a dark happy trail leading to...a towel that covers one of his best assets. With one finger, I could get that towel undone, take him into my mouth, and try to convince him that maybe we should stay one more day. Just one, because I haven't had enough yet. Carter grins at me, as if knowing exactly where my thoughts went. He walks over to his bag and takes a clean pair of boxers out. He's within my reach when he unwraps his towel and drops it to the floor, his glorious penis right in front of me. Unwittingly, I lick my lips, remembering the night before, the blow job and the amazing sex that followed. Carter groans and shakes his head.

"No time for that, Sunshine," he mutters, hiding one of my favourite appendages of his, second only to his tongue, away in his boxers.

After that, he gets dressed quickly and, before I know it, we're in the kitchen saying goodbye to everyone and having food before we head out. Without detours and stops, it shouldn't take us longer than four and a half hours to get to LA. Hopefully the traffic won't be too bad once we're in the city considering it's the holidays. Rey hugs me tightly.

"I'll see you in LA," she whispers.

I nod, not quite sure if she actually will but hoping that even if Carter and I don't work out, Reagan and I can stay in touch. Everyone hugs and Bella starts crying. It's the first time in my life I witness a mother reacting like that to her child leaving, and something in my heart breaks. I've never experienced warmth and love like that before. And the loss of everything that could be pierces my soul. The last few days with Carter's family felt amazing, and I nearly forgot how much I don't belong. This is just a vacation, a fantasy land for little old Sydney who craves love, craves a family. I look away just as Aunt Berta stands next to me, Gizmo on her shoulder. She squeezes my hand.

"Take some candy on your way out." She winks at me. I crack a smile.

"Thanks," I say, stroking Gizmo on her head. The squirrel seems to have taken to living in this house and the surrounding woodland area. She's also taken to Aunt Berta, so it was a no-brainer whether she should come with us to LA or stay here in squirrel heaven.

We say goodbye one last time and take our bags, along with snacks and hummus sandwiches, to the car. Carter snaps a photo of our stuff in the boot and posts it on Instagram. Then it's time to set off. It feels a bit like our first trip together, a little uncertain of what's to come and how to act. I fiddle with the stereo and put on some music as Carter focuses on driving us through the snowy roads. Soon, the snow turns to sludge then disappears altogether as the temperature rises. It's like we've been to a winter wonderland and now it's time to come back to earth.

I don't want Carter and I to end. I know I have feelings for him, but I just can't wrap my head around how it's going to work. I'll have to trust him. Trust in him. Which is hard to do when you have never trusted in anyone but yourself.

Even though we're silent for most of the drive, it feels a lot faster than it should. We're about half an hour outside LA, the traffic getting thicker, when my phone rings.

"Hello?"

"Hey babe," Hayley says cheerfully. "So your car is fixed and I'm driving it down to LA now."

"You're shitting me!" I exclaim. Carter lifts his brow, so I whisper to him that my car is fixed. "You're an angel Hayley. When will you get to LA? Do you still have my spare key? You should stay at my place."

"Planning to babe. I should be there in an hour, tops."

"I'll see you soon then," I say, my voice deflating a little.

"Aren't you gallivanting across California with Carter?"

"Not quite. We're outside of LA."

"All right, I expect a full report when I see you then. Better chill some wine."

We hang up and I take a minute to gather my thoughts before explaining to Carter that Hayley will be staying with me tonight.

"I was hoping I could see you after my meeting with Josh," he pouts. Me too.

The minute Carter's car disappears around the corner, my junk Honda speeds down the road and Hayley beeps the horn. My lips are still tingling from the goodbye I shared with Carter, and my heart already misses him, but seeing one of my closest friends stick her tongue out and wolf whistle at me as she slows down helps me get out of the funk.

"Baaaaabe!" she roars through her open window.

"Baaaaabe!" I roar back and laugh as she parks. "Ugh, it's so good to see you," I say as she flings the door open and launches herself at me.

We grab our bags and get inside my building. My flat, or apartment, as Hayley likes to call it, is on the second floor and is more like a shoebox with a bathroom and a kitchen, but it's all mine, so it's perfect.

Hayley makes herself at home, opening my fridge and pulling a bottle of wine out, then taking two wine glasses out of the cupboard. It's not even remotely weird. She's been here many times in the last couple of years. She always stays with me when she has a job in LA; it's our unspoken rule.

"So, tell me everything," she says, pouring a generous amount of wine into my glass then handing it to me. I take a large swig and then open my mouth.

"I should probably start at the beginning," I say then proceed to tell her everything that happened in the past week.

"Wow," she says as I get to the goodbye kiss we shared in front of my place just before she arrived. And how Carter said he'll see me tomorrow. We haven't made any concrete plans, or set a time, which annoys me to no end. I like to be prepared for things. I'm a planner, so this laid back attitude is hard to swallow. Now I feel like I'll end up sitting by the phone waiting for his call like the pathetic mess that I am. "Don't worry, we'll keep you busy." Hayley shakes her head. The rest of her group of friends is in LA too, having celebrated Christmas with their families here, so we make plans to meet them tomorrow at some point. I'll be putting my phone on silent and burying it deep inside my bag, because. as God is my witness, I won't be one of those girls who jumps at every ring, every buzz. Who am I kidding? I'll probably be one of those girls where Carter is concerned. He's got me wrapped around his strong forearm. And that's really what's unsettling me. The fact that although he hasn't been gone for more than a couple of hours. Most of my thoughts are about him. How did his meeting go? Is he thinking about me? Is he going to text me?

You see what I mean? Absolute dependability on a boy. Unacceptable.

Then again, is it really that or is it just that he's now a part of me? Lodged inside my soul, waiting for me to admit that. But I'm not ready. Not until I know that we can really make it work.

Chapter 31

Sit Down

When I arrived at Josh's office, he greeted me with a tumbler of whiskey, which I declined, then told me there might be a band interested in having me support them on their upcoming tour, and that they'd like to meet me tomorrow. Apparently, their supporting act can no longer travel with them. The front man checked himself into rehab. This all sounds like an incredible opportunity, doesn't it? And I'd be stupid not to do it, wouldn't I?

Thing is, there's a catch. There's always a catch.

Their tour starts on the second of January. Which means that I'd have a week to convince Sydney... What? That she loves me? That she should give us a chance even if I'll be gone for the next five months?

I wasn't quite sure why I needed to have that talk in person until Josh told me who the band is: Bleeding Hearts. Bleeding. Fucking. Hearts. Only one of the biggest indie bands at the moment. Josh told me how he found them and coached them over the past year and a half and how, once they started listening to his advice, their popularity skyrocketed. "It's all about the timing, mate," he said. "And your time is now."

I walked out of the meeting more confused than ever, uncertain about what I want from my future. A career in music is everything I ever dreamed of, so why am I hesitating?

My phone rings as I drive back home.

"Grasshopper!"

"Miyagi!" Jenny's voice comes through the speaker. "Where are you at, oh wise one?"

"LA, young Padawan. Had to cut my trip short for a meeting. Kinda got myself a label." There's silence then a loud shriek.

"You okay, mate? I think Jenny's wiring just short circuited," Aiden's voice comes on as Jenny screeches '*I knew it! I knew it! I knew it!*' in the background.

I laugh. "Aiden, good to hear you, man!" And it's true. The feeling of being the odd one out no longer hovers over me. The feelings I have for Jenny are crystal clear now. I love my best friend, she's amazing, but I'm not in love with her. Never have been. There's a scuffle, then my favorite person comes on.

"I missed you! How is my favorite brother from another mother? I was going to be the one to call you, but you know how territorial Jenny is." I can just hear the pout in his voice.

"Oh, bro, I can't say I missed you too," I say cheekily.

"Yeah, I saw your Instagram feed! Who's the Australian chick? Will I have to fight her for your affections?"

"Sydney," I say, my heart already aching for her. "She's English, not Australian. I'll tell you all about her when I see you."

"Give me that phone!" Grasshopper shouts in the background, then another scuffle ensues.

"Casanova, listen. I am beyond proud of you for signing with a label."

"I haven't signed anything yet."

"Potato—patato. You're as good as a superstar to me! Anywho, since we're all in LA, let's all meet tomorrow. And bring Sydney. We all can't wait to meet her." Some more fighting in the background, and something crushes to the floor. "Ohmigod, you're such a loser!" Jenny's huff is muffled before she says with resignation, "Jason asked me to tell you he loves you."

"Awww, tell my bud I love him too. Alright, I'm almost at the house, so text me with the details."

"See you tomorrow!"

"Later, Grasshopper."

It's dark by the time I arrive at the place that holds all my childhood memories. Usually, there's our housekeeper milling about. But tonight, the place is eerily quiet. It always felt just a little bit too big for our small family.

Shaking off the feeling of loneliness, I flick the lights on as I make my way through it. Once I'm in my bedroom, I collapse on the bed, my thoughts going straight to Sydney, wondering how her evening is going and if she's even thinking about me. I want to call her, hear her voice, but I don't, knowing she is catching up with Hayley.

I check my phone and reply to messages from my family about how the meeting went. There's nothing from my girl, though. *She's busy*, I tell myself, but the sadness comes anyway. I take a big breath and open Instagram. If I can't talk to her, I can talk to everyone else.

"How's everyone doing?" I start a story. "I'm back home in LA and have some potentially huge news coming up, so keep your eyes peeled for that. I have the evening all to myself as my girl is catching up with her friend tonight. What's everyone's plans? I think I'll go and write some new music tonight. I've been feeling quite inspired recently. Can't wait for you all to hear all the new stuff I've been working on. Have a good night everyone and wish me luck tomorrow. I have a big meeting!"

I finish the story and sigh, not feeling much better. Finally, I break and text Sydney.

ME: *Miss you already. Can't wait to see you tomorrow.*

I watch the screen but nothing happens. She's probably too busy with Hayley. I switch the screen off and hide my face in my hands, thinking of when exactly did I get so pussy-whipped that I'm sitting by the phone waiting for her to text me.

I go to brush my teeth and take a quick shower before picking my guitar up and playing a few songs I've been working on, but nothing really works, so I lie down on my bed and stare at the ceiling. Fuck, I miss her so much. Now that I'm all alone, I can feel the emptiness around me, the hole she's left behind. Can I even survive being on tour feeling like that? Does it get easier with time?

My phone buzzes next to my head and I blindly grasp at it.

"Hello?"

"*Hi.*" Sydney.

"Hi."

"*I just called to say...*" she trails off.

"Yes?" I hold my breath.

"*I miss you too, rockstar.*" I smile.

"Yeah?"

"*Yeah. It's weird. I've never missed anyone before. It's messing with my head.*"

"Is Hayley with you?" If she's not there, I'm getting in the car and going to see her right now.

"*Yeah, she just fell asleep face first on the couch,*" she chuckles. I groan.

"I need to see you, baby." She sucks in a breath. "Tomorrow I'm booking Hayley a hotel, and you're staying with me, or I with you. I don't care, as long as we're together."

"*Carter...*" she hesitates.

"Just think about it, okay?

"*Okay,*" she replies quietly.

"I miss you."

"*I miss you, too.*"

"I love you." She's silent for what feels like forever.

"*Goodnight, rockstar.*"

"Goodnight, Sunshine."

We stay silent on the line for a minute before Sydney sighs and hangs up.

I wake up in the morning with a new resolve to somehow get Sydney to spend all her time coming up to New Year's Eve with me, especially since, potentially, there's not much of that time left before I'll have to travel. I don't even know how I'll broach this subject with her. She's skittish about what's between us at the best of times, so if I tell her I'm leaving on tour in a week... I dread to think what her reaction would be. I just hope her feelings for me are strong enough that she'd be willing to give us a chance no matter the distance between us.

I get dressed and go to meet Josh at his house. As I drive

through the electric gate, I consider how surreal my life has become. If a year ago you'd tell me I'd be in love and on my way to meet with a music exec to discuss a potential tour, I'd laugh in your face. But here I am, doing exactly that.

I get out of my car and walk up the few steps to the huge double door entrance. A loud 'ding dong' sounds as I ring the bell and wait before an older looking lady opens the door for me. I can hear laughter coming from within the house as she guides me through the corridor and into a sitting room where Josh and the five members of Bleeding Hearts are sitting, casually chatting. I swallow the lump in my throat and put on a grin just as Josh looks up.

"Ah, good, you're here! Come, come. Sit down. This is Jack, Danny, Robert, Will, and Steven." He points at each member of Bleeding Hearts as if I don't know who they are. "Guys, this is Carter Kennedy, the guy I was telling you about."

They all say some variation of 'hello' in their English accents then start asking me questions. For the next hour, we chat about my music, friends, and aspirations. We listen to some of my songs and Josh plays a recording of the live performance from Lola's. It's weird watching myself through everyone else's eyes. The guys seem to be excited, and by the end I'm told the spot on the tour is mine if I want it. I'm shocked. Somehow, I thought it would be harder. When they get up to leave, Jack and I swap numbers and he tells me they'll be going to Stellar, a new nightclub in downtown LA, asking me if me and my friends would like to join. I nod, unable to believe that I'll be partying with Bleeding fucking Hearts tonight. So far, I have managed to keep my cool, but at this point it's a matter of seconds before I start jumping around, screaming like a schoolgirl losing her shit at the sight of her idol. Bleeding

Hearts is basically my Harry Styles in the early years of One Direction.

Thankfully, they leave shortly after I promise Jack to text him the names to put on the club's list. Josh smiles at me.

"So? What do you think?"

"Is this for real? This is not a part of some elaborate prank, is it?"

He laughs. "No, mate! It's as real as it gets. I believe in you. I believe in your music. Your original stuff is incredible. I want to start getting your name out there as soon as possible. In the meantime, I'll arrange for some recording sessions so we can get a couple of tracks down, start dropping them before we work on your album. I know this is huge. And not exactly in the right order, but I just have this feeling about you." I nod, not quite sure what to think. This has been too easy. "Obviously, you'll need to sign the contract I sent you over before, but other than that, it's as good as a done deal. You'll be huge, Carter. I'm sure of it."

"My lawyer is looking it over," I say.

"Good. Always get someone else to look at anything you're signing. That's rule number one."

The imposter syndrome is huge. Surely, this is some sort of cosmic joke. Surely, I don't deserve it. How the hell is this happening to me? But happening it is. After that, Josh and I head to his in-house recording studio and we spend a big chunk of the day recording a few of my songs. Just the acoustic versions for now. Josh has an incredible ear, and all his comments are insightful and helpful. Working with someone like him is incredible and truly a dream come true.

"This is great stuff already, mate. We will layer more instruments on top of them later this week," he says as we finish listening to what we have done. "You will also be able to use the instrumental tracks when performing before we get some people behind you."

Once I leave, I call our family lawyer who confirms that the contract is actually a very good deal. Coda Records prides itself on putting their acts first. I sign the paperwork, ready for the next time I see Josh. It seems like I really hit the jackpot.

Except I have this feeling that the other shoe is about to drop.

One person cannot be this lucky.

Chapter 32

Dickwad

Sydney

The day drags on without Carter, and considering the amount of wine Hayley and I consumed last night, I'm surprised we're both not dying of a hangover.

By the time noon comes around, we finally make plans to meet Carter and the rest of the gang for dinner. I was hoping I'd be able to see Carter earlier than dinner, but I understand how much he's got going on, especially since he spent the whole morning with Josh in meetings and in the recording studio. I'm so incredibly excited for and proud of him. Even if a small part of me thinks it's all going extremely fast. It feels like running with your blindfold on, exhilarating but dangerous at the same time. But I can't complain since apparently Bleeding Hearts, one of my favourite bands, invited us out to a club. I consider briefly if I should spill that I know them, having worked with Jack on a promo shoot before, but then decide it'll probably be more fun if I don't.

Seems hanging out with a rock band has its perks since, for the first time in what feels like forever, Hayley agrees to come out. I swear the woman used to be a hermit in her past life. Or maybe she just doesn't like to go clubbing? Either way, it's really rare for her to go out. We paint our nails and I tell her all about the book I'm writing, the romance about the busker and the introvert. I tell her about Darius cock blocking all my shoot opportunities and how I'm not sure how to proceed with it. There's not really that much I can do.

"At this point, I have enough saved up that I don't have to work for a year, so it's not a huge issue, but it still sucks. Maybe I'll get a job as a waitress?" It would be great for people watching and could give me some inspiration, get the artistic juices flowing.

"Oh, stop it! I'm sure he will tire of being a dickwad soon," she says as we lock up and make our way outside, the Uber waiting for us at the curb. During the ride, I start feeling nervous at the prospect of meeting everyone, especially Jenny. I kinda hope she's ugly and stupid, but I know it's unlikely. Hayley wouldn't consider her one of her best friends if Jenny wasn't a good person.

When we arrive at the restaurant, we're the last ones there, everyone else already sitting at the table, and as the hostess walks us over, Carter's gaze lifts up and lands on me. Time stands still as in one swift movement he stands up and closes the gap between us. Cupping my face, he captures my lips. The kiss, although not short, is chaste, which is probably for the best since it's a family restaurant.

"God, I missed you," he says as he touches his forehead to mine.

"I missed you too," I reply. And it's true. It's like my lungs weren't working properly since yesterday, only allowing for shallow, uneven breaths; and now that he's with me again, I can finally inhale. I take a step back, checking him out. He's wearing black jeans tucked into combat boots and a white t-shirt, a leather jacket hanging on his chair. He's got a five o'clock shadow on his jaw, and his dark hair is in its usual messy perfection. If you could spontaneously orgasm from looking at someone, he would be that someone. I can see his eyes travelling up and down my body, taking me in with heat in his eyes. I'm not wearing anything special, just a pair of ripped skinny jeans and a sparkly gold crop top underneath my jacket, my heels making me almost as tall as Carter. He lifts a strand of my hair, which I left down.

"How is it that each time I see you, you get more beautiful?" I shrug, having the same thought about him getting more and more handsome every day.

"Erhm," someone loudly clears their throat next to us. Carter reluctantly turns his head to his friends and sighs.

"Everyone, this is Sydney, my girlfriend. Sydney, this is Aiden, Jenny, and Jason." I don't miss the fact that he's called me his girlfriend. I suppose I think of myself as one too, ever since he told me that he loved me and that night in Bean Diggity where Reagan broadcasted to the gram that I am, in fact, his girlfriend. I put on my big girl panties, smile a huge smile, and hug everyone.

We sit down, Carter pulling me close to him until our bodies touch. It's comforting, the heat from his skin, the constant connection he seems to crave too. When we order our food, Carter surprises me once again by ordering a vegan dish. I tell him he doesn't have to, but he just smiles and tells me he likes it and is actually considering eating only vegan food going forward. Jason's eyebrows raise at that as my heart swells. I'd never make him change his diet to suit me, it's everyone's personal preference, but the fact that he has so easily taken to the idea makes me lo—like him more. Like. I definitely was going to say like from the beginning.

As Carter, Hayley and their friends catch up, they make sure to include me at every turn, explaining inside jokes, asking me questions. I hate to admit it, but Jenny is great. She's humble, funny, and she clearly loves her friends. Aiden is a fellow Londoner, so talking to him comes really easily. We laugh, trading stories of the place we grew up in.

Jason keeps eyeing me, narrowing his eyes until he finally bursts out, "What are your intentions towards Carter?"

I nearly spit my water out. "Excuse me?"

"Jason..." Carter shakes his head as Jenny starts laughing uncontrollably.

"What are your intentions?" he repeats himself, crossing his arms in front of his chest and cocking his head to the side.

"You don't have to reply to that," Carter says, shooting daggers at Jason. "Jase, stop it, man."

Jenny starts hiccuping, wiping her tears away. "You'll —*hic*—have to—*hic*—excuse my brother—*hic*," she tries to say through laughter and hiccups. "He thinks—*hic*—that Miyagi is the best thing—*hic*—since sliced bread."

"Speaking of bread, what's the status on Edward?" Carter tries to change the topic.

"Still looking good as new." Aiden shakes his head.

"*Forever young, I want to be forever young...*" Jason starts to sing then stops, looking around. "You devious beasts! Trying to make me lose focus. Intentions, Sydney! Intentions!"

"Admirable?" I ask. To be honest, I don't know quite yet. My intentions are not to get hurt, whatever that means in the long run.

This seems to placate Jason for the time being as he relaxes and joins the conversation until it's time to leave. When we pile into two taxis, somehow, he ends up in the taxi with Carter and I.

"I'm sorry about earlier," he whispers in my ear as Carter gazes out the window. "Carter is...well, he's the best human being I know. He'd do anything for the ones he loves and I... I just don't want him to get hurt."

"I'm not planning to hurt him, Jason," I say.

"Good."

There's a long queue in front of the club when we get there. As we walk past the people waiting, Carter takes a picture of us and posts it on his social media. I'm slowly getting used to this part of his life and, although I'd rather not be in the pictures, I know that social presence is incredibly important for him, especially at this time in his career.

The bouncer unhooks the rope for us, letting us through once Carter gives our names, and as we walk past him, I can't help but do my ritual, "I'm Steve Butabi." His lips quirk up as Jason stops in his tracks, his eyes large.

"I'm Doug Butabi," Jase says in a revenant tone.

The bouncer full on grins now. "You guys brothers?" he asks.

Jason and I look at each other and say in unison, "Noo. Yeees!" We hive five then burst into laughter.

"Thanks,"—I look at the bouncer's name tag—"John! I always do this, but you're the first person to get the reference."

"My pleasure," he bows as grinning Jason pulls me in.

"You know, Sydney," he says as we walk in, "I think I had you all wrong. Looks like we'll be bestest friends. Just promise you'll take care of my boy." Well, that was easy! I nod, which seems to satisfy him enough.

The club is maybe half full. There is still space on the dance floor as purple lights flash against the mass of dancing bodies. The music is loud, and the beat makes the blood in my veins pulsate as we make our way through the bar and up to the second-floor VIP area.

The guys from Bleeding Heart are already there, each holding a drink.

"Carter! Glad you made it, mate!" Jack stands up then does a double take when he spots me standing off to the side. I grin. "Syd? Fucking hell, it *is* you!" He runs up to me and twirls me around. Danny, Will, Rob, and Steven all stand up and come up to me. Everyone in our group looks confused. I suppose I could have said something. But what do you say? 'Hey, I know those guys. We bonded over our shit childhood and love of Yorkshire tea?'

"How have you been, babe?" Danny, the biggest flirt out of them all, puts his arm around me.

"Good, Danny. How are you? How's your mum doing?" A shadow crosses his face.

"Honestly? Not great. The cancer has come back so... Anyway, it's party time! Let's get you a drink!" he quickly deflects, turning around and pouring a generous amount of vodka into an empty glass then topping it with orange juice.

"How do you know Carter?" Will asks while Danny hands me my drink. I don't know why I say the next thing, maybe because I'm under a spotlight, maybe because I'm finding it hard to admit my feelings for him are stronger than I let on. "Ermm, we drove together from San Francisco." I regret it as soon as the words leave my mouth, then regret it even more when I see Carter's face fall and jaw tighten. "I mean, we did a road trip and..." I can't finish the sentence.

"She's Carter's girlfriend," Jason interjects, rolling his eyes. "Hi, I'm Jase." Suddenly, I'm glad that Jason is beside me, but not for long as Steve's attention goes straight back to me.

"Girlfriend?" He narrows his eyes as I repress the urge to groan. "What about your 'no boyfriend' rule?"

"Lads, that's enough. Some rules are meant to be broken, aren't they, Syd?" Rob, the sweetheart that he is, comes to my rescue and I squeeze his hand in a silent thank you. Thing is, when I had that shoot with Jack, Steve tried to get me to go out with him, and I just wasn't feeling it. I'm hoping this might have been part of the reason why I completely cracked under pressure when they asked me about Carter.

The night goes on, and, as we drink and chat, I relax a little, even though Carter seems to be quiet and keeps his distance. Girls join our little VIP area and hang all over the boys from Bleeding Hearts, one of them really flirting with Will, putting her hands all over him and whispering into his ear.

"Doesn't he have a girlfriend?" I ask Rob, who's sitting next to me, motioning in their direction.

"I guess..." he trails off as a sick feeling starts up in my stomach. The girl strokes her finger up and down Will's jaw as he laughs at something. His eyes are glazed over and movements not quite right. It's clear that he's drunk. I look over at Carter, who is chatting to one of the other girls. She laughs, throwing her head back at whatever he said. The spark of jealousy ignites flames as I narrow my eyes at them. "You know you'll have to trust him, love," Rob says, his eyes following mine. I sigh. "It will only be worse when we're on tour." I stiffen. What did he say? I glance back at Will and my heart stops when I see the girl straddling his lap, rocking into him and kissing him. My throat dries. Will, who's always talking about the girl he has back home. Will, who, when we met, told me he's never loved anyone like he loved his girlfriend. Will, who told me he's going to marry her, is kissing another girl. And if he's doing that, what makes me think Carter, who's been with me for a week, will not do the same thing? Maybe not at the first opportunity, maybe not for long. But I know girls will keep throwing themselves at him. Just look at him. Waxed vaginas will be offered to him on a silver platter left, right, and centre. He's bound to break.

"Your tour?" I croak out.

"Yeah, as long as he agrees, he'll be opening for us."

"Ah yes, he'd be silly not to." I swallow hard.

"Exactly," Rob smiles, oblivious to the cracks opening in my heart. "I know it starts really soon, but you can come visit us, love. You know we'll be more than happy to see you any time."

I blink. "That's great. Thanks, Rob. When again are you off?"

"We leave on the second of January," he says as my whole world collapses around me. Less than a week. He leaves in less than a week and he hasn't even bothered to tell me. Why would he keep this from me? Is it because he doesn't want to be with me anymore?

"Excuse me," I say and stand up. Like a robot, I walk out through the rope and down the stairs. I don't know what to feel. How to feel. Because, right now, a huge hole has opened up in my chest and is sucking all the life out of me.

All the happiness. How long will he be gone? Why hasn't he told me?

"Sydney!" A hand wraps around my arm just as I get to the entrance. I whip around, facing Carter. "Are you okay? You look pale. What's wrong, Sunshine?" My heart cracks even more at the sound of the nickname he gave me.

"Why didn't you tell me?"

"Tell you what?"

"That you're leaving on tour in less than a week, Carter!" My voice is steady, devoid of all emotions. He takes a step back.

"Who told you that?"

"So it's true," I laugh, but it comes out hollow. "Were you even going to tell me, or were you just going to string me along until it's time to leave? Silly, old Sydney, believing this was more than just a bit of road trip fun." I say mockingly.

"Sydney, you know that's not true, I—"

"Save it," I interrupt him. "I believed you for a moment. I wanted to believe you. Serves me right."

"Syd—"

"No Carter, I can't. Just give me some space, okay? Let's talk tomorrow." I turn around and walk towards the door. This time, he doesn't follow.

As soon as I'm outside, tears start to pour down my cheeks. I wipe at them with the back of my hand. Great, I left my jacket in the club. Thankfully, my phone is safely tucked away under my bra. I take a few steps down the street, remembering the face Carter made as I told him to leave me alone. Pain. Pain was the emotion in his eyes. Has he seen mine? Because it hurts. So fucking much. The possibility of not seeing him, not being with him. I wrap my arms around my waist, trying to keep the chill away.

But if he loves me... If he truly does, we could try to make it work? Would he still want to after my outburst? Why does this hurt so much? *It's because you love him, you idiot,* my inner voice says. And like that, things become clear.

What was I thinking? I need to go back. Of course we can make this work. We can make anything work if we truly want to. I love him for fuck's sake.

I love him.

I stop in my tracks. I need to tell him that I love him. I need to tell him I want to make this work. I want to be with him. Be there for him when he has a bad day and be there when he's got good ones. See him write music, be his inspiration. See his beautiful smile and laugh at his silly jokes. I don't care if he's going on tour. I trust him.

I trust him.

I don't know when and how it happened, but Carter Kennedy took over my heart, and he deserves to know about it.

I turn around to walk back to the club, resolved to tell him I was being an idiot when I bump into someone wearing a hoodie.

"Sorry," I mutter, not paying attention, trying to sidestep whoever it is. A gloved hand wraps around my arm. I look at it, not comprehending what is happening.

"Hello, Sydney." My heart stops as something stings my neck.

"Darius." I manage to say as the world turns blurry.

I take a few unsteady steps forward before I'm pushed into a vehicle. As my face connects with the cold leather, there's only one thought in my head. *Carter. I didn't tell him I loved him.*

Then the world goes black.

Chapter 33

This Guy

Carter

What the fuck just happened? One moment I was introducing Sydney to my friends, the next the whole of Bleeding fucking Hearts was all over her acting like they've just seen their long lost best friend. I saw how Steve and Danny looked at her like they had every right to touch her. And when she stumbled while telling them how she knew me. Well, that felt like a dagger to my heart.

So I gave her space, let her catch up with her friends while I watched her from the corner of my eye, trying to figure out how to tell her I might be going on tour very soon. Then Rob—thanks a lot asshole—seemed to have done that job for me. To be fair, Rob is not an asshole. But as I'm standing here, after Sydney ran out on me telling me we won't work, I have very little love for the guy.

My heart is in a million pieces, lying at my feet where she threw it and stomped on it with her high heels. The only thing stopping me from completely breaking down is the fact that she said we will talk tomorrow. There's a sliver of chance I can convince her to...what?

I am so fucked.

Maybe I shouldn't go on that tour; instead, I could stay with Sydney, finish off my degree. I've got one more semester to go, having taken extra classes the last few years knowing I could graduate early and focus on something I want to do. Because marketing and communications is not it. Who even chooses that as their major? This guy. I had no clue what I wanted to do, so I went for the easiest thing I could think of, coasting through years, sleeping around, and partying. Learning always came easily to me. Good grades were never difficult to achieve, so maybe that's why having the degree within my reach does not feel like an accomplishment. Because I've never had to work hard for it.

Music, on the other hand? Yes, writing songs comes naturally to me, music floating through my veins. What's difficult, though, is the performing side. Yet, once I'm done it feels exhilarating.

I'd give it up for Sydney, though. I can still write and sing, do small open mics in California. I don't have to go on tour, I don't have to be a rockstar. I could get a normal job, wear a suit to work, come home at the end of the day to her and kiss her each morning before going to work... If that's what she wants? I'd do it.

I'd do it in a heartbeat.

I walk outside, hoping that I can still catch her. I know she said to give her space, but I just want to explain to her one last time that none of that tour bullshit matters if she's not by my side.

There's a chill in the air and I remember she walked out without her jacket. I look around, but she's not outside. The queue to get into the club is still there, but other than that the street is fairly empty. I jog to the corner and look if she maybe took a turn, but she's not there either. Her blond hair is nowhere to be seen. She probably took an Uber home.

Resigned, I walk back into the club and up the stairs to the VIP area. It's just after midnight now, and I no longer feel like partying, or celebrating for that matter. I grab Sydney's jacket and say goodbye to my friends.

"You guys are going home?" Hayley asks. I hang my head.

"Sydney just left," I reply then tell them the reason behind her abrupt departure.

"Carter..." Jenny gives me a hug. "First of all, that's fantastic news! I knew you'd hit it big soon." I can't even smile. "I'm sure she'll come around. It's huge news, and it didn't come from you, so she probably just needs to process it. Give her the night to think it through." I nod. She's probably right. "Don't worry, you should see the way she looks at you. That girl is head over heels in love with you." The words are uplifting, but unless Sydney realizes it herself, they don't make much difference.

"I'm going to head home, you guys."

"Do you want us to come with you?" Jason asks.

"What? God, no! Stay, enjoy yourselves! I'll talk to you in the morning," I try to smile, but it comes out wonky. I'd truly rather be alone.

"Well, if you change your mind, we're only a phone call away."

I thank them then say goodbye to the guys from Bleeding Hearts, except Will, who's getting mauled by a random chick. I guess that's one way to get over a breakup. When Jack asks me if I thought anymore about joining them on tour, I give a noncommittal answer and tell him I'll talk to him soon.

"You know, if it's about Sydney, she can come on tour with us," he says as I turn around. "She could help with merch or just come as part of your crew. I don't care. It would be stupid to throw this opportunity away if a music career is what you want. Just think about it." I nod and leave the club. But that's a thought. Would Sydney even consider coming with me? I know I could definitely do it if she was with me, grounding me and making me forget about my stage fright. Would she want to though? Would she even consider it?

I guess I could always ask, and if the answer is no, I'll go with Plan B. Carter Kennedy the marketing executive.

It's seven in the morning when I wake up to my phone buzzing.

"Hello?" I answer groggily.

"*Carter, is Sydney with you?*" Haley's voice sounds panicked. I sit up in bed, fully awake.

"No, what's wrong?"

"*I just got to her apartment and she's not here. She's not answering her cell either.*" Fuck. What the fuck?

"Is there anywhere else she could be?"

"*Not that I know of. The only other place would be with you, but she's not,*" her voice breaks.

"Hayley, calm down. We can figure it out. I'm sure she's fine," I say calmly, but inside I'm freaking out. I'm out of the bed and pulling on any clothes I can find in three seconds flat. "Okay, I'm going to come to you now and you call Aiden, Jenny, and Jason to check if she's with them. Let's all meet at her apartment. Once you've called them,"—I take a deep breath—"start calling the hospitals." My voice doesn't falter at the words, because Sydney is okay. She has to be okay.

"*Okay,*" she whispers.

I hang up and run to my car, breaking all sorts of laws as I drive to Sydney's place. I try to call her every few seconds, but her phone goes to voicemail. I only bother leaving one, asking her to just let us know she's okay, as we're worried. Then I continue trying to get through to her, to no avail.

I don't think I even lock my car as I run out and take two steps at a time to her second-floor apartment. The door is open and, as I walk in, Hayley stands up, phone in hand, tears streaming down her face. She runs to me and, as I put my arms around her, she breaks into sobs.

"It's all my fault," she croaks out. "I should have come home as soon as I found out you guys weren't okay; instead, I stayed and flirted with Danny fucking Stephens." She starts crying again as I stroke her back. We all should have, could have, would have, but we didn't. I can't think about it because if I start blaming myself, I'll break down too, and my priority is making sure she's okay. Alive and okay.

The door opens and Jenny, Aiden, and Jason walk in. The relief at seeing them here is instantaneous. They can help.

"Okay," I say, going into boss mode. "Thank you guys. We can find her together. Let's just divide and conquer. You all have phones so let's start by calling LA hospitals, checking if she's been admitted anywhere." They all nod and get to work.

After an hour of futile phone calls, the atmosphere changes. Resignation is palpable in the air, and I pull at my hair.

"We're not fucking giving up!" I growl at them.

"Should we maybe try calling the hotels around Stellar? Maybe she didn't want to go back home?" Jenny asks.

"It would have been so much easier if she had a collar with GPS like Jake," Jason adds unhelpfully.

Except... The cogs in my brain turn.

Fucking hell, he's actually being helpful.

"Jason, you goddamn genius!" I exclaim, pulling out my phone and opening the Find My app. I can't believe I haven't thought of it myself! I pray to everything that is holy that her phone is on and not out of battery, that she still has the app, that she hasn't stopped location sharing.

When her face pops up, I exhale in relief until I notice where she is. She's in an industrial part of town. There's nothing there except storage and one small building where her face flashes. My heart stumbles. Fuck.

This cannot be good.

Chapter 34

A Little Too Late

Sydney

I wake up in a dark room, lying on the concrete floor. I vaguely remember the argument I had with Carter, but nothing much after that. I'm about to shout for help but think better of it. My hands and legs are bound, so letting whoever tied me up know I'm awake is not the best idea. I should try to get my bearings first. I let my eyesight adjust to the dark and look around. There's a bucket next to me. God knows I need to pee, but I'm not that desperate yet. I slowly sit up and take in the room. There's not much here, the small window is boarded up, but no light comes through it. Is it still the night? What time could it be?

I desperately search for something, clues, nails, anything sharp, but come up empty. Although the room is dark, I can tell by the bleached smell that it's been thoroughly cleaned. There goes my plan of trying to cut through the rope around my wrists and ankles. I test the bindings, trying to figure out if maybe I can wriggle my wrists out of them when I hear a sound. On a whim, I tip sideways to the same position I was in when I woke up. I bang my shoulder pretty hard, but at least manage not to hurt my head. I half close my eyes, steadying my breathing just as the door opens. Light gets inside the room and, through my lashes, I see brown boots walk over to me. One of the boots nudges my shoulder as I continue to play dead.

"You awake, little whore?" I almost suck in the air at the voice. Darius. Memories of last night flood me. The ambush, the sting on the side of my neck—which still hurts now that I think of it—the way he pushed me into his car. What a fucktard. If I wasn't bound, I'd knee him in the nuts. Except, he's much stronger than me if the memories from two years ago serve me right. What the fuck does he want from me?

I don't move. Instead, I wait as he stands there, still as a statue. I keep my breathing steady, as if I'm still asleep. Whatever happens, if I can make him believe I'm still knocked out, maybe it would buy me a few more hours. Maybe I can come up with a plan. Find out why he's brought me here. Convince him to let me go.

After a minute that feels like hours, he turns around and walks out of the room. As soon as he's gone, I get to work. I move my ankles up to my hands tied behind my back. My heels are gone, so I'll need to rely on my fingers to get out of this. I'm thankful for the hours of back bending yoga I've done because, for once, something goes right and I easily reach the rope. With my bound fingers, I feel for any kinks or knots, anything that I can grasp onto to loosen the bindings. After a while, I find a knot and nearly cry with relief. I break two nails trying to untie it but finally come up victorious. Once my legs are free, I sit up and consider my next move. I could try to move my hands from my back to my front. I try to move them over my butt, but the rope is too tight and I nearly dislocate my shoulder. Something else then. I stand up and walk over to the wall, sweeping my feet just in case there's anything on the floor. Once I'm by the wall, I move slowly, feeling for anything that sticks out that's even remotely sharp. Nothing. It's only when I come to the boarded up window that I finally luck out. I nick the skin on my cheek finding it, but I don't care, a small bleeding cut is the least of my worries. I bend over, lifting my wrists up and start rubbing them on whatever it was that caught my cheek. After what feels like forever, the rope finally loosens a little. I haven't cut through it yet, but the added length is enough for me to be able to move my arms over my butt and legs to bring my wrists to the front of my body.

I feel like I've run a marathon when I start rubbing the ropes against what appears to be a broken nail. The adrenaline is coursing through my body, and I know every second counts here. I haven't got a clue what Darius has in store for me, but I'm not just going to sit here like a little lamb and let him do whatever he wants. No way. If I'm going down, I'm doing it on my terms. And that means I fight. Like I fought my mother each time she locked me in a cupboard. Like I fought for every single meal. Like I fought for a better life for myself. This arsehole is not going to take any of this away from me. He messed with the wrong chick. If he thinks he's getting a repeat of the timid Sydney from two years ago, he is sorely mistaken. I'm awake, I know what's coming and I. Will. Fight.

The rope breaks, and I whimper with relief. I can still feel my phone against my ribcage. Thankfully, Darius was dumb enough not to check there. Now, if he was a woman, he would know that it's the best place to hide anything on a night out: money, phone, keys. Who needs a bag when you have a bra? I'm about to reach for my boobs to get my phone out when I hear footsteps again. I dive for the rope on the floor and run to where I was lying down, managing to arrange myself in a kneeling position, hiding my unbound wrists and ankle just as the door opens. Fuck, I have nothing sturdy enough to fight him with. My heart gallops in my chest as light illuminates the room.

It's such a contrast from the dark that it takes me a few seconds to adjust. I fight the urge to shield my eyes and thankfully win, as it would have given away the one thing I've got going for me.

"Sydney, Sydney, Sydney," Darius says. "Or shall I call you Sunshine?" I blink in confusion. "Tell me, what does that little boy have that I don't, Sydney?" Venom seeps with each word. "I could have given you everything. I wanted to, Sydney, but you chose to be a spoiled little whore instead. How does it feel to know you could have had the world at your feet and you threw it all away?"

Oh my god, he is insane.

"I'm sorry," I say timidly, playing into his hand, all the while thinking of the best strategy going forward. Thankfully, he's too absorbed in himself to even suspect that I've managed to get out of the binds.

"That's a little too late now, isn't it? I gave you all the opportunities to come back to me, beg for my forgiveness. Instead, you ignored me then decided to prostitute yourself to a wannabe rockstar."

"Instagram," I whisper, finally realising where he got all this information from.

He smiles cruelly. "Yes, Sydney. You may have stopped posting on your social media, making it harder for me to find you, but your attention starved 'boyfriend'," he says with a bite, "well, he couldn't help himself but to post everything for everyone to see. It was just a matter of time before I found you, and after that, all I had to do was to be patient. Imagine my elation when he posted a picture of you and your friends in front of a club mere blocks away from where I live. All I needed was to get you alone. So I waited patiently. Then at midnight, who should walk out, all by themselves, crying? Poor Sydney, did you and your boyfriend have a fight?" He mocks. "Do you even think he cares that you're gone?" My heart hurts as his words hit me right to the core. Does he even know I'm gone? I haven't even told him that I love him.

"What do you want from me, Darius?"

"So, so many things, Sydney, but first I'll enjoy finally having you."

"So what, you're just going to rape me?" I ask incredulously. "All that just to get your dick wet? Is that how you like your women? Bound, helpless, and sick at the thought of you?" I spit out. He roars, pulling his arm back. I know he's about to strike me, put me in my place, but before he does, I scramble up, grab for the bucket, and whack him in the head. I know the only reason he stumbles is due to the confusion. I have three, maybe five seconds before he comes back to his senses, so I don't wait. Instead, I duck and pump my legs out of the room and into a corridor. When I reach a door, I yank it open and come to a sterile looking room. There's a sofa, a table, and a couple of chairs in there. On the table, a tray with toast and a glass of water and a rose. He's lost his fucking mind.

A loud roar pierces the air as I run for the door. Hurry, Sydney, hurry! I reach for the handle, but it's locked. Key. I need a fucking key. My heart beats overtime as I scramble, looking around. I notice a basin in the corner of the room next to it, a key on the hook. I go for it, yanking it off as I run back to the door. I manage to push it in and turn it as Darius grabs my hair and, with a cry, drags me back. Tears threaten to break loose. I was close, so close. I'm not giving up now.

As he pulls me back, I reach for his arm, digging my nails in. It's not much, but it's something. It might not stop him, but at least I can inflict some pain on him...

I dig my feet in just as I decide to jump up and lean into him, hopefully making him fall over in the process, when the door bursts open.

Chapter 35

Say It Again

Carter

It's been two days.
Two days since Jason, Aiden, and I burst into that room to witness Sydney being dragged by her hair by a psychopath. The element of surprise was on our side. Because in the commotion, the asshole who held my Sydney let her go, allowing her to scramble away and run to me.

We were supposed to wait for the police, who I called as soon as I realized where Sydney was. We ran out of the apartment and drove straight there. The police weren't there yet, and when I heard a male roar inside, I couldn't not move, couldn't wait any longer. Sydney was in danger. I ran for the door, which was locked, but together, Aiden, Jason, and I managed to break it open only to be confronted with another set of doors. This one, thankfully open; although, with the sounds of a scuffle from the inside, I'd have kicked it in even if it'd made me break my leg.

And that's when I saw Sydney.

The moment she leaped into my arms, my whole world stopped.

My Sydney. She was barefoot, still wearing clothes from

the night before. Her wrists were bruised and there was a nasty, bleeding gash on her right cheek. If it wasn't for the fact that she was shaking against me, I'd have killed that motherfucker right then and there.

Instead, I held her tight as Aiden and Jason jumped on him, knocking him out just as the police sirens sounded in the distance.

"Sydney." My voice cracked as I lifted her up and took her out of that godforsaken place. I was never going to let her go ever again. Jason and Aiden stayed inside, making sure that the asshole could not escape.

As the morning sun blinded us, Sydney buried her face in my shirt and sobbed. My heart was breaking for her, for everything she must have been through.

"Baby, are you okay?" I asked like an idiot. Of course she wasn't okay, she was abducted and god knows what has been done to her. "I mean did he... Did he touch you? Hurt you?" She shook her head. That one small movement was everything that I needed for the tension to loosen just a little bit. She was okay.

I was so proud of her. It was evident she fought to get out. But it wasn't until the police arrived and Sydney gave a detailed account of what had happened since she left the club that I found out just how amazing and strong the girl I was in love with was. It was only when she neared the end of the story, when she relayed her conversation with Darius, that the wind got knocked out of me.

It was all my fault.

I've put her in danger.

Me and my careless Instagram account. I knew she was reluctant to post anything about herself, and yet I went ahead and posted all the details. Including the location of where we were, making it child's play for Darius to find her.

I was the one responsible for him taking her. I was the cause of all this. If only I stayed away from her, she'd have been safe.

And the past two days have made it even more clear that she felt the same way. She has been quiet and withdrawn.

After the police, I took her straight to my house, helped her shower, and dressed her in my clothes while Hayley packed a bag for her and brought it over. My parents and Reagan left Aunt Berta's as soon as I told them what happened. They arrived a few hours later and have been doting on Sydney ever since.

At least with them around, she seems somewhat alive. She talks, albeit in a small voice and in short sentences, but she does. When I'm around, though, it's a different story. She instantly closes up and looks anywhere but at me, usually down at her hands. At night, when we go to sleep, she curls into a ball, wearing sweats and a long sleeve t-shirt, and stays like that until it's time to get up in the morning, at which point she just leaves the room.

I'm starting to think she hates me for what I put her through.

I hate myself.

I haven't been on Instagram since that day. Not planning to anytime soon, either. But before I let her go, I need to try to tell her I'm sorry. Convince her that if she'd let me, I'd never let anything bad happen to her ever again.

If she just talked to me.

My phone buzzes in my pocket, and when I check the caller ID, I sigh. I have been avoiding this conversation for too long.

"Hi, Josh." I put the phone on speaker as I finish getting dressed.

"Carter, how is Sydney?" he goes straight to the point.

I run my hand through my hair. "I'm not sure, to be honest, still not really talking."

He's silent.

"Have you thought about your decision? Are you still set on pulling out of the tour?"

"I— Josh, I can't leave her like this." I won't leave her. Not if there's a sliver of a chance she wants me around. Not when she needs me.

"Bring her with you then. I talked to the guys, and they all thought it was a great idea." I look out the window as the morning sun rises on the horizon. The sky is blue with strings of orange running across it.

"What if... What if she doesn't want to come?" I lift the guitar pick she gave me for Christmas off my bedside table and turn it in my hand.

"If she doesn't? Well, maybe then it's best if you do come. Either way, let me know by the end of the day." He sounds irritated, and I can't blame him. He's putting a lot on the line for me. I only just signed my contract with his label a few days ago and I'm already this huge question mark.

"Okay." I nod to myself.

"I'll talk to you later, mate. And don't worry. It'll all work out." He hangs up.

I sit on the bed, tracing the scratched out 'rockstar' on the pick with my finger and trying to figure out what my next step should be when Sydney speaks.

"You're not going on tour?" Her voice is quiet as I turn my head to take her in.

She's leaning on the door jamb, her hair up in a bun, her face fresh and devoid of makeup. Even now, with her eyes sad and glistening, she looks beautiful. I fight the urge to stand up and take her in my hands. She probably doesn't want that.

"How long have you been standing there?" I ask, rubbing the back of my neck, trying to appear confident while inside I'm praying for this conversation to last longer than two sentences. What I wouldn't give for just one smile from her.

"Long enough," she takes a step forward. My heart speeds up at the prospect of her being closer. "You didn't answer my question."

"Yeah, I said I won't go." She takes another step forward.

"Because of me." It's not a question, more like a statement.

"Because I can't leave you," I reply.

She stops in her tracks. "I'm a burden."

"Far from it, Sunshine." Does she not understand? How can she think she's a burden when she's everything I ever wanted? I stand up from the bed and wait.

"Then what, you're just going to throw away your career?" she accuses me. I chuckle, shocking her.

"I don't want it if it means you're not there with me." She blinks then takes another step forward, as if pulled by an unseen force.

"And what's that about me coming with you? Why didn't you ask me? You don't want me to come?" She hesitates, stopping again. I take a small step in her direction.

"Sydney, I put you in danger." My voice cracks at the truth in that statement. "How could you ever forgive me for that? I didn't know how to ask this of you. It's a lot...and God, you probably hate me for what I've put you through. It was all my fault." Tears gather in my eyes. She closes the distance between us.

"I don't hate you, Carter." Sydney reaches out with her hand, but just before it touches my face she closes it into a fist and drops it to her side. "I hate myself." What? She must see the confusion on my face, because she continues. "I was so narrow minded, not believing in what you were telling me, thinking I'll be nothing more than a distraction, a burden. I didn't want to believe that we could make it work. And when I saw Will kiss a random girl that night, while his girlfriend was home... Well, it was like all my fears materialised right in front of me. Will, who has always been devoted to his girlfriend, cheating on her... I couldn't shake the feeling that it was only a matter of time before someone else would turn your head too."

"Sunshine, it was a rebound. Will and his girlfriend broke up," I say gently. She shrugs.

"Maybe so, but at the time, I panicked. And then when I found out about your tour, I ran and didn't let you talk to me. If only I stayed and told you what I was feeling."

"I shouldn't have posted on Instagram," I stop her.

"It's part of your brand, rockstar. I don't blame you for doing it, and I don't hate you. Not even a little." A glimmer of hope starts up in my heart. "What I hate is that I never told you I loved you." My heart stops. "I thought I'd never see you again, and the only thing that kept me going and fighting was the need to see you, tell you how utterly and completely in love with you I am." A tear slides down my cheek as I reach for her hand. The words I've been waiting for her to say are finally out.

"Why did you wait two days to tell me that?"

"I guess I thought you might have changed your mind. You kept your distance and I—"

"Sydney, I was letting you come to terms with what's happened to you. I didn't want you to feel like I was crowding you. Baby, I love you so much. Why would I change my mind?"

She cracks a smile. "Because I'm constantly getting into scrapes?" By the tone of her voice and the glint in her eye, I know she's joking. I pull her into me.

"Say it again," I demand.

She chuckles. "I love you."

"And you want to be with me."

"And I want to be with you."

"Forever and ever."

"Forever and ever."

My heart feeling full, I reach for her face and lift her chin up.

"I love you, Sunshine," I say before kissing her lips. After two days of being unable to do that, I finally feel like I've come home.

Chapter 36

The Kennedys

Sydney

We spend New Year's Eve in Carter's house—or mansion, rather. See, there's this little detail he forgot to mention to me. His family is very, very wealthy, not that it makes that much of a difference, except making me feel a little inadequate. But it's just the money. His family makes me feel whole. It has been as easy to fall in love with them as it has been with Carter. The Kennedys just creep up on you, I guess.

We welcome the New Year with family and friends, Aiden and I singing 'Old Lang Syne' at the top of our lungs when the clock strikes midnight. Before I realise what's happening, I'm swept away by Carter, who pulls me into one of the empty rooms and kisses me senseless. I'm drowning in this heady feeling of happiness as he licks my throat and lifts my skirt up. We make love in that dark room, drunk on vodka and each other, and when we come, Carter peppers kisses all over my face, whispering, "I love you. I love you so much, Sydney."

I no longer hold back. Instead, I tell him I love him too and wrap my arms around him. We stumble into our bedroom and make love again, until sated, then we fall asleep and in each other's arms.

I don't know when or how I got so lucky. Maybe the universe decided that I've had enough shit in my life. That finally, I deserved something good, something that makes me happy. And Carter makes me deliriously happy. It helps that yesterday we got a call saying that Darius has been incarcerated. With him being caught red handed, it was a no brainer he should be held in prison until trial. And there will be a trial, because as soon as news came out about what had happened to me, more girls came forward, and they kept coming. With stories about how he forced himself on them or drugged them before they woke up the next day, naked and alone in a hotel room.

I'm glad they came forward but sad that they had to go through it and kept quiet afterwards. It put a spotlight on the industry as well. There's more scrutiny now when it comes to male photographers, and the agency I work with started to make a point of having at least one extra female staff on set while shoots are happening. Hopefully, this will make at least a slight difference.

But I won't be there to see it.

I decided to quit modeling. I will focus on my writing instead. My agent told me the road is long and hard, but I'm willing to put all my eggs in that basket.

Speaking of all eggs in one basket, Carter stuffs yet another t-shirt into his suitcase.

"I don't know how you do it," he sighs. "Pack so quickly and efficiently. How are you done already?" He motions in the directions of the large suitcase in the corner of the room.

Oh, did I forget to mention? I'm going on tour with Carter and Bleeding Hearts. After we made up, Carter sat me down and told me how he didn't think he could do it without me. How he's terrified stage fright will take over and ruin this experience for him. I'll be honest here. I didn't need much convincing. As soon as I heard that idea, I was on board. I just needed to make sure Carter wanted me there. The whole thing with Darius made me realise how precious life and time are. And if that meant moving a thousand miles per hour with Carter, so be it. Just let me put my seatbelt on.

Carter will try to finish his degree remotely while touring, so it's not like we'll be partying for the next six months anyway. I can write when he studies. It will all work itself out.

I kept the lease on my flat too, although Carter insisted that, when we get back, we should just move in together. I guess I needed that security blanket, just in case. Even though I believe with all my heart that Carter is *it* for me. Old habits die hard. But he understands, and instead of making me feel bad about it, he just kept quoting Princess Bride 'as you wish', the goofball that he is.

"If you don't hurry up, we'll miss our flight," I smile, handing him a pair of jeans.

"Gah!" He runs a hand through his already tousled hair. "This is stressful. I already don't like going on tours. Not a good sign, Sunshine. I think we should stay." I laugh and wrap my arms around his middle from behind.

"Big breath, rockstar. It's just like a holiday. Except you get to sing on stage." He inhales then turns in my arms.

"I love you." He shakes his head. "How did I get so lucky?"

"You see, one Christmas Eve, you got really, really drunk, and you attempted to have a one night stand with this amazing woman. And even though that attempt failed, since she fell asleep on you, you still lucked out."

"Correction." I raise my eyebrows. "Even then, I knew it was more. It was never just a one-night stand for me. If you hadn't left, I'd have found a way to make you fall in love with me then. It probably would have worked too."

"Definitely." I laugh. I'm completely, undeniably, utterly, and irrevocably in love with Carter Kennedy, and I'm not even sorry for it.

Epilogue

Carter

6 months later

I run off the stage in Vegas and right into Sydney's arms.

"You did it!" she exclaims right when I kiss her. I drag her into my room and lock the door, adrenaline pumping through my veins, still high from the buzz of the crowd waiting for Bleeding Hearts to go on. The last six months have been crazy, touring across the US for three months, then three months in Europe. This was the last show of the tour before we finish off in LA.

Las Vegas.

And boy, do I have plans.

I lift Sydney's skirt up and drop down to my knees, kissing her until a moan escapes her lips and her legs start to tremble. I need her, need to be inside her. I get up, unzip my jeans, and in one swift motion, enter her. It's fast, hard, and needy. We can take it slow later tonight. I booked us a suite in the Bellagio. Once I'm spent, I clean us up and right her skirt just in time, as there's a knock on the door.

Sydney looks at it in confusion. I smile, shrug my shoulders, and open the door.

She's just on time.

"Well, that was a bit loud, wasn't it?" My aunt says, walking in.

"Bertie!" Sydney exclaims and runs to give her a hug.

"Is it me or does it smell in here like Carter's been giving you some writing inspirations?" Aunt Berta mutters as Sydney's face goes beet red. "Loved your songs, Carter, especially the one about naked lazy things. Very vivid imagery." Sydney goes even more red, if it's possible. It's a song I wrote when we did a John Lennon and Yoko Ono one weekend and stayed naked in a hotel room in Belgium for a whole weekend. I groan. Maybe inviting her wasn't the best of my ideas.

"I didn't know you were coming," Sydney says awkwardly. "I'd have come out to listen with you, or you could have come backstage..."

"Oh child, you'd have gotten crushed in the mosh pit. Better that you stayed backstage." Sydney holds in a smile. There was no mosh pit, but I'll let Aunt Berta reminisce the good old days. "Anyway, I'll let the two of you put yourself together, then let's go get some food." Aunt Berta winks at me. "I'll go see if I can sneak into that boy's, Danny's, dressing room. He is a handsome young chap, if I do say so myself. Reminds me of this band I had a sordid affair with." Band? She said 'a band', not one guy, didn't she? "Those were the times," she sighs and makes her way through the door, closing it behind her.

"Pretty sure your aunt just told us she had an orgy,"

Sydney laughs. "I can't believe she came to Las Vegas to see you. That's so lovely!"

"I can." I take a step towards her and grab her hands. "I invited her here."

"You did?" She cocks her head. "Why didn't you say anything?"

"Probably nerves."

"Nerves?"

"I had an ulterior motive." I wink at her.

"Oh look, he's got something stuck in his eye again," she teases.

"You." I smirk. "I had my eye on you since the first day I met you." She bites her lip. "Did you just swoon?"

"Maybe."

"Sydney, since the first time I laid eyes on you, I had this feeling like you were a part of me. I felt it then and I feel it now, even stronger. I think that maybe things happened for a reason. That first time, I wasn't ready for you and you weren't ready for me. But as soon as our souls got to that place, fate put us back together. What I'm trying to say in the most roundabout way possible,"—I kneel on one knee—"is that I love you, and I can't imagine my life without you." Sydney's hand covers her mouth as I pull out a small black box out of my jeans' pocket. "You are my sunshine, and without you, I'm just a man feeling his way blindly through the dark. Be my sunshine, always. Be my wife," I finish, opening the box.

It's a ring that Aunt Berta gave to me after Christmas, a family heirloom that was my great grandmothers.

Sydney launches herself at me with a gleeful yelp.

"Always and forever." She peppers kisses all over my face.

"That a 'yes', Sunshine?"

"Yes, rockstar. That's a 'yes'." I grin a huge smile and kiss my girl. My fiancée.

"Here's the thing, Sydney," I say, taking the ring and sliding it onto her ring finger. "I've got this crazy idea."

"How crazy?" She cocks her head as I slide her onto my lap.

"We're in Vegas, my aunt is here, and I just—" Oh God, what if she says no?

"You just what?" She smiles encouragingly.

"I don't want to wait. I want to be able to call you my wife." She opens her mouth, but I place my finger over her lips. "I know it's soon, and no one else has to know. We can have a nice long engagement where everyone else is concerned. Have a big wedding in three, five, or ten years. But tonight, just me and you, babe. Let's get married."

"Me and you...and Bertie," she giggles.

"Well, yes. She did say she has to be a bridesmaid." Sydney bites her lip.

"Let's do it."

"For real?" I can't believe it.

"For real. We're modern day Lola and Rico."

"Who?" I ask, confused.

"Never mind."

For What It's Worth

Want more of Carter and Sydney?

Scan or click the QR code to receive an EXCLUSIVE EPILOGUE straight to your inbox

Read on for a preview of Jason's story in For Heaven's Sake

And make sure to check out Rick and Lola's story in the Forever And A Day novella

For Heaven's Sake

Prolouge

Reagan

7 years ago
Freshman year

Pick up.
Pick up, pick up, pick up!

I growl in frustration at the absence of my broken-hearted brother. He was supposed to meet me almost an hour ago in front of my new dorm to help me move in. But he's nowhere to be seen. Ever since Jenny, his best friend, got together with Aiden, his other best friend, he's just not been himself. Carter Kennedy, my usually incredibly outgoing and self-confident brother, became withdrawn, locked himself in his house and stopped answering calls.

I'd worry about him on a normal day, but today of all days? I'm pissed.

"Corky, I swear to God, if you don't pick up the next time I call, I'll haul my ass over to your place and will castrate you with my nail scissors," I hiss into my cell, leaving him a voicemail.

"Rey?"

I whirl around and face the grinning blond Adonis. The guy who, frankly, I could lick up and down, were he not a part of Carter's tight-knit group of besties.

"Jason." I push my blond hair out of my eyes. "Can you help me?" I ask, motioning at my bags and the mattress, leaning against the post right next to me, where the delivery guy dropped it off. Normally, I would have asked him for help—by offering extra cash—but the guy looked really creepy and kept eyeing me up and down with a too friendly expression on his face. I made the executive decision to not die and instead, wait for my brother to show up in front of my dorm like he promised to.

"Depends... those nail scissors?"

"They've only got Carter's name on them," I reply. "I'll get you a coffee as a reward," I add as an afterthought—that should be enticing enough. I mean, who wouldn't want a free coffee?

"I don't drink coffee," he shrugs as my jaw hits the floor. Say what? He doesn't drink coffee? Is he even human? Who in their right mind does not drink coffee? Coffee is life. Everyone knows it. "I just don't like it." He blushes at my expression.

When I first met Jason last Thanksgiving, I honestly thought he was perfect. He had charm, good looks, and was funny. And even though my great aunt Berta felt him up under the table, I could look past that. I could look past the fact that he was my brother's best friend. I could look past the hordes of women he flirted with. But not drinking coffee? The nectar of the gods? The freaking ambrosia? Well, that will be a hard pill to swallow.

"So what shall we do first?" he asks, pulling me out of my downward spiral.

I shake my head, trying to wipe the image of Jason hating on my beloved coffee and sigh. "Is it safe to leave my things here while we take the mattress upstairs?" I ask.

Jason looks around, his eyebrows scrunched in thought, then reaches his hand out, stopping a girl in her tracks. "Hey, beautiful." His gravelly voice makes her doe eyes dilute. "Could you watch our bags while we run the mattress upstairs?" She blushes, twirling her brown hair around her fingers as his baby blue eyes focus on her.

"Sure... You won't be long?"

"Just a few minutes, I promise." He grins, booping her nose. My eyes widen, seeing the effect he has on other women. It brings me back down to earth. As gorgeous as Jason Cowley is, he is also a huge player, and it would be wise to never forget that. The girl who changes the player? She doesn't exist outside of romance novels. And even if she did, she certainly isn't me. I like my guys nerdy and safe, thank you very much.

Unaware of my thoughts, Jason motions at me and we grab the mattress at each end, lifting it and walking it up the few steps towards the dorm entrance. I'm late to the party, so there's no welcome committee, no dorm or floor reps. It's just me, my mattress and the hunk in front of me. His muscles ripple as he shifts the mattress above his head and calls the elevator. I'm low-key drooling, ogling his perfect body before I'm brutally ripped out of my daydream when he asks me for the floor number. I mutter the answer and watch him press the button, his calloused fingers drawing my attention. Without a sweat, he lifts the mattress all by himself, propping it against the elevator wall, allowing me to take in the sight in front of me. He truly is stunning. Tall, tanned and blond, with those bright blue eyes, he's what you can find under 'perfect surfer boy' in the dictionary. Wrapped up with a bow of a sculpted body.

I lick my lips as my eyes trail up over his chest and stop on his face, his gaze intense as he watches me appreciate his body. Our eyes lock as the air grows thicker. He steps closer to me and brushes his rough fingers against my cheek. There's a rush I've never felt before. Desire mixed with a hint of inevitability. And just like that, I don't care about any of the things I listed before, the ones clearly stating that what I am about to do is a bad idea. With my head tilted upward, I lift on my tiptoes, moving as close to his face as I can reach. Without hesitation, Jason closes the distance, pressing his lips to mine. The heady feeling of passion and yearning comes over me. The kiss is everything I imagined and more. His breath mingled with mine, the sparks of electricity, when his hands slide into my hair pulling closer. I want more. More of this feeling. More of Jason Cowley. And as if he can read my mind, he swoops in, prying my lips open with his tongue, forcing himself in without waiting for my permission. He takes, takes, takes. Demanding my all. Molding me into him. I have never been kissed like that in my entire life. Never have I felt this primal need to taste someone, to let them in, have them claim me in such a masterful way. I wrap my arms around his neck and pull him in closer as he assaults my mouth. God, if he fucks like he kisses, I'll have to build him an altar or something. My body tingles with the need for him and my heart pumps to the rhythm of... catcalls?

Shit! In my lustful haze, I didn't even realize the elevator doors opened and we were giving my entire floor a show. Reluctantly, I pull away from Jason's lips, his taste lingering on mine. The way his head follows mine a few inches, wanting more, and his groan of disapproval make me smile.

"We better get that mattress in." I wink at him and grab the huge thing. I'm all for more kissing, preferably without an audience. He bites his lip and readjusts himself before lifting his side. As we walk through the busy corridor, passing students milling, I say a little prayer that my roommate isn't in, that maybe we can grab the rest of my bags and run back upstairs to test this new mattress. Brothers, coffee and heaven be damned. I want to burn in hell if it means more kissing with Jason Cowley. The thought makes me walk faster and before I know it, I'm wrapping my hand around the doorknob, turning it and pushing the door open with my hip, all the while balancing the mattress on my other side.

"Back so soon?" my roommate, who didn't get the memo of staying away, says. I don't really mind though, I'm happy to meet the person I'll be living with for the foreseeable future. I peer over the mattress, propping it down on my foot as I grin at her. She's gorgeous, in all her disheveled glory. Her confused expression as she processes my face, clearly having been expecting someone else, turns into a wide smile when it finally clicks. "Rey? Are you Rey? My new roommate?" I nod, my smile matching hers. "Oh my god! You're finally here! I'm Sarah! Girl, I thought you bailed on me!" She rushes to me, pulling me in for a hug. I let go of the mattress and hug her back as she goes on talking a hundred miles a minute. Then she stops, her gaze focused on something or someone behind me. "So, you *did* come back. And you brought my new roommate with you. Thanks, babe." Babe?

I untangle myself from Sarah, stepping back and trying to understand what exactly is happening. My gaze bouncing between my new roommate and the guy holding my mattress up. The guy whose passionate kiss still lingers on my lips. The guy who I threw myself at in the elevator. The guy who clearly is dating my roommate. I look around the room. The bedsheets are all rumpled, the nest on Sarah's head screams sex hair and Jason? Well, Jason is unusually pale. Oh fuck. Fuck, fuck, fuck.

"You know Jason?" I stumble through the words, praying for a miracle.

"Oh, I *know* Jason," Sarah smiles a coquettish smile and saunters over to him, tracing her finger up and down his chest before lifting on her toes and assaulting his lips. The lips that were on mine not even a minute ago. I stiffen as Jason kisses her back. He doesn't pull her closer, but he doesn't push her away, either.

I shake my head, trying to comprehend the scene unfolding in front of my eyes. Jason is looking at me as Sarah continues to kiss him.

Red hot jealousy mingles with disbelief in my veins. I'm hurt. So hurt that I'm just another conquest to him.

But what's worse is I'm a fucking home wrecker.

I sway on my legs, needing to sit down as the reality settles on me. I have thrown myself at a guy who has a girlfriend. I basically made him a cheater, made him into everything that I despise.

But no, it takes two to tango. I might have thrown myself at him, but *he* didn't stop me. Not once did he say 'I can't', or 'shouldn't', or that there's someone else. Fucking guys. There's a reason I stick to my usual nerdy guy type. And this is it. Situations like this. The feeling of being deceived, the feeling of being less than... I just kissed someone else's boyfriend. Me, the person who lives by girl code.

This means one thing and one thing only. The two-timing bastard is off-limits for life. It will be hard, considering he's part of my friends' group, but I'll just avoid him. I'll avoid him and let this feeling of betrayal fester. Let it turn to hate if it'll make staying away from him easier.

Probably for the best, too. Nothing good could come from it. Jason Cowley is Trouble, with a capital T.

For Heaven's Sake

1. Defective Rod Stuart

Reagan

Am I forgetting something?

Keys.

Phone.

Purse.

I check the items off in my head as I run through my apartment in downtown LA.

I'm definitely forgetting something. But to hell with it. I will not be the person who holds up my soon to be sister in law's dress fitting. At breakneck speed, I run out of my apartment and barely manage to stop in time before crashing into my yellow VW Beetle. This thing should have a human imprint on its side, considering the amount of times I *didn't* manage to stop. As it stands, my trusty Ol'Rusty is pristine and dent free. Well, except that one dent on the side where I backed into a fire hydrant, and the scratch on the passenger door from when I misjudged a barrier, but who's counting?

Not this girl.

This girl is late, and doesn't have time to do any counting. Especially since math was never my strong subject.

Give me arts any day of the week, but trigonometry? I couldn't even tell you what that was about. Triangles, maybe? Sounds about right.

I wipe the sweat off my forehead as I slide into my car and press the start button. A low hum starts up as the electric engine comes to life. I call my car Ol'Rusty for shits and giggles. In fact, it's only a few months old, which says something about my driving. What, with all the dents and scratches... Fine, there might be more than just a couple. But like I said, who's counting?

The mellow sounds of alt-J fill the car when I plug my cell into the sound system. I crank up the volume and lower my windows, letting the vibe out onto the streets of LA as I drive to my destination. On the freeway, I stick my left arm out the window and let it float in the air, making waves as the song plays on repeat. Just for a second, I close my eyes, pressing my foot down on the gas pedal.

Tempting fate has become a sort of a game to me over the past couple of years. Normally, I'd keep them closed for as long as I'd dare. Seeing which one of us will win. Not today. Today isn't about me and my abundance of issues. Today is about Sydney, my brother's fiancé. My sister from another mister. My favorite human, right after my brother, Carter.

I don't see either of them often enough. Their schedule doesn't allow for that. Eight months of the year they are on tour, Carter singing to the masses and Sydney apparently helping him with stage fright, which is ridiculous if you asked me. The guy is a freaking rockstar who has been performing in front of huge crowds for the better part of the last six years. But I get it, I wouldn't want to spend any time away from the person I love either, if I were in their shoes. Just one look at them makes it obvious how utterly gone for each other they are, even after six years of being together. The four months they're not touring, they spend holed up in a little mountain cabin in Yosemite National Park. I say 'little', as it used to be small when I was growing up. But Carter and Sydney have made some changes since claiming the place. Considering all the additions, including a recording studio, that cabin can no longer be called 'little'. Or a cabin, for that matter. The place is pretty huge now. And considering they like their space and privacy, I'm glad they have everything they need right there, even if it means they're not in LA as much as I'd like them to be. But I see them every day anyway, just over FaceTime.

You know those kids who don't have any friends and always say that their mom or sibling is their best friend? Well, I'm kind of that kid. Except it's true. Our small family is close, and I consider their overbearing asses my closest friends. Carter leading the troupe as my 'BFF'. I'm the first person to hear his new songs, the first person he talks to if he and Sydney have a fight. He plays me unfinished tunes, asking for my input. Not that he needs it. Ever since he signed with Josh Coda, Carter has been recording hit after hit.

My brother, the wonder kid.

Have you ever felt lost in your own skin? In your own family? I do. All the time.

Although I love my family with all my heart, I sometimes wonder if things would be different if my parents never had me. If all they knew was Carter, the golden boy who could do no wrong.

Ugh, it sounds resentful, but I swear I'm not. And he truly can do no wrong, aside from the times he pisses Sydney off. He's crazy, impulsive and often a liability, but he's my big brother, and in my eyes he will always be perfect.

There's ample parking space outside the bridal shop and I snag a spot right by the entrance. With a sigh, I step outside, holding the door to my car as I rearrange my face, stretching my lips into a huge smile and crinkling my eyes.

Carefree Reagan at your service.

I stop on the sidewalk, gazing through the glass window into the shop beyond and spotting a familiar silhouette—my great aunt Berta, Grandad's sister, and my third favorite human being.

On an inhale, I square my shoulders and take a confident step forward.

It's showtime.

The doorbell jingles as I walk through. The place is everything you'd imagine a bridal shop would be. Plush blush pink furniture with white, pink and green floral arrangements all around. There are white wedding dresses hanging on display on each of the four walls. I pass the reception desk and head toward the side room, where I can hear voices. Just as I am about to walk through the doorway, I pause, listening in. I've been doing that ever since I was little, always expecting to overhear something I shouldn't, something that would or could destroy my life. It hasn't happened yet. The worst I've ever overheard was when Carter was talking dirty to Sydney one day. I bought noise canceling headphones after that and have used them at family gatherings ever since. This time my habit is not fruitful either. I can't make out the words, just muffled voices, Aunt B grumbling something and Sydney bursting out laughing.

I take a deep breath. No time like the present. Taking a step forward, I say, "Hi."

Both Sydney and Aunt Berta snap their heads in my direction. There is a cat carrier right next to the chair where my aunt is sitting, a small squirrel stretched out on her lap. "Gizmo!" I say excitedly and rush over to the little critter my aunt adopted after it joined us for Christmas the year Carter brought Sydney home. Honestly, I have no clue how my aunt convinced the owner of the bridal shop to let her in with a squirrel, or to let that squirrel out of its carrier. I suppose I shouldn't be surprised. She has her ways of making things happen. If someone turned around tomorrow and said to me that she heads up the Italian mafia, I'd just nod and say, "That makes total sense." I lean over and scratch Gizmo on her tummy, getting a little happy chirp in return.

I give Aunt B a kiss and turn to my sister from another mister.

"Reagan," she beams.

"Sydney." I tip my imaginary hat to her before laughing and enveloping her in a hug. "I missed you," I whisper into her hair.

"I missed you too."

"Can you not just stop touring and stay in LA for the rest of your life, please?" I ask.

"I think... We actually might do that after the wedding... For a little while," she says timidly as I suppress a squeal.

"They'll finally start working on those great grandchildren they've been promising me for years," Aunt B mutters. "I'm starting to think Carter's Rod Stewart is defective."

"Berta!" Sydney gasps.

"What? I'm just speaking my truth," she shrugs as I try my hardest to contain my laugh.

"What's your truth?" Jenny asks, walking into the room. She holds a bottle of Champagne in each hand. Oh fuck!

That was it! I was meant to bring Champagne. Thank God someone else remembered.

"That Carter's Winky Dinky ain't working," Aunt Berta says, checking her nails. I tried, I really did, but the laughter bubbles out of me all on its own.

Three pairs of eyes turn to me. Quick Reagan, deflect.

"Hi, Jenny," I wave in her direction. "You brought Champagne! Yay!" I love Jenny, I really do. But she's related to public enemy number one, Jason, the two-timing-sex-on-legs-with-washboard-abs enemy number one, so we don't get to spend much time together. Especially since she lives in London and her visits to Cali are few and far between. With trying to avoid her brother at all costs, I skip a lot of events she and her husband, are involved in.

"Rey! It's been ages. How have you been?" Jenny squeals and rushes over to me, giving me a side hug with the Champagne. I hug her back, then take the bottles out of her hands and put them down on the floor. One thing you should know about Jenny is she is clumsy to her core. Pretty sure she tripped and slipped out of her mother's vagina when she was born. That's how clumsy she is.

"Did someone say dress fitting?" Hayley, Sydney's and Jenny's best friend walks in wearing a huge grin and her trademark black leather jacket.

It's surreal. Having all of us in the same room. It's been years since the last time that happened, definitely before—

"Hayls!" Jenny squeals, jumping up and down, then throwing herself at Hayley.

"We saw each other this morning, babe!"

"I know, I know, but I'm just so excited about the news. Can I tell them the news?"

Hayley shrugs and nods.

"Hayley is moving to Cambridge!"

"Massachusetts?" I ask, frowning. Hayley already lives in Cambridge in En—

"England!" Jenny exclaims. "She's moving to England!"

Sydney and I both look toward Hayley, confused.

"I got offered a permanent position," she explains. "I'll be working at the Cancer Research Hospital in Cambridge." My jaw hits the floor. Both Hayley and Jenny are incredibly smart, working for various research institutes, helping beat diseases. I don't quite get the details, but I know that their work is important. But Cambridge? Cancer Research? That's huge, even I know that. Hayley moved to England a few months ago to help in some research project, but that was always going to be just a short-term thing.

"Oh my God! That's amazing!" Sydney exclaims. I nod in agreement. But inside my world is spinning. The thing about having friends that are so incredibly accomplished, it highlights how far behind you are in your own goals and dreams.

I bite my lip as my Aunt B sidles up to me, grabbing my arm and pulling me closer.

"My friend Eunice's grandson has recently divorced," she whispers in my ear. "He's a doctor, well, an orthodontist, but that's still a doctor, right?"

Oh God, here we go again.

**WANT MORE
FOR HEAVEN'S SAKE?**

READ NOW
just scan or click the QR code

About The Author

Jo Preston writes fun and sexy romance books.

She lives with her husband, son and a dog (that doubles as a teddy bear) in the UK, where she wraps up in warm clothes and hang out under umbrellas, dreaming of warm destinations.

When she's not writing, she enjoys a glass of wine (or two) with a good book or a favourite Netflix show and coming up with terms like #SmutCom.

Want to be a part of an exclusive smut loving community?

Become a member of the smut tribe

Scan or click the QR code

- facebook.com/authorjpreston
- instagram.com/authorjpreston
- goodreads.com/jpreston
- bookbub.com/authors/j-preston

Acknowledgements

There's always a ton of people to thank and this time is no different.

First of all thank YOU, the reader for picking up this book! Without you there would be no point to it, so once again thanks! Hope you liked it!

My alphas. You guys are my freaking rock. Don't ever leave me! I wouldn't let you anyway :D

My beta team. Thank you for your invaluable feedback and support!

Special thanks to Bri, Deb, Kirty, Chelsea and Carissa. You are amazing and I can't even begin to express how much you've helped me on this journey. Thank you!

Thank you to all my author friends, who support me, read my stuff and sprint with me! Heather, Kristin, Rhylie ad Chelley you guys are amazing and such a huge part of my journey!

My editor, Addie - thank you for tidying up the huge mess I give you!

ARC team - thank you for giving me your notes and spotting last minute edits!

My husband, for being so patient and supportive each time I said I needed to write or edit. Thank you for believing in this dream of mine!

THE FALSE STARTS SERIES

For Crying Out Loud

For What It's Worth

Forever and a Day

For Heaven's Sake

THE HOLIDATES SERIES/ THE FALSE STARTS CROSSOVER

The Sexiest Nerd Alive

HEART OF A WOUNDED HERO/ THE FALSE STARTS CROSSOVER

Nothing Left To Lose

CURVES FOR CHRISTMAS/ THE FALSE STARTS CROSSOVER

Frost My Cookie

Printed in Great Britain
by Amazon